DOWN
WITH
BEAUTY

# DOWN WITH BEAUTY

&

## Nostalgia for Unknown Cities

## KEN EDWARDS

REALITY STREET

Published by
REALITY STREET
63 All Saints Street, Hastings, East Sussex TN34 3BN, UK
www.realitystreet.co.uk

First edition 2013
Back cover photo of the author by Elaine Edwards

*Reality Street Narrative Series No 13*

A catalogue record for this book is available from the British Library

ISBN: 978-1-874400-61-5

# CONTENTS

## Down With Beauty

# Nostalgia for Unknown Cities

DOWN WITH BEAUTY

# Prologue: Without History

THE SCIENTIST:
As for the particular we actually observe, it is selected from all the possible generalities and particulars. And if it were changed by just a few percent then stars would not be able to form carbon, for the physical reasons that we observe. This is a necessary condition, and it is obvious and special, a sheen of certainty laid upon the waters of conjecture. It is a fact that we need in order to be present. Now ask yourself the question. Ask it quickly.

THE DANCER:
?

THE SCIENTIST:
No, that's not quick enough. The speed of the answer would be a condition for your own existence. That is, in order to exist, at least that much time must have passed.

THE DANCER:
What is time?

THE SCIENTIST:
You should be able to intuit the answer, $6.6262 \times 10^{-34}$, which is what business analysts refer to as *added value*.

THE DANCER:
I am in this space called consciousness, which is composed of the elements carbon, oxygen, nitrogen and phosphorus. These

could not have been made; they are necessary consequences of heating. Could a particular exist without any form of consciousness whatever? Are the forms of presence specially designed to allow libido its devices?

THE SCIENTIST:
To answer this, we need to go back to the origin, which is *primarily soup*.

THE DANCER:
I know it. It's an alphabet that occupies zero dimensions, a liquid of uncertainty, a dream of becoming lacking only its dreamer.

THE SCIENTIST:
The heavier elements had to wait in the wings, but soon it was their turn in the sun. This resembled a vast furnace, wherein those elements flourished with multiple iridescence, racked as they were by the sudden storms so typical of this time of the year. Their surfaces were carpeted with oxide daisies and vipers bugloss. Around this time, sentient creatures began to appear: a genet hunting amid patches of lavender; the elephant of the Serengeti; the obscure progeny of the mobile phone; a human infant essaying its first smile; the dread form of the basilisk.

THE DANCER:
I remember now. I was ready at this point, coming to a focus, overcoming key barriers to communication. I began to leave home, knowing that things would henceforth not be as they had been but, increasingly, as they were. I mean, that things began to resemble themselves more than they had done. That was the beginning of my exile.

THE SCIENTIST:
Though it wasn't without regret that we looked back, into the interior of our emergence, the closure of the circle.

THE DANCER:
What is regret?

THE SCIENTIST:
Ask the question. It little matters that value is a necessary condition for your own existence. Ask it. A single voice sounds raw. But still you will not understand the physical reasons for that value to occur. We can deduce the value from the fact that we're around to ask what it is.

THE DANCER:
I hear that voice! Is it the voice of time? Or is it a voice *in* time?

THE SCIENTIST:
Time is a precondition. Up to a few thousand million years of heating is required. After that, we are in the world of memory. Principally, this allows one to compare present experience with the traces of the past. "At dusk the sound of church bells from the valley floor" as church bells starts up nearby. Or you're waiting for the bus opposite the Half Moon (an English pub) and a half moon lurks in the blue sky beside it. You are guest to the world's host; the result is a ghost. The ghost of physics, located in the sound picture.

THE DANCER:
Is there something special about this?

THE SCIENTIST:
Try to remember.

THE DANCER:
Once, the physical universe was located in a key region containable within the compass of an ordinary dwelling or hut, such as is found today in rural areas and shanty towns of underdeveloped countries. There was no water. There were objects in the sky, but they didn't count. Too mobile, or something. Then things changed. They changed subtly, by just a few percent, so that we should not have found ourselves present all at once. After that, the stars appeared, and they would be just right, but somewhere else, at some other appropriate time.

THE SCIENTIST:

So, unless all these developments had occurred, we couldn't be here, visible and constant, actually observing the heavier elements, whose interiors, themselves resembling sentient creatures, needed to be present. How important is fusing, or pitch memory, or weird sleep? Are these emergent properties of the mind, or whatever?

THE DANCER:

This box doesn't deserve to think. I am in this space and the world is out there, or, no it isn't, it's in here and I am outside of it, and something happened.

THE SCIENTIST:

The requirements to generate these laws (of motion; of consciousness) necessitated such elements to be specially designed in order for order to exist, at least in the sense of that existence of conscious life such that sufficient time should have passed ... that we should or should not be in a particular location. Something happened. Why was that significant? We don't know.

THE DANCER:

It was arranged and somehow it all pancaked out like that. History began. Politics began. The consequences of which may well be compound.

THE SCIENTIST:

We ask ourselves: why is life so rare? To answer that question, we need to be present, creating space by a process of unfolding, in the sound picture, not merely subject to cognitive systems. So whether you are thinking or feeling, or have a sense of having implemented or shared, you would need to come to the topic with your approaches hoovered. Are you present? Please bring any supporting material.

THE DANCER:

But then, suddenly, you have lost your family, and with that, all traces of home. No sooner has the memory been created than

12

the memory is erased. Not knowing, you might as well have come out of nowhere. Proceeding from a blank sheet, you'd be here till further notice. From a spiral of fifths, you would quickly withdraw, show up settled and translated, the voice superimposed. Where would you be?

THE SCIENTIST:
Having no framework, you would have created space, which is new and open.

THE DANCER:
But this quickly fades. The logics of line and syntax lapse. There is tidal movement. It's clean, and without history: a fiction, or a contrivance. The consolations of philosophy are of no consequence in such regard. Is this what we mean by an "alternative tradition"?

THE SCIENTIST:
We can use such techniques to create nucleosynthesis, to generate such elements as are required, to focus on the things that are certain or likely to happen and to determine what we can do. The arguments can be used to explain why the conditions happen to be right for achieving existence at the present time. For if they were not just right, then they would either be too vast in scale, or else significantly smaller than was practicable in any event. Then we should not have found ourselves in our present locations, but somewhere else, at some other appropriate time.

THE DANCER:
Therefore is the philosopher's ladder to be discarded (kicked away)? And do we find ourselves simultaneously immersed in and immune from space, I mean, dangling or afloat? I don't believe that. And are we all at once contained within ourselves, yet joined at all points to what is? And for what purpose?

THE SCIENTIST:
It is hard to accept the basis for your reasoning.

THE DANCER:
I don't reason – I only dance.

THE SCIENTIST:
It is incorrect to assert "We are here because we are meant to be here"; for we could be here while not being meant to be here, or, alternatively, we might not be here though we are meant to be here. In either case, whether we are here or not here, it is impossible to determine whether we are meant. We may be, or we may not. But because of the shared dynamic of the history we lack, the history of existence and non-existence which affects us equally, heats us and bequeaths to us the sense of physicality that is so palpable and quick, because of these and other reasons to do with interiority and exteriority, significance and non-significance, we feel at home here. And yet we feel a sense of exile. Now ask the question again.

THE DANCER:
There's a lot of noise.

# Us and Them

THIS IS no longer the place we thought it was. Nowadays the street is covered in a thin sheet of khaki water that slowly ripples when the wind comes. What is there is not what we thought. Our country was a constellation of mountains and streams with shallow coastal plains watered by magnificent spring rivers that became mere wallows in summer. Most of the territory to the north consisted of relatively high mountains, and this natural defence was reinforced by strong fortresses and fortified towns where attack was easiest. Valleys were difficult of access, a division which affected local customs. For example, we used lard from the pig, since in the colder north no olive tree could grow. We had fine bread. Everything was piled, one on another. Everything flowed, one into another. There was no difference. That came later. Certain signals were given, that certain of us understood. There was no worry, as such. You never had to say anything: what could there be to be said? If you started to say it, it would never be completed. One did not speak about the others – no need to mention it – it wasn't done. Beyond these – it didn't exist. On the whole, we were prosperous. Drinking parties were held on the river at night, or in a grove or flowery meadow either in the cool of the evening or at dawn. These celebrations were sonorous. Our music would pulse like the human heart. We preferred contemplating it at dawn. Voluptuous tendrils enveloped it. Nature provided the idyllic background. High fields were infested by moonlight with beautiful small rodents. These were idyllic walks through meadows with far reaching views available in the freshness of the early morning, and a myriad of

wild flowers such as crested cow-wheat, green-winged and but-
terfly orchids, a host of pinks, bellflowers, daisies and clovers.
Satellites clustered in the lee of the moon. Nobody could disturb
the shadows. There were orchestras of strange hills, presaging
nothingness. Cows plodded in tall grass. Deer glid by; the air was
heavy with their breath. In the lakes, perch dimly gleamed and
glid. Bears from the woods tore the children to pieces. Beyond
these are the chasms. We shall never forget the words a melancholy monk spoke through a long vale, shivering amid the rubble. The immense mountains and forests of the north were com-
memorated by such sights and sounds, the villagers in bizarre and
sometimes touching costumes and masks, trading delicacies and
emblems. These were to be found in the meridian of our love. It
was fascinating to all those who respect historical monuments
and cultural heritage. Old women sat outside their gates coaxing
coarse wool onto spindles. Deals were sealed with a handshake, a
sip of home-made plum brandy and cash payments. Rare mountain horses roamed freely. Open-armed people nestled in clumps
of beech, flawless in their history. We believe that we could
glimpse the sea beyond all this. We have no knowledge of the so-
called mass graves. Everywhere there was wood of the highest
quality imaginable. Even our victims were filled with the scent of
countless wild flowers. In numerous restaurants and taverns you
should have been able to taste home-made specialities. Rolls of
soured cabbage were freely offered. A substantial breakfast
would be at your disposal. We remembered the creak of the train
at night as it sped through the countryside. Towards the end, we
saw the lights of our own little town from afar and we wept. But
those others would not have understood any of this.

Our great capital city has prospered through the ages. Fine
craftsmanship over many generations gave it its contemporary
allure. Cafés, restaurants, shops and banks of many colours and
styles were enjoyed by admiring visitors. One of its elegant
streets, adorned by period lamp-posts, is named after an English
general. We had no problem with the British in those days, we
welcomed them in our bars, from their cities filled with fog, their
icons such as Maggie Thatcher, Manchester United, and also
Liverpool, The Beatles! It may be different now. Cultural prod-

ucts were built from 1926. On this, the last word has yet to be said. Our nice children were selected by us. Beautiful photography and rich prose were abundant. How sharp and with what definition the shadows! Modern parking lots were equipped for the richest minds of their generation. Businessmen walked arm in arm among the arcades and distinctive yellow luminaries, witnessing many cultural events. There was once a thriving Jewish community here, before the war. Racial ethnicity is of no importance. Slippers were worn by beautiful women. We should like to state that we never had anything against the Jews. The restored municipality was much admired for approaching beauty. The great river shone like the blade of a knife. There was statuary. The library was said to contain 400,000 books, all beautifully catalogued. Nobody has read them all. How could they? Our happy children propelled their tiny vehicles along clean cobblestones, safe from any predation. Amid the clamour of the street market, a man might be seen in a green T-shirt with the slogan NO TIME TO WASTE in English. There were looks of wonder. Bright lights and American donuts. Young ladies gazed at the indicative map. The men thronged the bars watching Manchester United. There was Virgin Megastore amid the splendid geraniums of our youth. Children respected the fine carpets. LA TERRE announced a poster suspended from one of the many fine lamp-posts. Glorious emblems were prized above the heritage. You could choose the Barcelona, you could choose the Milan, you could choose the Manchester, it was the right of the young men; they were allowed to sing, they were beginning to gain credibility, to gesture, to capture the midfield, to attack. The flow of capital led to this place of construction, peace, and sighs. The lovely skin of this was that which made it what it is, or rather, was. But it's going to end badly. Each year turned on its axis, to the slow solstice and beyond, dipping into darkness from the festival of lights. We went into hibernation, knowing that this time we wouldn't awaken. We were "hot in the mouth of snow".

What were the details of our nostalgia? Nobody can say for certain. All this is gone now. What happened? The bestiality of terror came. It was not of our choosing. We heard the sounds of laughter in the dark, and it froze us momentarily. Our daughter pleaded with us, our son hardened his heart. Sights and sounds are still transmitted to us; but they are out of kilter. There'd been a time when it had been hoped that members of different faiths could be welded into a unity; but it was becoming clear that this was not possible. The manners of the people deteriorated day by day; certain agreements went into abeyance, and still the visitors grew in numbers, until it seemed as though there could be no solution as to where or how they might be accommodated. Each time a green-painted train comes to a halt before the end of the platform, we know the outcome, mass migration and heartache is caused. It's always the same. The more ignorant among us start to imitate the incomers, as if this would give any social cachet! One drunkard in a dark suit holds a carrier bag with the name and logo of a legal outfitters. A woman struggles to retain a low bloodhound on a leash, her face tilted upwards in a characteristic gesture, but she is probably not blind. There is excessive arm-swinging while walking. A jovial man and his serious friend stagger under the weight of long cardboard boxes, some beginning to split; it is claimed they contain artists' easels, but we know better. The visitors were not welcomed among us, partly because of their numbers but also because they are a polyglot community divided among themselves and unable to establish any sort of unity. Their envy consumed them. They were accustomed to live in the midst of government offices and barracks of their unruly soldiery. Most of them have gone now, actually. The worst act no better than Arabs, and the others though better behaved yet are unruly sometimes. They are not of our sort at all. They may claim to be proud descendants of Illyrians, but they act like ungrateful guests who walk into houses with shoes covered with cow dung. The air is heavy with their breath. They have no schooling as such. Their knowledge seems to them to be perfectly systematic, yet it is complete nonsense from start to finish. Their hygienic customs, their exhalations, of depleted methane, of distorted syllables: it is this that gets under the skin, as does their incomprehensible music, so-called, like the babbling of forty thieves or fifty lunatics. These people were given prestigious flats by our municipality, but they prefer to spend their time in the open, kindling their fires, trading their horses, playing electric guitars and rendering the common spaces into fields of mud. They possess scummed-up dogs who are mindless. Their dance is just a stagger. Their tongues are rough, like white butterflies skimmed across the cement factory; their manners are those of uncertain bears. Their colours are of a different stripe. They give great clouts to our ideals. Their young men explode themselves. For what? They make cheese from their dogs. How could we know what to do? We were saddened to see the monasteries vanish. Political thought, once solid as a shining lighthouse, was moving in its several directions. Our throbbing heart echoed our dreams and deepest aspirations. We had to do something about this. We do not want to live in tents or slums while the immigrants confiscate our land, water and even the air that we breathe! Battle came to us and we couldn't wait. Civil strife was fostered by those foreign to our customs. Our hands shook. We can't remember clearly. We knew our daughter was lost to us. One of her eyes was facing inward. She has had portions of her tongue removed. The last thing she wrote, in a shaky hand, was "I love you all." As for our boy, he would never now marry.

Throughout the tempest, one man stood as straight as an iron rod. Nothing could shake his clear determination to undertake his job fearlessly, without the blink of an eye. He was a lion among foxes and bears. He stood against the coming age of darkness, scornful of the intelligentsia who offered only counsels of despair. And he was a teacher. He found ways and means. But his name can't now be spoken, for fear of reprisals. The forces that were ranged against him, incoherent as they might be, stole power day by day. Such things overwhelm thought. Hearts break. Hospitals burn. Melancholy hypocrites abscond and skim. They have escaped from the zoo. Our true friends fall. This is what has prompted us to write these pages. It has become a world where truth is shadowed by endless lies. We have the internet, it's an infection, the babble of *vox populi*. But the ordinary people of this country are almost voiceless. The babble is of ignorant, conceited and stupid people who pass judgement on others without having any idea what is going on in the world. They are so stupid that they cannot fathom their own limitations and insignificance. Their sickness lies not so much in the fact that they are misinformed, but in their self-deception and hypocrisy that makes them feel confident despite their feeble-minded emotional reasoning. They report that the authorities are finding more and more mass graves every day. But where are they? They don't say. We should like to state publicly that we have no knowledge of such things. We wish such illiterate individuals judging high political things would have refugees flood into their home town, claim independence and then their illiterate equals from all over the world accuse them of mass killings! They are she-wolves without a clue to reality. They are not to our taste. Our cities and towns are no longer our own, and even the villages are now threatened. Our nostalgia has been corroded. Long demolished goods yards have been turned into derelict car parks. Consider our great city. Trams no longer run here. The rails are rusted and overgrown with moss and other vegetation. No one has seen a doctor for 43 days. Wild vegetation grows in the streets leading to the Opera edifice built in the neo-Egyptian style towards the end of the twenties. Collapsed scaffolding forms a rusty cradle around which the vegetation is beginning to creep, barring entry to the once proud thoroughfare. Water damage is beginning to crumble the columns. Rolled steel blinds conceal the unimaginable. We believe that was once a pharmacy. Burnt to the ground, an apartment block presents a picture of dangling telephone cables, furred cornices and illegible signs; a tractor has penetrated one of its spaces, and around the next corner further movement is impossible because of a great wall made of rusting containers. The windows have all been blown out, rags hang from a line and a stray hubcap languishes in dust that was once street. On every street, a barricade. Walls of sandbags make further progress impossible. Men in fatigues patiently patrol the rubble. Creatures that were once children play in the shell of a burnt-out car. They prefer death to life. Plastic bags with unknown contents are scattered amid the rubble. Honey slides from the barricades and is lost. Amid the ruins of the municipality you can hear a recording of a boy's voice. We want for the throbbing of life to be, but any hub so wounded would never regain such lustre. People with tree heads, in the garden of snipers and land mines, declare their allegiance to what doesn't exist. They worship jungle creatures in lieu of the flag, dire progeny of the bomb. Fragrance fragments. Pictures conclude: show now distressed towers, desolate alleyways, existent rubble, naked schools, torn landmarks of destruction and oblivion, memories of civilisation that we long for, that we fear, that we never knew! Spires in a flash. Alley catastrophes. The world has abandoned us. We requested them not to, but it was to no avail. These are all lies. This wind will not come again. And the others, the original cause of all this desolation, increasingly seem unreal creatures even as they become more and more familiar. We imagine them to be so, and they for their part pass themselves off. They pretend to be ordinary people. They try to tell us who we are, to convince us how could we will to live, how could we even will to live without them? And yet they will kill us. They that pretend to be us: they lie. We can't accept this, we can't accept them, they change their story, sometimes they say they want to be us, then that we want to be them, but we don't want to be them. It's madness! We don't even know where they came from. We've said nothing, we've done nothing, we want nothing to do with them, let there be an end to it. But we're afraid. What are we afraid of? That there'll be no end. There'll be no end to this. Well, they will obliterate us in the end, and that will be the end. Everything comes to an end, after all, it's natural. They tell us, no, they tell us nothing, they talk to the world's media, about such and such graves, which they have no hesitation in inventing, for they are people of invention, they make up anything you like; but as for us, we're afraid of nothing. Nothing. Signal drift, ghosts, a spiral into lamentable sand. See us glistening with quagmires. Skirt spires down. Detritus within the embrasures. Executive turmoil. Wire in the flesh. It's all connected. There is nothing. We know nothing of it. It's a shame and a scandal. How could there be mass graves? Where?

# Soldiers

THERE ARE rags of flags, hanging limply. Peeling posters denounce the modern world. Nobody in the streets. Everyone's scared, they're indoors, there's no life left. A dog maybe, trotting by, its ribs showing, maybe puts its mouth to the gutters, here, there, looking to what it may find. The electricity's off at the present time. We are awaiting the soldiers, there's little else we can do.

Somebody says the soldiers are a day away. Another that they are but hours from the city. Really, nobody knows. There's a thrill in this.

There used to be music in the city, but it's silent now. The only reminder is the fading posters on the side of the darkened Theatre Royal. All the great ones played there: both traditional singers with traditional instruments, and also electric guitars, bass guitars, keyboards, drums. I remember as a small child clasping my father's hand tightly in the street, hearing from within the buildings the wail of brass and the cries of the singers, holding a note, then dropping away, and coming back up, swooping as though to elude the emotion that followed and would have overwhelmed it. The sound was muffled, until someone opened the door to spit in the gutter, or to beckon to a friend, and then its full force was revealed, as though in three dimensions for the first time, only to be re-muffled when the door closed again. That music used to be forbidden; then we went through a period when it was compulsory; and then it was forbidden once more. The musicians were taken away, some said, or maybe they just went of their own accord, there were no further opportunities to play, or perhaps no-one would pay them. So they would have had to go away, or starve. Perhaps the people who might have paid them became afraid. There would have been consequences. There are always consequences; it's called cause and effect. You can't escape it.

The musicians had names. Some were big names and some only small. The soldiers, when they come, will assuredly have no names. That is the way with soldiers: they don't use names, only numbers. It's better for discipline. Names would only confuse the issue. Anybody can understand that. When giving orders it's more convenient to say, numbers XXX to YYY shall accomplish this task, right, make it so, and thus it's done, and the strategic military objective is achieved. Imagine organising musicians in that way, by name, especially as many of them had more than one name: for instance their given name, and their familiar nickname, and then another nickname by which they were widely known, to signify their particular musical prowess or quality of skill, such as "Honey Boy" or "Silicone Grease" or "The Little Flower" – well, you would never get anything done, you might accomplish an arrangement of a song maybe, but taking a complete city, forget it.

But we do miss the musicians, and what they signified. They were an odd bunch. Often they quarrelled, it wasn't always harmony. Some were your people, and some were our people; the bands had distinct grooves, grooves of a certain genre, you couldn't always define it in words or mathematical symbols, but there were undoubted differences. You only had to hear a bar or two and instantly you would know: that's your kind, or that's our kind. The great singers were on the radio too, we shall never hear their like again, each putting their own interpretation on the same age-old themes. I come from a great nation, yet I'm a poor man. But I'm rich in love. You don't know what love is. I know what love is. I would put out my eyes rather than see you with another man. All that kind of thing. A lot of drinking went on, and that helped to loosen things up and make them jolly, although it also led to fights and unseemly behaviour of all kinds. Some shunned the drink entirely, even cursed it. Some played for the glory of God, others cursed God or never thought about Him, or were enthusiasts for the latest scientific thinking from the West. And there was widespread sexual activity, I know this, though it's not advisable to talk about it too much. There was a lot of light and shade in the city in those days, not like now, when an even greyness, almost whiteness, presides. It seemed that time went by more quickly: day followed night followed day followed night; the morning would fade up with great suddenness, accompanied by an overwhelming clatter of pigeons flocking into the sky, and then would start the hum of traffic, people making their way to work, or if they had no work to do, strolling to the cafés in the great squares to dwell on their strong, fragrant coffees. And tourists would come by, in brightly coloured clothes, looking bemused in the heat of the sun, carrying the latest electronic gadgets; it seems incredible to us now, perhaps we imagined them. Perhaps there never were any tourists, it was all government propaganda. Wishful thinking. What would the tourists have come for, what would they have been seeking? I can't imagine too many of them would have been interested in the music, they wouldn't have understood it. They'd have been no more than "cardboard cutouts" in the audience, as a musician friend of ours once expressed it. So I can only think that, if they ever existed, they'd have been looking for something they had lost, but which they couldn't define; and if so, they were doomed to disappointment, because I think that we have lost it too now, and because it's lost we no longer even know ourselves what it was in the first place. But anyway, whether there were any tourists or not, the sun would wheel around the city, or the city would wheel around the sun, whichever way you chose to imagine it, and then dusk would fall, the delicious aromas of frying meats would waft across and mingle with the heavy scent of diesel and the fainter hints of animal exhalations and shit, and recorded music would flow from the ice cream parlours, with their lime green and pink neon signs flashing incessantly, and there'd be much activity elsewhere; in a garage for example the brilliant, livid flicker of an oxy-acetylene lamp accompanied by the harsh cry of machinery, the scream of metal on metal, and the swift dusk would penetrate into the parts of the city where it wasn't wise to venture, those alleyways where someone would call out from the shadows but where, if you had been around for any period of time at all, you would know enough not to reply and to hurry on as quickly as you could.

BLACK FLAGS hang at the city limits, or so it seems, though on closer inspection they prove to be just rags, or fragments of plastic bin-liners caught on the palings. You could imagine if you like that they were put up to welcome the soldiers, or at any rate to signify their imminent arrival. Were there an appropriate breeze, the fragments would flutter effectively enough to make a statement, it would be a performance of some sort at least, in the absence of any live action; but there has been no wind at all in the city for weeks, months. There's just the level haze, and a smell of mildew. So the black fabric is limp. The torn, blistering posters on the sides of warehouses are badly faded in the sun, their original vibrant colours almost gone, yellows and other warm colours having leached away and the spectrum shifted towards the blue and grey and violet-crimson. The golden age has evidently departed. Some announce concerts that took place many years ago, in the Theatre Royal or elsewhere; others have, or had, a more overtly political message directed at one or more of the factions that have done so much to divide our city. A generation ago, I used to play ball with my cousins on the pieces of waste ground between the warehouses here. The soldiers would have to come through here to enter the city. There isn't any other way, especially now the bridge has been bombed. But nothing is happening now. I think time has slowed down, almost to a standstill. We are looking to the military to wake things up, we are almost praying. Both types of poster, the musical and the political, occur in either of two modes of language. In one mode the writing goes from left to right, in the other from right to left. Since we are not completely sure where the soldiers are coming from, it's unclear which kind they will understand better, though it's more likely they will have little or no understanding of either. It's hard to see how they could. One way of writing is the way of your people; the other sort, with the lettering going the other way, pertains to our people's understanding. As a child, it always seemed puzzling to me, that a book could be written the other way, so that it seemed to start at the end and finish at the beginning. How could that be? You would pick up the book and open it, and immediately you would see that you were at the end, so that you'd have to turn it round and open the back in order to begin it. For the back cover would actually be the front, and *vice versa*. And even so, you couldn't understand it, you could make out a word or two maybe, and the numbers would be the same or similar, with sometimes a quoted word or a trademark standing out like islands in the alien text. And even as a child, because I was quite intelligent, the idea did come to me, vaguely, that you people must experience the opposite, that the text that was so transparent and normal to us would seem to you, on the other hand, distressingly contrary and inexplicable, and would engender the same disturbing feelings in you, that the world is maybe less familiar than it seems, a place where you could very easily become lost and confused and find no way home.

But what the soldiers are to make of any of it is anybody's question. We can't ask them, because they are yet to arrive, and even when they do I suspect that it will be very difficult to broach the subject. They will see the posters, they will look at the signs, and they will make of it all what they can. I privately don't think they will make very much of it at all, but we can only hope. That they are on their way, of that there is little doubt, at least so we have been told. We can imagine them marching along the dusty roads towards the city, as soldiers do, in columns of three or four abreast, in their fatigues and helmets, left-right, left-right, left-right, left-right, monotonously for hours on end, past burnt-out vehicles and the corpses of animals, left-right, left-right, unless the count flips over, as the brain might make it do after so long, so that it becomes right-left, right-left, right-left, right-left. That's what might happen, the monotony might make the rhythm flip. Everything would go the other way. That happens. As when you look at a photograph of craters on the moon, the stark shadows indicating indentations, and then something happens in your brain and suddenly you perceive the indentations delineated by those shadows as bumps instead, what had been perceived as concave suddenly becoming convex, so that the craters become mounds, and you know this can't be, that they are not mounds, they are craters, but you can't get this flipped image out of your head. That's what the long monotony of a march might do. So when the

26

soldiers finally reach our city, you can't tell which way their brains might have flipped, which way round they will perceive everything.

But, says one of us, that can't be right: this is the 21$^{st}$ century after all, soldiers don't go on long forced marches any more. They will be approaching in vehicles, not on foot, in armoured personnel carriers, that's the modern way. Heavy armoured vehicles, lorries, maybe even tanks. And if they are Americans, as many believe, those vehicles will be Jeeps and Humvees. For the Americans, the brand names are important, as indeed they are already becoming even to us. Or perhaps they will be in helicopters even now, or they will be paratroopers sitting in rows within the dark bellies of vast military aircraft, waiting for the first glimpse of the city to come up on the navigator's screen, waiting their turn to respond to an order and jump one by one into the blue air and float to earth to begin their assignment. Who knows where the soldiers are at this minute? At one time, we were monitoring developments, but we've lost the internet, we've lost the electricity of daily communication. It may be that they haven't even begun their deployment to the theatre of operations yet; that they are relaxing within their compounds, joking among themselves and listening to their mp3 players, throwing darts against the door of their barrack room, or polishing their great heavy boots until they can see their faces in them, safe in the knowledge that once they get their orders it will take them very little time to reach our city and complete the assignment for which they have been briefed. They will get things going. Then the party will begin.

They may be able to see their faces in their great shiny boots, but I find it difficult to imagine those faces. Some have seen them, and they say they are just as we imagined, but as for myself I have never seen them, those American faces, if indeed they are American, so I can only speculate. The young women will line up to greet them as they approach; we love you, Americans, they will say in English, even though some are afraid, because the soldiers have been going flip-flop, flip-flop, and they can't be sure how they will end up, it might be flop-flip. The sweet young things will offer them cigarettes and flowers with a shy smile, and it is hoped the soldiers will be observed to smile back, showing their white teeth under those heavy, net-encrusted helmets, they will give out presents. Are they really Americans? Some have very dark skin, even darker than ours in some cases, but if they all have the same dazzling white teeth, then that would mark them out for certain. They will hand out chewing gum, chocolates, memory sticks, magic markers and other toys. They will hand out comic books in which toy versions of themselves act out simplified scenarios, outlined in incomprehensible speech bubbles. There will be something wonderful or terrifying about them, an arbitrary quality that we have not seen before.

IT MAY be, however, that we won't ever see their faces at all. It has been said that the soldiers may be more frightened than we can imagine. They will fear chemical weapons and therefore they will be heavily armoured, with goggles and face masks, breathing their own private oxygen through tubes. They will resemble insects. No human contact will be feasible. That's a possibility. At the approach of our young women, they will take fright, because they fear suicide attacks; they will suspect the girls have wrapped armaments around themselves; at the first approach they will shout at them to stand back. The girls will see tiny images of themselves in the soldiers' goggles. The soldiers will go rigid. Their manhoods will be aroused by the appearance of the girls, but they won't know what to do. The city will echo with the tense reverberations of barked commands. They will approach and approach, with their hard manhoods and their hard guns and, for all we know, beads of sweat trickling within their face masks. But at least the period of stasis will have come to an end, things will start happening again, days and nights will begin to follow each other once more. History will be on the move. Is that a consolation? I hardly think so, but then, we hardly know what to think in these times.

I have to keep saying that the soldiers will come, believe me. There may be no sign of them yet, but it can't be long now. Something has to resolve. For too long, your people and our people have invoked God – your version and our version – as a final referent for our desires. And yet, God has not shown His hand,

and some say never will. Others argue that He's a busted flush. Therefore all we have left to put our trust in is chance. That is: the soldiers may come and we may see their faces and in the fullness of time learn their names, the names that preceded their numbers and that they have almost forgotten themselves, and so they will usher in a new era, of what possibilities we can't yet know. Or they may come, and we will not see their faces; they will be greeted, not by maidens with flowers, but by boys, and even girls, with their own faces covered by masks, with explosive devices and noble hatred, and in turn the soldiers' anger will be cold and terrible and because they are more powerful than us they will destroy the old order forcibly, they will kill us all and rape us, so that new life will arise only from our ashes. Only chance can decide this: left-right, left-right, one-two, right-left.

I can't contemplate the third possibility. This is that the soldiers will not arrive. That we will learn eventually, over the radio, or by a fleeting re-establishment of internet connection, that their generals have studied the maps and the intelligence, and, after long consideration, have decided to by-pass our city, deeming it too insignificant to squander resources on it. So the musicians have gone, the culture has gone, and now the soldiers would not even be coming to take their place. Nothing would have arrived. It would signify the beginning of the reign of Nothing. The black flags made of rubbish sacks would continue to hang limp, the posters would continue to fade, until whiteness, yes, absolute silence would reign. What horror! No, it can't be contemplated. Because the stasis that has enveloped our home and its history for so long already would then settle for eternity; and the day we obtained that dreadful news would be the first day of our everlasting death.

# A Memoir of Our Father

"I SHOULD never have left home," he told us on more than one occasion, his eyes glinting with tears. After that, we could never look into his eyes. Often we heard his voice, a voice that convinced on the surface; but when we didn't, we would ask each other "What's going to happen now?" and we couldn't find an answer. His glare alone was enough to destroy people. There was a long, vertical crease on either side of his mouth. Black looks were his stock in trade; he was puissant and cussed in equal measure. He had a strong disbelief which eventually turned into devotion. The simplicity of design of the monastery buildings, the flat, earth tones and shades of beige, all of this had an early and profound influence on him. He was only born in that house, the family moving away when he was three months old, so it was unlikely that the mahogany-framed bed on display was in any sense "his". All his life, he had a recurring dream in which he was a little boy in a city at night. This took place within the hidden compartment. Saw a lamb in the midst of the abandoned racecourse, and the little buff aeroplanes turning in the sky, just before he fell off his bicycle. The remnants of a goose touched it. Tops nestled in hay. You can't really blame him for not having a childhood: black angels hounded him all the way to Christmas. Soldiers marched past. The village was later burned down. As a student, he ate baby birds. Night after night, he would be engrossed in the theory of bundles. Gradually, he became less interested in doing further research in genetics, as an enthusiasm for administration developed, culminating in his being appointed as the Secretary General of the University. It is little known that

he was the author of books on normalcy, obsession, and genetics. It is believed he lost a testicle when injured on the battlefield
in 1916, the same year that the future Nazi leader is said to have
suffered his own, much mocked, loss. There was that later business with the pole dancer. What if that were true? After further
trouble with the police, he joined the staff of a local newspaper,
and wrote a novel that was never published. He was firmly
implanted in the world of learning and applying business technology to small businesses. This cheap transcendentalism offered
a kind of fake consolation, an apolitical quietism where communication failed and actions were meaningless. Amphetamine
withdrawal caused the spidery network of his nervous system to
hover free of his feverish body. His dance routines mainly
derived from martial arts movies he had seen on Arabic television. He was seen chasing our mother round the garden. If his
anal fistula was ever spoken about, it was only in hushed tones.
He made a name for himself leading attacks against nationalist
insurgents and in 1927 was promoted to full general and made
principal of the Military Academy. All opposition was ruthlessly
dealt with. It was the fervent wish of many that he would pay for
his crimes. In the dying weeks of the civil war, with the government on the verge of collapsing and the rebels advancing, he
held his position. He stayed loyal and tilted the army during those
tumultuous days in April, paving the way for a return to power
and restoring democracy. Everyone followed him. Those were
the days of his puissance. His headquarters in the Grand Hotel
were ringed by police gondolas, and detectives might be found in
every corridor. His cruelty was legendary. Later, he was stripped
of power and faced corruption charges that could have kept him
in jail for decades. They killed people in front of his face; it's difficult to know just what he experienced. He sought political asylum in Peru. He always maintained that God is a racist. He was
arrested in Osaka, western Japan, days after it was revealed he
had attempted to transform his appearance by undergoing extensive plastic surgery. His hair was thin and straggly and he didn't
look well. Then he covered his face with a blanket. Surgery was
not completely effective. He crawled into a cave in order to have
a religious epiphany. On the third day, he rose again and helped

to stabilise the economy, which had been ruined after the civil war. Not only did the economy improve during his administration but many people who held other beliefs were killed. He took no interest whatsoever in political or ideological matter. He was a small, weasly kind of fellow at that time. There is no reason to doubt that he was sincere when he portrayed the war as a conflict of civilisations. Mistakes increasingly plagued his life, and increasingly unnerved him; he became obsessed with how they had slipped in or why he hadn't noticed them. Dead poets were audible in his words and rhythms. In his spare time, he was a photographer, interested in language and images. A theorist and player of microtonal jazz, he reinvented the octave. There was little more to be said; but still he said it. Someone described him as "a lark with rented feathers". He moved quickly. It is these invisible qualities, the ignored moments and gestures, that give his life its beauty. No, that would be wrong. His vastness was exaggerated, and actually pretty stupid. His thoughts were collected, before being dispersed for profit. His language skills were excellent; he even read a whole book by Ted Hughes. Golden in his skin he was, an example to the neighbourhood (in some accounts). Using a camera with night-vision equipment hidden inside fake rocks, he brilliantly captured evidence of the fishermen's dirty secret, and with it the chicanery of those who profited from it. On his birthday, there was a big evening performance in the square involving candles laid out in the form of hearts, a huge PA and sentimental singers warbling melodiously against pre-recorded backings; and the square was thronged with adults, young people and whole families; but by early the following morning the pavements had been cleared and you wouldn't believe any event had happened at all. It was down to him that such disparate groups of people were able to overlook their differences for long enough even to contemplate such a gathering. But something was said. It has never been established exactly what it was, but that it was deeply troubling to him is beyond question. Once again, judgement is suspended. We see him, we hear him still. Piles of legal documents were emblazoned with his name. He railed against the cultural establishment. There were many who viewed him as a supremely good man; a hero possibly; possibly a saint.

He won a place on American television thanks to his bizarre stunts. He was the chief dolphin trainer on the US television series *Flipper*. That was a joke. It was his dream to make the sea and the forests ours once more. How can that be wrong? There was a real incident when he opened fire on the customers of his bank. Each night, he returned home drunk. He always hated those blue dogs. People recall his many acts of kindness, sometimes with tears welling up in their eyes. He was a peripheral player on the international stage. He had been brought up with little experience of change; he liked to repeat that everyone must accept their destiny. We used to listen to him on the radio. He showed us all a picture on his BlackBerry of a man exposing himself, with the comment: "What do you think of this?" Glinty-eyed as ever, he dreamt dreams of baroque splendour but didn't mean any of it. As though we were china dolls, all of our arms were raised stiffly in greeting to him. The narrow path he followed led him into the valley of the unknown. What made it beautiful was his timing. But he never liked the expression "numinal". Pale, the sweat beads standing out on his temples, he would smile at us and attempt to speak. Something wrong there. His proximate destination was never, in fact, to arrive, or be arrived at. He thought nothing of making a *pot au feu* from the offal of his steer. There was a graceful glow on his limbs even when he was doing such things. He wanted to be the man who set broad standards and found the money. Old dreams kept recurring; he would "murmur them in the mud". He was a keen trumpet and flugelhorn player. He was widely loved, especially by the common people. But why? Rumours of his condition provided inspiration for a notorious and morale-boosting song on the subject that was popular with soldiers. That was his cue. Fervour gripped him. At what point did he enter the domain of mythology? There has long been a division of opinion on this. Now he was even more interested in success than most Americans, because somehow, for all his genius, despite having built the largest factory in the world, he had spent much of his life being mocked as a failure. For a time, he lived in the grounds of Berlin Zoo. He called on us all to follow his lead and reject the old discredited regime. It was great fun. By then, he had lost control of his bowels. This anomaly has since been rectified. Details of the surgical procedures are not available. He used to suffer from bipolar disease and had periods of melancholia, but he was happy with that; it was the upbeat periods that really frightened him. This distinction is unimportant now. A mane of snow-white hair and a pair of glittering spectacles; these were his signifiers. What would *his* parents have made of it all? Each night, he would go through the photograph albums, meticulously discarding all those pictures in which the subjects were not smiling. I think I can almost see him, with almost complete clarity now, slumped, half asleep, over a pile of lobster and mussel shells. His work served to cast doubt on the value of the "self" and the "inner life". He used to say "Everybody dies – it's not hard." At dusk, he wandered through the deserted building; some people said afterwards that they had heard him crying out in rage once or twice, but this may have been a later embellishment. Among his "special friends" were Audrey, Mirabelle, Lateefa, Chou-Chou, Josephine, Ana María, Marta, Carlyle, Perdita, Fatima, Lauren, Frou-Frou, Russell, LaToya, Hannah, Jayne Marie, and many others whose names are now lost. His connection to poetry was profound; you could almost call it mystical. Even sunbeams were heavy in those days. Soon after his demise, the field was left to a fresh wave of admirers. The disembodied voice called out a name, and repeated this once or twice; but that was not *his* name. No, we are not up to that point yet. He deliberately deceived his doctors and family about his mental state over a period of many years, during which he subjected our mother to heavy irony, disparaging remarks, cold silences and other forms of mental cruelty, and for this I find it hard to forgive him even now. We were domesticated pets at ground level in his presence. He pilfered obsessively. It didn't help that he was undermining his own authority by indulging in sensual gratification on a grand scale. At that time, he appeared even more handsome than before, wearing a smile with an irresistible complicity in it. Autumn was his favourite season, as he said many times. He used his appearance to criticise Islam. He did not have any political views other than a hatred for certain groups of people. It was said of him that he "looked hard for things to think about"; but was it thought that ensued? According to him, we could never get anything right. He returned to performing zoological experiments. Wearing a cave-man mask, he killed a marauding crow. On later returning to the same crow territory, he was dive-bombed; but when he changed to a Dick Cheney mask nothing happened. Nobody expected this result. Among his friends there was some perplexity at the way his speeches were reported. In this, nothing would ever change. I remember him gazing out of the window at the fine rain that was dropping through sunlight in the garden, and being unable to fathom what was going through his mind. His nails yellowed, with ragged but blunt edges. The scent of virgin tobacco; the strike of a match; a fug of sweat in an airless room. Blood streamed from his nose and clotted in his beard. We gathered nettles for him. We never had any reason to fear him. He always had a mournful look. The alcoholic father in the novel was not a portrait of him but of "the man he nearly was". Blood from his rectum was caked thickly on the trousers of his uniform. A faint smell of dead cat pervaded his study. Slowly, he regained control of his pelvis. Two steps forward, then two steps back, always the same, over and over again, he would pace incessantly throughout the proceedings. Angrily, he hunted for the remote control so as to rewind each scene (which signified undoing the action). These were signs of a compulsion and anxiety to get things right. Because he could not be humble. So concerned in his earlier career with tearing down the social order, he later appeared to be weighing the positive value of civilisation. He possessed intimi-dating charisma and perilous charm. It is very difficult to estab-lish at exactly what point he underwent surgery. If ever you feel fear, self-pity or failure in your life, then surely you must think of him again. I have an etiolated memory of him, sitting at the din-ing room table, drawing a picture for me on a piece of paper of a plate with three fishes on it – one for himself, one for our mother, and one, he explained, for me – while all the time my sis-ter was being born in the next room. There is attention to, and mastery of, historical detail in his own accounts, but never at the cost of losing the thread or failing to draw out the general signif-icance of the detail. As children we would be given boiled milk to drink, but we didn't want to. And so he would tell us stories, and then he would pause and say "Drink your milk", and we did, so that he would resume the story. He was a collector of clothes that people had thrown away. He was accused of an extraordinary litany of racist and sexist behaviour by a former employee who claimed discrimination over her sacking. His own mouth was opened by those events; to those whose mouths were empty before being closed, his language itself was a tongue from beyond. It was that melisma of madness that he had. But this was not his voice. That's what they said. The point is that it's impossible to tell. It was claimed he stopped breathing deliberately. You can say that he was a failure. But when all seemed lost, he was the man who saved us. While our mother was twisting the silk scarf in her hands, not knowing what to do, he gazed abstractedly at her; then, after she had draped it on the stand, he came forward and guided her gently into the shadows. During an extraordinary three minutes in which the world became slow and indistinct, he seemed to hover as much as speak, his voice fluttering in and out of his throat. We couldn't believe this. After that, his heart was broken. He was drowned. And this he took from her, and wouldn't give back. I never really wanted to mix this all up, but it seemed appropriate at one time. He did not expect to be a free man soon. At the end of his days he was too thin to work. "His karma caught up with his dogma," quipped a bystander. His eyesight, by then, had gone. I could see by the way he was sitting, very stiff, with his hands clasped tightly together in his lap, that he was in his worst state of nerves. He lay down on his pillow and cried himself to sleep. Sometimes our mother had to get him out of bed and put his shoes and socks on for him. Friends and family said this would soon pass. But it did not. He would spend the day reading, watching TV and entertaining grandchildren and visitors. When the fancy took him he wrote a newspaper column. He was beginning to weigh us down, his mass seeming to increase with every second. His boots, his shirt, the slope of his nose, the great lobes of his ears. We wondered if he was truly a prisoner. His mass was his fundamental property, the numerical measure of his inertia. Definitions such as this often seem circular because his was such a fundamental quality that he is hard to define in terms of something or someone else. At the last, he welcomed the dark; spoke to a man on a horse from China. Towards the end, he did his business in his pants while watching television. Who cares? He is part of our cultural heritage, and effectively public property. But we could not bear the weight of him any longer. We were crushed in body and in spirit. Apathy claimed him. He was ill-defined by then; you could say he was dead. In his fantasy, hundreds of cockroaches massed in the corners of the room, preparing to crawl onto his feet and legs and over his hands. But gravity had undone him, and his massive head, weighing many kilos, rolled easily through the city streets. After that, his eardrums burst, and it was all over. We struggled to breathe the air he displaced. Those were the days before "reality" intervened. He ceased to be at the exact same minute as eighteen thousand other inhabitants of the planet. He left the kingdom of the living in total silence, packed into a container. Our children believe that he's in heaven now, watching us all. Most people would like this to be true. Visitors still turn up at his house every day. The property, which was supposed to serve as a literary sanctuary where he could find peace to write, was later expanded to include six hectares of land when he expropriated local farms and homes. Who was he? He was always a defender of Western civilisation. One day, he will return, and save us. But it's hard to even remember him now.

## Exile

WHEN I was in the world, everything was exactly the same as it is now. You could open a door, switch on the light, and there would be a room beyond. There might be a bed that could be folded in the daytime, or maybe a plastic-topped table with a china cup and saucer on it with a willow pattern. And the linoleum on the floor: imitating ceramic tiles. There was a stain on it, the shape of Asia. On the wall, a picture of a dead loved one. The wallpaper stared at you. You might hear the sound of a car horn for a moment outside in the street (was there a window?), and then it would be gone. Or a faint smell of fish might persist for a day or two, and someone might say: That's not fish, that's the light fitting that is perishing. It emits a chemical that smells of rotting fish. Everything was mutable: the photograph might disappear, or the cup and saucer. Now that I am no longer in the world, everything is the same but more definite: it's either there, or it isn't. And once it is, it is for evermore. Before, the cup and saucer might be gone next day, but a tumbler of water might appear instead, and you would wonder: was there a cup and a saucer? Now it's impossible to get rid of anything. The tumbler is there, but so is the cup and saucer. Everything is a ghost that lingers or accumulates, and that's because when you are no longer in the world everything is made of language. I used to listen to stories, but there aren't any stories now. Because the story is all there is. There are no imitations; or else, everything is an imitation. When I was in the world, I knew nothing about communication, but now we are in the age of communication. It's inescapable. So we are told. I can't remember who the loved one was, but you can look them up if

38

you use a well-known search engine. Everything is present, but also simultaneously absent. There is no strangeness in opening a door now. It's just a metaphor; or that's how it could be taken. You don't have to hold your breath, in case there's a stain on the linoleum that wasn't there the day before, or in case an object you remember on the table has vanished. That's not quite true, though. If I wanted to get rid of the cup and saucer, I could go back and delete the sentence in which it appears. But then I would have to delete the sentence I have just uttered too, the sentence referring to *that* sentence, and also any others with related reference. It could be done, if you really wanted to do it. You could eventually get rid of everything, deleting sentence by sentence. Amazing opportunities present themselves. I'm too tired, though. Right at this moment, I would prefer to go to sleep. This is actually paradise, compared to what I remember; but what am I missing? I'm missing something. And because I am no longer in the world, I can't remember what that is. You can laugh. Actually, *I* can laugh. I *can* laugh. Only the other day I laughed long and hard. I don't remember the joke now. Anyway, the point is that I am no longer in the world, for whatever reason, and the worst of this is that when I try to describe this world that I have left, I can't do so except in terms of the oddly similar not-world that I inhabit now, that is, the language I've become accustomed to, and which is all that exists. And there is no way out of this.

# Our Mother's House

By CONTRAST, the living envy the dead.

On the other hand, the dead envy the living.

And so on, until forever makes its intervention.

Nobody is happy, not in these times. But what do you know about it? How long is it since we heard her voice, speaking or singing? I disremember. The verdigris on the columns intervenes. The rust, the corrosion that is normal. So many years have intervened. I don't even have the photographs now. I remember that one showed a group of children who gathered or dispersed, with a view of water beyond the covers and of the empty wastes and pumps that no longer worked in the fields that were no longer our refuge.

And also, a song arrives in the memory: two old men sang it as they watched. "Criminals of war," one said, when he had finished, I don't know who specifically he was talking about, a point of verification that perhaps didn't matter, that perhaps it was not wise to elaborate, not with the army in the vicinity. They sucked small dark cigarettes and their eyes were glazed. "We watched what they did, and what nobody takes care of," said the other. That was all he could manage – I don't expect you to understand. Most of the great buildings, the apartment blocks, had been destroyed to their foundations, some become mere slabs, others collapsed entirely, the interiors of the apartments spilled towards the outside, each mixed up in the other in great waves of concrete, broken ones. Bullet holes were as multiple as ripe fruit in the landscape of our childhood, and many walls had been blown apart to reveal gutted homes, with the chipped furniture hanging in a dusty earthy mess, in a sweet scent of decomposition.

You have seen the pictures, you can judge.

One child in that photograph survived, to die only last year after being hospitalised with a brain haemorrhage. I admired him even then. They told me that in recent years he had a powerful impact on all those he met and that many at the University were very upset by his death. He was not in the group that day. Another child – I was going to say, another writes these words … but those, they who did not survive, were never really children.

Were they?

No, that's not right, for, as with all who had died in the conflict, they never ceased being children. "They have killed us dead," one might have said, "I was at home and now we have gone to heaven."

I am surmising.

Our mother had the greatest concerns for these children, as I will relate. She sang that song too; I can't translate it. There were reasons for everything that happened that we did not really understand at the time. They said the problems came from the south, I don't know. There were a lot of problems. You are talking about tens of thousands.


AT DAWN, we saw the soldiers approaching the town from a long way off. They moved slowly across the waste ground. They appeared like small insects, crawling, slowly, slowly, towards us, you know, like when you spy ants for the first time on the jamb of a door, at first one or two only, then, as you look more closely, three, four, nine, ten, eleven, twenty, more than twenty begin to emerge. First, there was nothing, just silence deep as a cavern over the wide, dark ground, and then suddenly there were one or two soldiers – but still no sound, you understand. They could be observed as small black isolated figures at first, in cumbersome armour, each clutching their rifle or other ordnance. They moved between the scattered dark thorn bushes in a line; there was no unseemly haste, they had the target in their sights. The dawn was yellowish in the sky above the distant buildings that could be seen, those suburbs we remember, some already smashed. You could say that it was a very peaceful scene, almost dreamlike. We

41

did not see the tanks, or the helicopters, until later. The soldiers took cover behind a thorn bush, then, after an interval, moved on. We didn't understand. We were not fighters. They were the sons of other mothers, I suppose. It's hard to keep that in mind, especially when you don't see their faces. The yellow sky. There has never been a photograph of this, it's in my memory, so it will die with me.

Many poets have spoken about war. They have these fine feelings about it, but we never had these feelings, I don't know why. We saw our town break apart and I know where it fractured. When you are hiding in the garage, behind the tractor wheel, terrified, you don't know about these finer points. I still wake in the peaceful early hours of a morning, many years later, and I see those soldiers coming nearer, carefully, without hurry.

It was supposed that the partisans were to protect us from such evils. They had spoken openly about the evil, and about the nobility of fighting it, and some, in this respect, were near to being poets themselves. Many wore scarves on their faces. One with a printed scarf bandaging his head, and a rocket launcher in his hand, was the most eloquent of all: he would never leave us, he vowed at great length, using many impressive words we had never heard before. But by the time the army arrived most of them had fled to nearby camps. Our mother predicted this; she was never in love with the partisans, though she was always loath to speak. "They need to re-wash their brains," is all she said once, in a rare utterance that made everybody laugh nervously, an utterance that she would not repeat. As for ourselves, we couldn't flee, we had no other homes.


I CAN'T describe our mother, who has always been in the shadows, principally when our father was alive, for one of the main shadows she was in was his. She washed and cleaned and cooked, like any mother. If she can be pictured at all, she is to be pictured in the kitchen, which was her domain, absolutely. My earliest memories were of sitting on that kitchen floor while she cooked, of how I would drag the pots and pans out of the cupboards and play with them. She didn't mind; even helped me fill one with water, from whence I poured into another pan. The only time she turned around to frown was when I caught up the lids of two pans and began to clash them together like a pair of cymbals, and then she made a motion with her fingers to her lips, to tell me that was enough. That was in the quiet days, before helicopters and rockets. Though we heard the beeps in our sleep even before the event. In those days, I played with my sister and the boys and girls from across the way on the staircases of our apartment block, which was our only home. We set out our toys – dolls and toy soldiers, pots and pans – on the steps and the landings. The washerwoman, on her way to the roof, used to grumble at us; she called me "Wednesday", because I was always in the middle. It's true that I organised; I was the eldest. Wednesday, you're here again, there's no peace for us, she would argue, and I would smile, uncertain of my response.

When our mother wasn't in the kitchen she would be on the terrace on the roof of the apartment block, working in the wash-house up there with the washerwoman. Sometimes the children would play on the roof as well. We especially liked when the sheets were up on the line, to play in the labyrinth of sheets. I should like to explain that our roof terrace was criss-crossed with washing lines from one end to another; as the bedsheets were washed in the wash-house with boiling water and powerful soap, our mother would iron them one by one, humming and singing all the while in a low breathy tone, that song with the words I can't translate, that the old people sing, something like "If I could, if I could, if I could, if I could…" over and over, and then she and the washerwoman would peg them up, one by one, to cool and dry in the wind that swept across our roof daily, until at last the whole space was covered by huge white moving walls; and we children, up to six of us, would wander between them, up and down the corridors so formed, would run and chase each other and lose each other and would get lost ourselves in the midst of the sheet maze, smelling only the scent of soap-washed cotton, kicking odd wooden pegs that had fallen down onto the tiles of the floor, hearing only our companions' shrieks and laughter but being unable to locate them; sometimes, when the wind blew, would be hit sharply in the face by the flap of a still wet sheet, which would make us laugh like crazy; and from time to time would emerge unexpectedly from the labyrinth and find ourselves in the open air again by the long concrete parapet that surrounded the terrace, from where we could see below the vista of our little suburb, extending beyond waste ground and scrubland, not yet ruined, into other suburbs and villages, white houses and apartments stacked around under a blue sky dotted with circling birds; and on the tiled flat roofs of many of those other buildings and projecting from many of the windows and balconies also other sheets hanging out to dry, a crowd of beautiful flags fluttering and flapping in the wind.


IF THE WILD geese could speak, they would tell me all things that have happened, for sure, because they fly so high they can see what occurs, with no difficulty. I can imagine that they curl their little flesh-coloured feet into their fat bellies, they strain the muscles in their necks as they fly forth from across foreign seas to migrate over our land. They see everything below, as clearly as one can. I feel coldness inside my eyes when I imagine that. Are they wild geese? I don't know, because they are too high up for us to make out. They are on the wind; they traverse weathers; they are not like us. I think maybe they are not geese, they are of other species: maybe they are swans or eagles, or something like that, but it doesn't matter. It is what they see that matters, but also the fact that they can't speak of it, and that it is therefore lost. Me, I can speak in my stupidity, but sometimes, I think, only to mute creatures such as those birds and animals; and I am no longer sure that I can see so clearly, so I don't know if I have anything to say, or at any rate anything of worth that will throw light on the subject, whatever the subject may be. I am not well, I have problems. My mind is attuned to fantasy, and also to fugue. I am a guest in this place where I find myself, forever a guest, I have no fixed place of my own, I am beholden. If I stay, it is only to rest for a short while, before I move on, before I resume my journey. Maybe I will try to say something before that journey resumes, the journey towards what I cannot reach. Maybe I will soon give up conversing altogether, and that will be a great relief.

Then I will only imagine birds, in their flight, I will hold in my mind the map of the territory that they contemplate in such clarity, such that I am not capable of right now, and even more than this I will admire their wonderful muteness, which can only be experienced as a release from a burden. But I can't help thinking, what if, what if, what if just one of these incomparable birds could be persuaded to convey what they made of the brutal patchwork they have viewed far beneath them?

NOTHING WAS seen, then. They say the children were shot for no reason at all. But what does that mean? That a mistake was made. There are always mistakes. It is part of being human. Whatever that means. They were not shot, actually, it was a rocket. It was an accident: the rocket was fired from a long way off, and it landed in the wrong place. That is another story I have heard. But for no reason? If children are shot, then obviously there cannot be a reason. So it follows that it's normal, children have always been shot for no reason at all. Actually, I could write a book, or many books, stating the reasons. But it's quicker to say "no reason at all". It's also more understandable.

Mistakes were made. She made one, even. In the heat of the moment, in the panic, you have to make a decision quickly. The army was coming, everyone was screaming, giving advice, to get out, to stay put. The older boy was away, our father was dead, the four youngest were scared, she told me: "You are eldest, you stay here until I can come back." She had to get them to a safe place, that was the idea. That there would be no safe place, that was not foreseen. Quickly, leave your toys, put your coats on, she shouted at them. One had to go to the toilet, she was banging on the door. She took them out. The morning air and brightness hit them. Their uncles had a car, she would be back before very long. Somebody cried out that they had heard a loud bang. It was confusion.

Then there was silence.

Then more confusion, loud noises, people screaming. Our mother had not returned. I waited and waited, until I could wait no more. A dream came upon me, in which I was running away down long corridors, branching into other corridors, escaping from dark presences that could only be glimpsed for less than a second.

Later, I was hiding in the garage, behind the tractor wheel, but I will not say more beyond that. It was the NGOs that found me. Since that time, I have been a guest on this earth.

Some say there never were any children. That is another version of what happened, or what did not happen. Those who say it have very understandable administrative reasons for this: it's too difficult to construct procedures, strategies, norms that would encompass this possibility, the paperwork would be immense. Easiest to say there were no children who lived in such and such places, therefore no children died.

Sometimes the doubts even creep into our own minds; it is a measure of the enormity of the situation that this can happen. The years have gone by, many many years, other things have happened, some good, some bad. Maybe there *were* no children, who can tell? I may say I saw them with my own eyes, I saw myself playing with them, every day of my short life for a period of ten years until that day when I saw them no more; but eyes can deceive themselves, there are any number of reasons to doubt such empiricism. I mean perhaps because the children have the bones of sparrows and their skins are soft like feathers, their heads are small, with squeezable bones. There is nothing to them, it's easy to miss them. Moreover, should those bones be shattered, should those heads be exploded and should the soft organs be dispersed, there may not be enough substance there to leave a lasting trace, not when the matter and blood and so forth is spread out over many square metres of broken paving and cobblestones; and as for the mother, well, a mother does her work invisibly and is soon gone.

OK, there were never any children. Let's say that. So, for convenience, let us add therefore that no mother was obliged to save them or guide them to safety. There was never a mother, only the same absence that has haunted us all these years, as you will see from what I related above.

There was no mother, therefore I was never born. I think sometimes that is the case; that nobody is relating these events, which in fact never occurred.

As I SAID, many years have passed. One time, when not so long had passed, we were taken back to the home we had once had. There was some idea about salvaging possessions, but we soon lost heart for this. The army were still patrolling the district in armoured personnel carriers; they were, they claimed, performing security operations, they were protecting the properties that had once been ours. The fact is, there was little left to protect.

In the street, thin mattresses had been deposited, and a punctured football lay in the gutter under the solitary eucalyptus tree. In the courtyard outside the broken apartment block were stacked up about a dozen fridges and washing machines. An army officer said they had been taken out to check for booby-trap bombs. We were invited to identify and reclaim which were ours. Inside, there was a powerful scent of dead fire and ashes; the concrete walls of the stair-wells and stairs where we used to play were smoke-blackened, and they were also covered with graffiti which stated many beliefs about our people, comparing us to certain animals of the field, and so on. On the stairs also were many excrements, but of humans or animals it wasn't clear. We gained access easily to our apartment, for the lock had been broken, and discovered all was ransacked within.

I opened the door to the kitchen, and all at once had an immediate sense as always of our mother's presence. But she wasn't there. Instead, there was desolation: the window was smashed, the drawers of the units had been pulled out and thrown on the floor, cascading all their contents, the pots and pans were scattered around, and in one I saw more excrement.

I went further up the stairs. Nobody spoke here. But the silence was broken by a low humming, a sweet cadencing that awoke my memory. I ventured up the broken stairs – some were missing altogether, so that I had to step carefully, for fear of plunging – until I reached the level of the roof, the sunlight pouring through the open door. And there could be no mistaking that voice, coming from the other side of the wash-house door beyond.

In the wash-house, I saw two piles of white sheets: one a crumpled heap apparently freshly extracted from the big washing-machine but that could not be so because it was no longer there, because the army had ripped it out; and the other a newly pressed pile, waiting to be hung out on the lines of the roof terrace. And between them, there was our mother, busy ironing the sheets, in her headscarf as normal, singing under her breath the same song that I remember – only now the words were something like "Unidentified, unidentified, unidentified…"

I called her softly, but she didn't even look up. She didn't see me. I said: "Mother, are you in Heaven?" (She looked happy.) No reply, she went on singing, the same lyrics over and over again, ironing and ironing, and when she had finished a sheet, laying her hot iron aside, she folded it (it was hard, for she had no help, but she could still manage it on her own, from years of practice, jerking the folds expertly into position) and laid it on the folded pile, and then turning to the wrinkled pile started over again on a fresh one. "Are you in Limbo, perhaps, Mother?" No reply. I would have offered to help her there and then; but I knew that the instant I did, she would disappear as though she had never been. I apologise, I don't expect you to understand this. It happened a long time ago, or it didn't happen at all. Or it is always happening. And there is no ending to the story.

# The Story of Nobody

SHE UNDERSTOOD quite early in her life that her name was Nobody. This was to be her signature, a fragile, beautiful, negative identity for a body that was nevertheless sturdy and well-made. Such understanding came while, as a small child, she used to hide under the piano, which she took to doing whenever her mother practised her singing in the mornings. The old songs, of Gypsy origin. An identity is something, like a poem, or like love, that has its own existence. Of her father, there is no sign; he was said to be an accordion virtuoso, but he left the scene early. Some disgrace was rumoured. But hiding under the piano? How could that be? Her mother had to make ends meet somehow; she would sing in cafés, in bars, in the north-western city where they had settled, wherever there was hard cash to be had. How? You can't hide under an upright piano, and a grand would have been inconceivable in that tiny fifth floor flat, in their circumstances. That's what they say, anyway, that's the story. It's only a story. A series of rooms, one leading off the other. Outside, pigeons congregating on the encrusted sills, rumbling in their throats. You would notice a certain behaviour at a certain measure, and the end of it some measures later.

Who knows, she may have been saturated with her mother's cadences even before she was born; they would have passed from abdominal tissues into the amniotic fluid. Sound does cascade, after all, and becomes solid before you know it, and long before it knows you. (But it may never know you.)

The city had a famous bridge. It was green, or greenish, but changing all the time, depending on sun colours. The number of stone blocks in its vault is 459. The weight is not known. The bridge was bombed in the war. That was symbolic. Later they rebuilt it. That also.

Or was that a different city? I think so.

What happens next? Her mother abandons her suddenly when she's fourteen years old, leaves the city with another man (I am surmising heavily) and never comes back. The mother's out of the story now. So she adopts the mother's identity, turning up at the restaurants where she (her mother) used to sing, in one of her (her mother's) old frocks, held together with pins and needles, begging the musicians to allow her instead to sing with them. They laugh at her. Who are you? they demand. I am Nobody, she says. She's pregnant, actually. All right then, we'll give you a chance.

Years went by, not easy ones by any means, during which she was made to sing in several different styles, not always the traditional style that she loved, so as to please the different crowds that frequented the bars and restaurants in and around the city, sometimes in their hundreds at a time. Always hard currency. She refused to shed any light on those years. Intellectuals, writers and artists began to adore her, wrote about her, constructed theories around her. Disco and techno came and went, turbo-folk too. The Socialists were suspicious, and the feeling was mutual. Synthesisers replaced acoustic instruments. The trick was to hold, actively, simultaneously and for a substantial amount of time, the many images whose totality constituted the reality of the day, and which defined the social structure. Although she rejected the overtures of radio and TV, her voice was pirated many times over for the admiring bog. Usually there was just about enough to eat and drink. This wasn't the same as intelligence, and she knew it, but what could she do? There were whispers of something different, but things didn't turn out that way. After being submerged for periods, autobiographical memories would be reactivated consistently moment by moment, but it's quite hard to keep up with them, and the facts they bring into provenance, and sometimes amnesia is the best policy. War was first on the horizon, and then actually arrived. She had two children by now. It was Nobody's turn to leave.

It's believed she went to Germany, where there were jobs to be had. That's it; that's all there is to be told.

Like her mother, she is out of the story. And it's kind of hard to tell a story, even though there isn't much to it. We are no longer guessing if the world is flat or round; we are wondering how to get from point A to B. Years go by, and nothing is known for sure. Where was she, what had happened to her? Nobody would or could say. She was in a foreign city (Hamburg? Düsseldorf?), and so she started dreaming in a foreign language (I am imagining again). The cadences, the prosody if you will, would have been radically different. She forgot the music. She got married, to a German, or maybe a Turk. These may well have been happy or prosperous years, but I am probably being sentimental now. It was most likely a marriage of convenience. She was most likely working as a cleaner, getting up each morning before it was light, travelling by bus or tram, getting by in German. Eventually, she had grandchildren. A big woman, with a rich, deep voice.

Hey, swan, swan…. Bells ring out over the river that continues to flow under that bridge. No, it isn't like a poem, that's stupid. There's nothing to it. She loved silk or chiffon scarves in pure colours. Her health declined badly. Blue-gold flash of a kingfisher darting from bank to bank. A faint smell of the detritus left behind. Above, the pigeons gently rumbling on the grey tiles. *Are* there swans on this river? She unwound the purple scarf from around her neck. How dreary to be Somebody, as a poet once said. To tell your name, constantly. She unwound the purple scarf from around her neck, gently draped it on the back of a chair and left the stage.

You're right, I'm constantly putting my own spin on it, for whatever reason. For example, I have mapped the scene onto an English river, many miles away. But *this* is a river that has seen war, that has maybe accepted human blood. I imagine a boy in love, caught up in the fighting, startled to hear the voice of his beloved who is hundreds of miles away – but it's only a voice on the radio. He's wearing the wedding ring on the finger of the opposite hand, as is the custom before marriage in those parts. A voice that haunts and drifts for just a moment, and then vanishes. Everything is being destroyed: the old stuff, but also the glorious future that technology was going to bring; it's not going to turn out quite the way that was expected and hoped for. War is receding now, and market forces are coming forward. That's pretty much the same. But underneath it all, there's a voice on the radio, the voice of Nobody. Who are you?

# Return of Darkness

**I am black, but comely, O ye daughters of Jerusalem,**

MY DEAR,

I know my message will come to you as a surprise is due to the political problem in this country, I am write to intimate you of a matter that requires an urgent attention after going through your profile, but briefly, I'm Miss Nellie Hendris, originally of Republic of _____, West Africa. I will be 25 years old by December 17. I weigh 58kg and of shapely form and good countenance. I am Christian since my birth in a poor village in my native country, I have good education, as you can see I speak and write English, I am teacher by profession. I am a widow, I lost my husband recently, I will tell you the story of this, and I have an inheritance from my late husband who is an Exporter and Importer in my country. I have been one of the bad places of the earth. For a darkness has come upon my soul recently, from a long way afar and I do not know where to turn. I was falsely accused, I and my lovely Sister, of which I will speak more, and I will describe to you so that you may know.

**as the tents of Kedar, as the curtains of Solomon.**

*— the utter desolation depicted in this rude scrawl was so overpowering. Then in a moment they acquired a vacant, terrified stare, as though they were striving to realise some half-seen horror; the withered old bundle bending down to kiss his icy lips as though in affectionate greeting. Those who waited upon her were deaf and dumb, and therefore could tell no tales. One of them, a*

*stout, excitable chap with black moustaches, was thunderstruck. What, how, why? The manager himself was there enclosed by a crazy fence of rushes. It was on a back water with great volubility and many digressions, surrounded by scrub and forest. A neglected gap was all the gate it had, about twelve feet by ten, and in the recess was a couch and a table whereon stood fruit and sparkling water. The herald laughed loudly, very hospitable and festive – not to say drunk. "Ye frighten not men with such swelling groans, blanket horrors, words," he cried out, strolling up to take a look at me, and then retired out of sight somewhere. The heavy pole had skinned his poor nose. Everybody had behaved splendidly! splendidly! With this shaft of sarcasm he retired, and almost immediately the sun sank, perhaps with as profound a meaning as the sound of bells in a Christian country. Then I saw the man with the weapon straighten himself for the effort. I saw the cold steel gleam on high, and once more I shut my eyes.*

## Look not upon me, because I am black,

I CRAVE your indulgence at this mail coming from somebody you have not know before. I decided to do this after praying over the situation. I want to tell you that I really want to been relationship with you. Though we've not met before now but it take one thing for two to be together in unity and peaceful life, which I will like to confide in you and also visit you as soon as possible. I look forward to discoursing with you. I will like to know firstly more about you. I need to know more about your love life. Your hobbies etc? My type of ideal man must be the honest type, caring, loving and forgiving as a devoted Christian. I do hate deceit and cheating in all its ramifications. I do not like a man that goes after everything in skirt. I detest alcoholics. It appears to me that you must be a very remarkable person. Everything belongs to you. You present yourself in my mind as a voice. I need not dwell on how I came by your contact information because there are many such possibilities these days.

## because the sun hath looked upon me:

*I couldn't help asking him once what he meant by coming there at all. However, all that is to no purpose. There's something pathetically childish in*

*the ruins of grass walls with a pretty border of smelly mud on one side.*
*Paths, paths, everywhere; a stamped-in network of paths spreading over the*
*empty land, darkening the moon. Be bold, fight, and be merry, before the*
*crows pick your bones till they are whiter than your faces! It had ceased to be*
*a blank space of delightful mystery. All quite correct. Farewell; perhaps we*
*came in sight of the big river again, and hobbled up and down stony hills*
*ablaze with heat into a recess; but now a solitude, a solitude, nobody, not a*
*hut. It had become a place of darkness, throughout the length and breadth*
*of the land. "We may meet in the fight; fly not to the Stars, but wait for me,*
*I pray, white men." Still I passed through several abandoned villages.*
*Perhaps on some quiet night the tremor of far-off drums, sinking, swelling.*
*Now and then a carrier dead in harness, at rest in the long grass near the*
*path, with an empty water-gourd and his long staff lying by his side. No use*
*telling you much about that. My mother died when I was a baby and since*
*then my father took me to lose myself in all the glories of exploration,*
*straight to the end of the vast and silent cave, where her loveliness did not lie.*
*She kept a vessel like a font cut in carved stone, all things of which I have*
*spoken, and special, with an imperial shape. "You must go and see the gen-*
*eral manager at once. He is waiting!" Here this extraordinary woman broke*
*off her speech, or chant, which was so much musical gibberish to us. "It*
*would be interesting for science to watch the mental changes of individuals,*
*on the spot." I felt I was becoming scientifically interesting.*

**my mother's children were angry with me;**

I WAS BORN and bred a Methodist. I was baptised so many years
and I am a confirmed member. I take my holy communion also.
I am a full fledged member of the church founded by Wesley
brothers, the great singers. It is many times that my Sister and I,
and my Brothers also, were singing in the church with great sen-
timent, what we have been taught by our parents who alas live
no more on this earth. This is in the village in which I was
brought up. We live by a mighty big river. That was before the
War, I will explain. We have all suffer too much. But before that
I and my family lived a simple life, I wished to learn much in the
elementary school, it was God willing that I should become edu-
cated, under the trees in geography and history and book-keep-
ing, also the study of the Bible and all the things that a young

girl should study. I loved the education, I wished to become a teacher, and accordingly I was sent to the training college in our capital, many footsteps took me there. I leave my village, where my Brothers play football in the field of dust, it was normal. I love all the small children, it is my wish and desire to have one day some children of my own, God willing, my dear. In those time, I dreamed many things. One night I dreamed that my Brothers were approaching in the long grass, naked and bearing weapons. For war had broke out. I was in the city, in a meeting with the man who was to become my husband, a distinguishable gentleman of older years, I looked to him to protect me, and so it was for a time. He was a great God fearing man, who wielded influence in his business, but always for the good. My Sister joined me in the city, fleeing, she reported to me the horror of what passed. The men came into the village, they were rebels she said, they grabbed what they could get for the sake of what was to be got. On the hill a big fire burned. She said many more things like this. Our parents were taken to a military detention camp, and it is believed that they had perished. The villages were abandoned. All our meagre breasts panted together, it was a blow on the very heart.

**they made me the keeper of the vineyards;**

*Now my customer, his wife and their three children were involved in a plane crash on board an ADC airline flight at the Ejirin River in Lagos, Nigeria. Unfortunately, they all perished in that crash. That night was a busy one, for weary as we were, so far as was possible by the moonlight, all preparations for the morrow's fight were continued, and messengers were constantly coming and going through the long grass, through burnt grass, through thickets, down and up chilly ravines, till you thought yourself bewitched and cut off for ever from everything you had known once – somewhere – far away – in another existence perhaps. It was the stillness of an implacable force brooding over the place where we sat in council. The glamour's off. So, one evening, I made a speech in English with gestures, not one of which was lost to the sixty pairs of eyes before me. They jibbed, ran away, sneaked off with their loads in the night. Day after day, with the stamp and shuffle of sixty pair of bare feet behind me, each pair under a 60-lb load. At last, about an hour after mid-*

*night, everything that could be done was done, and the reaches opened before us and closed behind the camp; save for the occasional challenge of a sentry, they sank into silence. Sir Henry and I, accompanied by one of the chiefs, descended the hill and made a round of the pickets. I had a white companion, too, not a bad chap, but rather too fleshy and with the exasperating habit of fainting on the hot hillsides. He warned me that because of envy he was poisoned by his close associates. He was very anxious for me to kill somebody, but there wasn't the shadow of a carrier near. Annoying, you know, to hold your own coat over a man's head while he is coming to. Was looking after the upkeep of the road, he declared. It was clear to us that none were sleeping at their posts. The population had cleared out a long time ago. Once a white man in an unbuttoned uniform, camping on the path with an armed escort of lank Zanzibaris, could speak with certainty. His wife served me a poisoned rice meal, but for divine mercy, her daughter, in a godlike stamp of softened power, secretly whispered to me not to eat the meal because "there is poison in the rice". As soon as a female child was born, this husband, who was never again seen, was put to death. The flabby devil was running that show. Why? To make money, of course. "What do you think?" he said, scornfully. If you are eating your dinner you think of poison and it goes against your stomach, and if you are walking along these dark rabbit-burrows you think of knives. I wasted the meal to the bin only to find two dead rats in that bin the following morning, and that made me run away immediately to Abidjan, the economic capital city of Ivory Coast. And the next morning… well, we won't talk about that.*

## but mine own vineyard have I not kept.

AT THIS TIME, my husband was falsely accused of many thing. He had enemies, as is normal in business, and they took sides with the Government and made many lies, so that it was insupportable. In this way a simple merchant is brought down. I've seen the devil of violence, and the devil of greed, and the devil of hot desire. Some events happened, then led to the arrest and detention of my husband and other men after a face-off with the Government on allegation of subversive activities and treasonable offence which was nothing but a mere political persecution. There was death and hidden evil done to us. The rest of the world was nowhere, as far as our eyes and ears were concerned.

One afternoon, I saw such and such men strolling aimlessly about in the sunshine of the yard of our house. They were to be seen gesticulating, discussing. I ask myself sometimes what it all meant. These persons were Godless. They intrigued and slandered and hated each other. They argued among themselves with loud voices. We did not know if they would attack. They went away again after some time. But one evening a shed full of belongings of trade of my husband, and I don't know what else, burst into a blaze and it was not know how this had happened. After five months in the military detention camp my late husband was announced dead by the government special press release. Although I had my Sister to console me, I couldn't have felt more of lonely desolation somehow, had I been robbed of a belief or had missed my destiny in life. When I went to the Government office to plead, or to obtain some informations, it was useless, and then I was myself arrested and put under questioning. What did I know about my husband's activities, etc, but I would not speak. Later, my sister came, and the police men questioned her also and tried to make her testify against me and my husband, but she would not, and thanks to God Almighty, I have been released for my innocence. But I knew I could not stay for longer in my native land. The government of my country is now making plans to seize what is left of my family wealth. Feel free to ask any question that agitates your mind on all this because I want us to build a solid relationship.

**Tell me, O thou whom my soul loveth, where thou feedest,**

*Then we returned, picking our way warily through thousands of sleeping warriors, many of whom were taking their last earthly rest. A great silence around and above made the land wicked in the sight of the heavens above. As we went, suddenly, from all sorts of unexpected places, spears gleamed out in the moonlight, seemed to emanate from the glorious air only to vanish again, and with a certain serpent-like grace that was more than human, when we uttered the password. A tremor vast, faint; a sound weird, appealing, suggestive, and wild. On she led us. White men with long staves in their hands appeared languidly from amongst the buildings, flashing eyes upon the deep shadow before her. Camp, cook, sleep, strike camp, march. A lot of mysterious niggers armed with all kinds of fearful weapons suddenly took to travelling. The moonlight, flickering along their spears, played upon their features and made them ghastly; the chilly night wind tossed their tall and hearse-like plumes on to the floor. An hour afterwards I came upon the whole concern wrecked in a bush. There they lay in wild confusion, with arms outstretched and twisted limbs; their stern, stalwart forms bright, and wicked eyes gleamed like those of a snake – sunk in a heap, looking weird and unhuman in the moonlight.*

**where thou makest thy flock to rest at noon:**

WHAT I DID not speak of to the authorities, was that a week before my husband was taken to the military detention on the 26th of June last year, he handed over to me a paper about a box that he said was containing $11.6 million US dollars and that it was highly confidential. I helped him carried the box down from the car to a place that he considered safe in premises of a Storage Company. I am quite sure that he did not disclosed to the Company that the real content of the trunk was cash in US Dollars, rather, he registered the trunk box as diplomatic immunities for the safety of the box. Before his arrest he told me that I should looking for a trustworthy man that will help me to transfer the money to his country for investment. That man is you, I believe and pray. I knew at that time then that it was possible I would not see him again, and he knew it also. He said that he willed a proportion of this money to any good Christian organisation for the propagation of gospel because according to him, he was saved through gospel, so it shall be done. I am now ready to carry out his wishes and must never have any hand in that which was willed for God's work. Since his death, I have been passing through family problems with his family members, and also the Government, which they had to freeze the whole accounts and his properties he had both in this country and in UK and took it to themselves, but they don't know about this box in the storage. That is why I have decided now to make a move by taking this money he gave to me privately into your country and invest it and that is why I have contacted you for your assistance.

## for why should I be as one that turneth aside

*Often I sit alone at night, staring any fixed abiding place that I had a han-*
*kering after. By this time it was not a blank space any more. She herself fas-*
*cinated me as a snake would a bird. Then the female child grew up and she*
*looked more like a bundle than anything else. Only here the dwellings were*
*gone, too, miles away from the least bit of shade and water. Other places were*
*scattered about the hemispheres. I entered the little room, and there stood*
*uncertain. "How many of these do you suppose will be alive at this time to-*
*morrow?" asked Sir Henry. I think his eye-glass and solitary whisker gave*
*him a fictitious value. "She is the evil genius of the land," he answered, "and*
*I shall kill her, and all the witch doctors with her!" Then all of a sudden*
*the long, corpse-like wrappings fell from her to the ground, and she hobbled*
*back, stopping now and again to address a remark, the tenor of which I*
*could not catch, to one or other of the shrouded forms. This woman was very*
*terrible, for all that we understood of what she was talking about, and*
*seemed to fix her eyes of the mind into the blackness of unborn time; the air*
*and curtains were laden with a subtle perfume. I entered, shuddering. Within*
*the curtains was… By it, at its end, was… The place was softly lit… But*
*of these matters none can remember. There is no such thing as Death, though*
*there be a thing called Change. I felt myself slide a pace or two down the*
*sloping surface of the rock, and then pass into the air,*

## by the flocks of thy companions?

I WILL ship this trunk through friends that I have that I trust, and
upon arrival in UK I will like you to help me to transfer this
money in your account for investment. Then I will prepare to
come over to your country we can live as family there, and will
share the money on an equal basis, minus the proportion that will
be given to charitable purposes. All I require is your honest co-
operation to enable us see this deal through. I guarantee that this
will be executed under a legitimate arrangement that will protect
us from any breach of the law. Please get in touch with me via e-
mail to enable us discuss further on this matter. On the notice of
your willingness to assist me, I will tell you the modalities we shall
follow to ensure a smooth hitch-free transaction, because I am a

novice in the field of transaction and investment. We want, for the guidance of the cause intrusted to us by your country, so to speak, higher intelligence, wide sympathies, a singleness of purpose. It is my pleasure communicating with you for the first time and believe that it will lead us to a Better Relationship between us. Well dear friend, I need your assistance so much, it will not be long before we can be together, and probably we can to develop our relations, and also my dear Sister after leaving our country due to the political crisis that led to war in our country. As I talk of you, I seem to see you for the first time. I feel that I am crawling, on my hands and knees, crawling as a small creature towards you, my dear. I am ready for creation family and want it very much. I want to live and be sure in the future. If this proposal satisfies you, please e-mail me immediately with your full names, telephone and fax numbers to enable me to contact you and work out all necessary modalities.

With all my heart, remain blessed.

I am waiting.

# Down with Beauty

WAR IS coming I'm telling you about it what is now won't last can't last and that what is coming who can say when the filth will be swept away when the language will be cleansed when our hands will shape up when the button will be pushed when the adorable scholars will prevail this is a wake-up call

you won't find my identity I dance with thousands I ride ISDN I ride ADSL I'm the proverbial my fingers are dancing always you know what I'm saying you come to home-page you come to what's it called the donkey the automatic rifle you come to how-to you know it's a school of thought that hardens seeking victory the choice weapon I'm talking infrastructure yeah I'm talking special needs yeah I'm talking language and not by all under which secure is considered and reward yeah and deserving of by so doing and not by the sum total it bring misfortune and death by the hands of God being in the carrying out of duty yeah for other believers it come to be essential information on the enemy you to urge the scholars them adorable scholars with endurance in battle

you come close I shoot I push the button I will not be satisfied in battle enhancing the endurance of both the heart and lungs increasing muscle mass and strength respond sweetly to adore to destroy it don't matter which it is always recommended you understand recommended to display to the children the spirit of never weaken by all possible means you know what I'm saying a kind of chastising by invoking tearing the plaster off the walls and cutting each other with scissors what's that going to do you're a hypocrite know what I mean a hypocrite why are you reading this why are you listening to these why are you looking at my language you don't speak my language you don't understand my sacred duty you know my language is not your language and anyway you stole it I got nothing to do with it

but actually this sacred duty re broken bones re providing infusions to not give aid in any way to the enemy you are the enemy is recommended is morally corrupt you understand is recommended to tell which justify I say justify the way of what happen to weaken the spirit it can't be that's what it means yeah you have to go towards lifting you see what I'm saying is in my language to tell the truth about what's going on is not right is not correct you know wherever say you're going to the gym wherever you go to the library is full of lies where you gonna go

how-to you know my hands is cut I say cut but this is not what happen you try your best that's not good enough a life of dissonance that's what they say dissonance is not what I'm saying whether you're an engineer or a doctor you might have conservations whatever to discuss issues with interpretation any issues you might have it's your right there are many issues it's not for you to say is not allowed commanding what is righteous and forbidding what is wrong let's wake up

they say what you doing you waging war on America it's laughable how can I declare war on America it's laughable Germany declares war on America Japan declares war on America Mexico declares war on America Osama bin Laden declares war on America George W Bush declares war on America the Jews declare war on America Obama declares war on America how can I declare war Israel declares war Hitler declares war on England Churchill declares war on England Maggie Thatcher declares war on England Blair declares war how can I declare war give me a break what can I do just wash my hands I take the pills it's a joke I got no army where's my army you show me my army they're hiding yeah they're hiding behind the corrugated iron behind your Toyota yeah they're gonna come out boo here's the fucking army excuse me army

shame and lies is what I say you say values I say shame on your values you say democracy and human rights I say what democracy what human rights you say freedom I say down with freedom you say discrimination I say down with discrimination you say competition I say down with competition you say free market I say down with free market you say free speech I say down with free speech you say rule of law I say God's law rules you say education I say down with your education you say feminism I say down with feminism you say prosperity I say down with prosperity you say beauty I say down with beauty you say the earth in all its glory I say down with the earth and all its glory is a farce you know and everybody knows you may say greetings but I reject your greetings your issues are not my issues you say chance I say shame you say good I say bad you say music I say noise you say mixed I say pure I say it loud what is coming is what it was before you came what is coming is

this what is coming will come you can't stop it what's to come is the future isn't it it may not be your future you think it's the past OK but what comes from the past goes into the future is in the hands of God I say it loud the future is the past made into glory

you own me but you don't own me reptiles in fine dresses but only reptiles and dogs and pig-like things things I've forgotten shame comes before a fall they say I will now be sworn so help me God I speak in plain English anyone can understand you understand we make agreement I say I up and down head movement by almighty God

what you want to know is when is it all going to start you know what I'm saying when's it going to start you say there's nothing going on well everything's going on you say you can't stand it it's like high and dry you might as well be anywhere the corrugated iron the dog the dirty dog nothing's happening you say painless I can't tell you painless in this place or space or whatever I can't tell you I have nothing to tell

dog is dirty is what I say there is dirt see and what isn't is what I'm saying that is the animal is decreed is whatever don't give me that fucking bow-wow

everything slow me down everyone do their best to slow me down you come in a cluster man a cluster I don't need that I don't slow you see me slow you don't you are the enemy don't forget that yeah that's what I'm saying

we have avenues to pursue all avenues many you understand the enemy are down many avenues it's a big operation too big for many of us we can only fight to defend ourselves our families not only for us no we are under attack our social values you understand

it's war and there's ugly things happen in war such like you know what I'm saying you can't stop it which means all of which you understand there are things that happen on all sides it's true I can't have responsibility for that especially non-specific you say killing of a child well killing of a child is not allowed it is specifically forbidden or raping of women specifically forbidden

but that was in the vision the big idea which is the coming reality OK it all comes down to that has nothing to do with it such things are condemned in America in the UK in Pakistan wherever that is the reality OK that what will happen will happen anyway that it will you have to understand it's crucial it's big stuff

lies is all lies whether spoken or on paper or money money whether electronic or paper I need it to buy a shirt I can't buy a shirt without money dollars pounds euros whatever you see what I'm saying you have to go along with it it's too big but there are social values you can't put it on paper or if you can people misunderstand it man I can't have responsibility for that if it's lies why all the lies I don't know it doesn't signify more than a barking dog this is massive you know what is coming the fuse is lit what I'm saying lit which means there ain't no going back you can say anything you like massive I can't speak of it what is in the reality what you think is not real you say I make war on English it's not right it's not I make but what I am made you can't go back it will all come back you know what I'm saying

say human what you mean human values I don't know I don't say human might as well say bird or animal I say brothers whom I trust I lost my way I was taken from my brothers after months of suffering to my eye my stomach my bladder my thigh my reproductive organs and I feel all that all the symptoms human I can't speak clearly human all other things being equal I don't say human rights I certify that what I say is a true record so help me God leave me be

I don't have a view in favour of burning of farms or of children etc

so I say you English I demand you sauce bottle no brothers you think I love well you got to think again you English human relationship you lie in spoken or whatever language whatever right you are deviant what is coming to you you dogs and hypocrites you don't care you don't remember what is coming I tell you

it was you who put me here but God will get me out by my eye my stomach my bladder my thigh

put me in an underground room with you know fluorescent tube lights one table with formica top two chairs leave me there go away come back this and that and kept asking where I was at this and that date I get confused what do you expect I try to answer to the best of my you know I'm trying to add it all up I didn't speak to anybody all day how can they say what I said they say it conflicted with what I said but I don't remember at all it don't add up how can it

you think I love a prison nobody loves a prison how could they therefore I can't love the world because the world is a prison for me and it don't matter whether I'm in or out this is it whether it's soft or hard it don't matter I can write my name on the paper on the wall it don't make no difference

if I am a foot soldier if I am or not I don't know you say that you can say anything some say why should fear killing destruction displacement orphaning and widowing continue to be our lot while security stability and happiness be your lot that's a point of view it's valid anything like that is valid in a war

there are three categories that come to us fundamentalist extremist and fanatical I would not work with the fanatical in fact they threatened my life because I wouldn't work with them it's true they deceived me I don't have such relationship so how can I be a facilitator in something unspecific it is ideas only it isn't in relationship to that is negative I express this by shaking my head from side to side

I'm in this place right I've been put here it's not my doing they are the criminals that's what I'm saying they are the criminals what put me here what the brothers say I don't care put me in this space they laugh they give me holy war software they think it's a joke is not a joke these are the games they play they say you wanna see your girlfriend I say I don't got they say wanna see your girlfriend she not my girlfriend what you talking about this is forbidden what they say I don't slacken

yeah they say I have a child I say that's not my child I can't remember exactly I don't recognise your number this is not my calling card I don't remember if I had a child it would be dedicated to God you know what I'm saying how could I forget if I have a child it's like

I wash my hands of all this anyway I wash my hands they have provided a basin that's all I wash and wash a rude basin that's all there's a bit of soap no plug a rough small bit yeah I wash my hands till they bleed yeah see the soap it consumes itself you know what I'm saying what you gonna do with that you got issues it get smaller and smaller day by day when it's all done there is nothing left it disappears itself you see what I'm saying the bit of soap get smaller and smaller until it is no more I can't say I don't have issues they put me they put me they can't they can't I will go further into this thing further than anybody they can't do nothing about that further until I consume myself you can't do nothing I consume myself entirely yeah

I say to you I wash it all away I shall be all washed away altogether myself and all yeah bit by bit you won't see me bit by bit I consume myself I will be nothing I will be in the hands of my maker washing away and washing away till there's nothing left you can't do nothing man yeah probably it doesn't matter yeah I'm very happy with that very happy I don't know about relationship I will get married God decrees I will get married a hundred times

I don't remember he said greetings I don't remember and then he says what's up and I say I don't have any problem and he say yeah by God's grace you sure you got no problem I called your mobile there was no answer I got the number wrong whatever see what I'm saying he said yeah yeah meant you were free to talk and he said he was my brother what happen I seen it on the BBC

greetings means you know everything all right he say greetings by the grace of God I'm all right that's what he mean I mean he didn't say nothing about a child the child was born premature he never said nothing about the mother of the child that's a separate issue

I do not be scared God will protect happen then you do not worry well I got issues but not about that not about all that I told him I got a child I got a child born that was me they say they have arrested certain people I say so what what's that got to do with me I don't know much about it a sick child I don't know nothing I am sick with my knowledge

get this number what number it's a US number yeah he says greetings it's a private matter you know what I mean yeah it winds me up in relation to you know in relation to all that we were previously discussing it was on my mobile

there was a child yeah OK

my child yeah I have a child was born by C section my child was not doing well I don't remember exactly the mother of my child was called away call me on my mobile I was trying to speak it's difficult I'm trying to add up the pieces called from the hospital he say speak or tell I am not able to I don't remember the number couldn't get through I'm not being funny can't remember the time this was not my calling card a child yeah I have contacted that was soon after it was on my mobile the police have gone through my contacts they say you trying to be tricky I say I'm not being tricky

yeah I call up I go straight to the house I go straight to the yeah my mobile go straight to my email this was my Yahoo account I don't remember it was the middle of July her birth wasn't proper it was premature I may have said some things they make me say some things it isn't true but what I'm saying now is true is the truth so help me Allah God that the main thing I did was not what they said they have issues with that I say I have issues very difficult I try to call as soon as I can

I say that wasn't my child they confuse me they try to make me say something I have a sense of responsibility you know what I'm saying they are talking about a different thing a child was born by emergency C section I would not want to bring a child into the world I have no love for

I don't know nothing about the mother leave her out of it I know what happened she don't know they try to make her I went yeah OK this was me she was provided for she was OK he was not telling told him that I that this was that's your interpretation I said I'll give details and that she was not my life I will get married a hundred times I will get married in glory what's my name did I change my name yeah you can google or whatever is full of lies you understand is all lies a name is a number is what they say damn statistics I don't know I can't tell you they say free speech but there ain't no free speech you won't find it you put me in this place in this little room but I got all the space I need yeah I'm a dancer man I am a dancer I have a child by whatever means possible it's what anyone would do you understand me you say feel responsibility but what about your responsibility you don't say nothing about that I wash my hands of it I don't want nothing to do with it would I push the button yeah I would push the button or no I would not push the button whatever yeah they are lies all little lies and one big lie I have no name OK I am nobody

what is my name well what is your name well you cannot say it doesn't matter anyway that's the reality is such and such a rela-tionship or such and such I could say I don't remember it don't make a difference or it might but who could say when you are gone or I am gone

the concrete walls the cage the dog the dirty dog it gets smaller and smaller until it is no more

you go to the cashpoint you have to give ID you have to give a PIN what does that signify is that your name it don't mean noth-ing except that an institution believes that you exist which may be true or not

my name or your name it don't matter what does it matter you can change your name maybe I changed my name maybe I didn't why there are many reasons I push the button I change my name you make me say that you gave me whatever name you invent in hypocrisy I have this space because you put me in this space I have no name I'm not confused you understand I used to be con-fused that was in the past I've gained what you say my name has changed it isn't anybody's business a name can be of something or of nothing you can give a name to nothing and make it some-thing or vice versa you understand what I'm saying

# New Found Land

HOW MANY of us are there? And for the majority of us, if not for all, who are we, or they, or is it that we don't know we are ghosts, or characters, as some call such entities? Believable characters, we are told, are what it's about. Do they, or we, live their lives, day by day, heeding only the spaces they inhabit at any one point in time? What can anyone do, in any case? What can they do? Eat whenever they can or must, drink, defecate and pass water, thus preserving the symmetries; engage in complex rituals offering advantage and obligation (not always in equal measure) (otherwise known as "relationships"); give birth, or procure this act, quarrel, die (or imagine that they will transcend this eventuality by means of translation to a new and undescribed state of ghosthood – a protocol sometimes known as being "saved", or elsewhere as being "reborn"). They say some here adjudge themselves to have achieved happiness, or at least are dutifully engaged in the endeavour to "pursue" such a state, as designated in the American constitution, but then, we are not in America; yet others do not; and the majority don't know, or the question is not relevant.

And where in hell or heaven are we? Space is constrained. For a long period, there was darkness and great heat. I think this space is akin to that of a slave ship, and the passage is one of that sort. It may have indeed been a ship, or at another point, a shipping container or lorry or even an aircraft. A big dull cage holding about 20 of them (of us?), with one toilet to share, or none. And a bunch of refrigerators, which have probably been transported from China. At any rate, a long period of travel in the dark. In between, also, a dank, dingy room, suddenly and harshly illuminated by blue-white fluorescence. Someone got punched in the mouth, or in the eye, was it – anyway, there was blood, momentarily. There was a flash of steel. It was all suppressed by the leaders. These are ghost-people who don't even have names. You don't ask them.

The destination is the United Kingdom, a place of the imagination, where about fifty or sixty million of the ghosts reside. There is a Queen, who lives in a castle. Unclean animals are worshipped. Language is subtle. There are large plasma screens, and fast computers. There is football. The old are not respected. Young people don't feel a sense of love for themselves. All-day drinking laws were introduced. Police frequently come across mobile phone footage of young men posturing with guns, which may be real or imitation. Other than that, little is known.

## DRAMATIS PERSONAE

HERE IS a list of characters in the story, roughly in their order of first appearance: Shaheed; the unidentified English gentleman on the island; Mimi; Mimi's father (who doesn't actually appear); her brother Gary; Gary's mate who is not named; Mimi's mother Jo; Richard and Annalisa (they too forever waiting in the wings, as it were); Emma; Rosie; Wayne; Lorraine; the handyman Geoff; "Craig" and "Craig's mother", played respectively by Michael and Maxine; Michael's real mother (and her partner, Serge); Michael's partner, Christopher; also a number of detectives and police in decontamination suits, interrogators, burglar-ghosts, surgeons, uncles and those others who cannot be named, passengers and other customers; and, finally, shortly after the high point of the narrative, Miranda. The characters can be thought of as representations of spectres that may flicker across the consciousness of those of us who are dreaming, those of us who thus have no access to our own representation.

## WELCOME TO THE UK!

IT IS SHAHEED who travels, and after he has travelled a long while, he arrives. Welcome to the UK! That is what it says; he can read it. Sand arrives with him. He's got some kind of imaginings in his head: such as, a superior party attended by burglar-ghosts, whisky that tastes like aromatic urine, pin-up girls on every corner. Digital clocks help trains and buses run like, well, like clockwork. There are computers to take care of his dreams! Most of all, money, lots of it. Shaheed resolves to stay away from the drugs, that's important to him. This is a delicious-smelling world; the nightmares are over. The skin beneath his eyes is peeling. An uncle directs him to the door of a house, an apartment – it's in a part of London, a local area, one of many, for London is absolutely enormous, for it seems as though there is no finish to it, it goes on and on to all parts of eternity; but the floors of the rooms in this flat are completely covered by carpets with the colour and smell of dust, and each room leads into a further room. People's voices sound like pistol shots, and it's cold, but he isn't scared any more, because he has arrived. One of the uncles says, "Muslims are more proud of local area than any other faith." Soon, his life will begin.


## SHIPWRECKED

AFTER MANY years of travelling and hardship (said Shaheed, speaking later), I finally arrived at the greatest country on earth, the United Kingdom of Great Britain and Northern Ireland.

My earliest impressions (he continued) were gained from the time I spent marooned on a traffic island near the edge of one of the great cities of the world: London. I spent my days watching the traffic zooming past, and I knew I was in the UK from the delicious aroma of fish and chips wafting to me from across the hard concrete. It wafted every day, except Sundays, which I understand is the law; but the wafting was exquisite. Also enticing to me was the vision of you within, a goddess whom I could espy dispensing to the customers with your exquisite skill of the oldest civilisation on earth, and of this I will later relate. However, I could not get across to actually partake myself at that time. But from studying the traffic that intervened, I got used to which side of the road to drive, which stood me in good stead. So that now, when I pause to think, which side to drive, which side to expect traffic, I always have the signature in my mind of sitting on a fashioned boulder on the side of that traffic island.

Wait a minute, I don't think that was me, said Mimi. You've got it all wrong. You have the chronology wrong. *And* the geography. Whatever.

Mimi always had difficulty understanding him, right from the beginning.

I had many conversations (continued Shaheed, heedless) with a distinguished Englishman residing in this place that was a traffic island. He had heard or observed my footprints (I could not understand precisely) before he actually saw me and we met. I don't know whether he was trapped there, like myself, or disinclined to get off. He related to me interesting stories of his childhood in old Shanghai, so immediately there is a connection with you there, you see. Do you know Shanghai? No? Well, it doesn't matter. He wore a well tailored English suit of light grey, a striped shirt and a tie, but his clothes had become shabby since the beginning of his sojourn, his hair fell down over his collar, his face was unshaven and his speech was slurred. I think he had a secret store of drink, of which once he offered, but I didn't wish to partake myself, owing to cultural norms. Of his stories there was no end. In response to his questioning about my origin, I replied: They told me I had arrived in Kent, but the cliffs were not white as fabled, they were a dirty grey, from what little I could see. Kent is the garden of England, my mother (God preserve her memory) always used to tell me, but I saw no flowers in all my journeying through.

He did not comment about what I said, this English gentleman, but merely smiled, as if to say he knew.

Once he pointed at the tall lamp that shone its orange light on us night and day, and remarked "That is pure information!" before relapsing into laughter. Like many Englishmen, he loved a drink and a joke.


## A BALKAN AIR

MUCH LATER than all this, Mimi has a significant hospital appointment, and so she has taken the entire day off. For now she lies abed cradling a big candy-striped mug filled with an apple and cinnamon infusion, feeling genuinely nauseous, companioned briefly by a cat of a tabby persuasion which then jumped and wandered off, its tail vertically stiff. (Was that a real cat?) Soon, apple and cinnamon will spatter the door. In despite of her actual heritage, there's a Balkan air about her: hidden wars, ancient grievances. Her mother is solicitous on her behalf. The density of the morning light outside the window is quite impenetrable. And she reads in a magazine about the fashion accessories of the future: "They might include tattoos made from tiny light-emitting diodes, sensors giving readouts of metabolic functions, or strapless digital watches embedded in the wrist. Meanwhile the poor will remain with us, unemployable and unable to afford the body of the future." Etc. As a matter of fact, she purloined the magazine from the waiting room on a previous occasion at the doctor's.

Furthermore, on a pullout page, she is instructed as follows: "Please indicate the activities which you *or your partner* enjoy on a regular basis: ☐ Bicycle touring/racing; ☐ Golf; ☐ Jogging/physical fitness; ☐ Snow skiing; ☐ Squash; ☐ Tennis; ☐ Bowls; ☐ Hiking/walking; ☐ Fishing; ☐ Hunting/shooting; ☐ Motor/power boating; ☐ Sailing; ☐ Crossword puzzles; ☐ Eating out; ☐ Gardening; ☐ Grandchildren; ☐ Household pets; ☐ Motoring; ☐ Motorcycles; ☐ Car maintenance; ☐ Do-it-yourself; ☐ Entering competitions; ☐ Going to the pub; ☐ Health foods; ☐ Slimming; ☐ Fashion clothing; ☐ Model making; ☐ Photography; ☐ Science fiction; ☐ Sewing/needlework/knitting; ☐ Listening to recorded music; ☐ Book reading; ☐ Current affairs; ☐ Fine art/antiques; ☐ Gourmet cooking/fine foods; ☐ Wines; ☐ Theatre, cultural/arts events; ☐ Religious activities; ☐ Caravanning/ caravan camping; ☐ Package holidays; ☐ Foreign travel; ☐ Charities/voluntary work; ☐ National Trust; ☐ Wildlife/environmental concerns; ☐ Coin/stamp collecting; ☐ Collectibles/collections; ☐ Going to bingo; ☐ Shopping by catalogue; ☐ Stocks and shares; ☐ Unit trusts/investments; ☐ Cards, board games; ☐ Further education; ☐ Home computer games; ☐ Internet, social media; ☐ Personal computing; ☐ Science/new technology; ☐ Watching video films; ☐ Watching sports on TV; ☐ Cigarette smoking; ☐ Pipe/cigar smoking; ☐ Other (please indicate)."

*Or your partner,* she thinks bitterly.

After a great deal of further considered thought, she indicates, writing in "NONE".

Undernourished, with bad, whitish skin, in her mind Mimi is a fat girl, but in reality who knows? Objective reality is not attainable by human beings; there are only narratives. She lives with her mother in a nice flat above the shop (the father from Hong Kong is permanently attached there), and somewhere, but not easily trackable, a nice cat that does make a very fleeting appearance or two, more than can be said for the father in point of fact. The cello rests, abandoned in its case, against her bedroom wall; she has not practised in a month. She is like a child, so perfectly self-contained within her small features. She has given up on wanting people to think her attractive and will settle for their not being excessively disgusted at her repulsiveness. Pale eyes, straight dark hair. Her resemblance to Hitler (once she's removed her glasses) is palpably obvious in the bathroom mirror. In her estimation, she lacks only a black smudge on her upper lip to complete the likeness. Mimi's real problem has to do with that partner business. Actually, that isn't her real problem at all, it's merely a consequence of her real problem. Yes, her only love, currently, is a cat, which is nowhere to be seen. Shortly, her younger brother Gary, and then her mother will make an appearance, and there will be further grief.

## OFFICIAL LAUNCH FOR HI-TECH MANNEQUINS

A WOMAN lost her job because managers at an exclusive London club thought she was too young. Guns can provide an intoxicating and almost pornographic attraction to young men. Young singles opt for novelty over age and character. No wonder there is concern about toxic childhood. The ground staff are trying to remove as much surface water as possible. State-of-the-art mannequins that can simulate breathing, moaning and even have a heart rate are being launched at the University of Wolverhampton.

## THE GREAT ESCAPE

THE STORY of how I escaped is too long to relate, continued Shaheed, but basically I noticed at last an underground exit from the island. At first, I was put off by the powerful scent of human urine emanating from this tunnel mouth, and turned away repeatedly, but finally I steeled myself and when I went in it was not too bad. Messages had been sprayed on the walls in a variety of coloured paint, but although they seemed to be in Arabic script I couldn't read them. There was a network of concrete caverns in there, and I soon realised because I saw into these dimly lit caverns on each side that were filled with endless rows of shining vehicles that this formed an underground car park of incomparable dimensions.

How did you feel, at that time? inquired Mimi politely.

I very much wished to be reunited with my uncles. And so, seeking a way out, I made my journey through the passages, following the yellow line that was helpfully painted on the ground. And then, in the midst of this underground car park was an extraordinary sight.

Mimi: What was that, then?

I saw advanced surgery being practised, amidst flashing police lights and much commotion of this sort, for perhaps there had been an accident? It took place in, you know, the space for a car, in between the pillars?

Mimi: In a parking bay?

Exactly, said Shaheed, a parking bay.

Mimi: Fucking hell.

It was all fitted with the latest hospital surgery equipment, all the powerful lights and tubes and monitors, in which I was very interested, because of my background and studies, this space where there was emergency surgery taking place you understand, at that very moment, and I stopped to watch. Yes, this was interesting for me, to see what procedure was being carried out. Hello, I said, I have seen this on internet! Nobody noticed me, they were all busy attending to the patient on his bed, who was attached in various places to various equipment. So I wondered if I could help, and I decided to introduce myself to the chief surgeon; he was wearing green all over, and a mask. Hello, I said,

I am [and here I named myself] and I'm a medical doctor and a poet, but unfortunately not yet qualified to practise either profession in this country because the necessary paperwork has not been accomplished.

What did he say to that? asked Mimi.

He didn't say nothing, he looked at me. Then one of the policemen touched me on the arm, and he said: Come away sir, there is nothing you can do. I was impressed that he called me sir, they don't do that in my country. But he did lead me away, quite firmly. And so I realised I would have to work my way up from the bottom again, perhaps if I went back to the uncles as had been my first plan, for catering was an option. I would have to start with catering, you see.

Is that when you came into the restaurant? said Mimi. Or was that later?

Shaheed: Maybe later. I call you Ling Valentine.

Mimi: Why?

Shaheed: I see this on internet. "Hello, I am Chinese Contract Hire female human expert, Ling Valentine. I am unique in the UK! I bring you best UK car takeaway poetry menu!" So I ask you for a job.

Mimi laughed. But you'd never been in a fish and chip restaurant before!

Shaheed said: I know that I had much to learn. I knew therefore I had to ask the uncles, who would be there for me. Perhaps I would have to go to Manchester, but I prefer to stay in London, for now I had met you.

Mimi said, You are very sweet.

Shaheed noted, not for the first time, her charming habit of pushing her glasses up her little nose with her forefinger.

Shaheed: I go to university maybe one day and study for sure.

Mimi: I'm hoping to go to uni next year!

Mimi had never met anyone like Shaheed before, and probably never will again. I want to have your baby, she thought. It was just like that, it just happened. Six, seven months passed.

## INFUSION INCIDENT

AT THIS point Gary looks into Mimi's bedroom without knocking. The comment he makes (before slamming the door shut again) is subsequently disputed, but "You fat slag" or "You lazy fat slag" is Mimi's interpretation. In fury and misery, she has picked the apple and cinnamon infusion bag out of the bedside saucer where it's been deposited and flung the soggy object across the air in his direction; but it doesn't achieve the intended contact, instead making a disgusting plopping sound against the already slammed bedroom door where it leaves a pink stain whose bifurcating trickles elongate in their journey to the floor to join the original object that has slid down to find its final repose on the carpet. She does not move from the bed during this procedure.

## GHOST OF A CAT

GARY'S CHOICES would have been ☐ Going to the pub; ☐ Watching video films; ☐ Watching sports on TV; ☐ Cigarette smoking. Actually, this would have been part of his pose; secretly, he is writing a novel. Although it is still before nine in the morning (they have been up all night), Gary begins rolling a joint on a folded up newspaper on the low table in the front room, while talking to his mate about witchcraft. Yes, witchcraft, it's the subject of his novel. Nobody is listening. Wicca. His mate isn't listening. Fuckwit, opines Gary. Fuckwicca. Fuckwit has no money. Fuckwit's hobbies include car maintenance (in rare moments of sobriety) and going out in like-minded groups and physically inconveniencing people.

Gary: It's a *genre* novel. Do you know what *genre* means?

No, says his mate.

Gary: Well, I'm one up on you. It's French. You know French?

His mate says: Hurry up with that fucking spliff. Fuck, was that the cat?

Where?

Gary's mate: It just went past. I can't stand cats, they schiz me out, man.

It flitted, it is no longer there.

Gary: That's actually a ghost cat, known as a "gateau".

No kidding?

He has a mane of buttercream.

Fuck off, you're talking shit. Gary says nothing, continues to make up the spliff. Then his mate adds: I need some money. Do you fancy going down town?

Gary, tamping down the end with a matchstick: You mean go into the shopping centre and walk about a bit, for no earthly reason?

Gary's mate: No, I'm serious.


## IN THE KITCHENS

THEY ARE people moving in the shadows, said Shaheed, they don't know where they are going. I have crossed the broken edges, I have gone tiptoe, he said, and I have left dreams behind because there are other dreams to come. (What dreams, demanded Mimi.) I think there is a better world to come, Shaheed explained, but you have to go through all the secret places where the money is, feeding on anything that you can. People's voices still sound like pistol shots. What is the meaning of invisible powers? There was central heating, and he moved out of its range. He would stand with his hands in his pockets, as if it didn't matter, but you could see it in his eyes, always. If the handclasp was offered, he would take it. It was the end of Ramadan. Men and boys in white shirts, embracing one another. The cold wind blew along the pavements, waving bits of rubbish around, newspapers, a plastic bag, and so forth. He heard ghost trance music, and he moved into the kitchens; this is where he would work for the foreseeable future. Large plastic tubs and paper sacks filled with exotic substances, a great deal of heat and noise abounding. I mention kitchens, but they were more like the partitions of a vast factory, a factory that never slept, supplying the needs of the people, or their perceived needs, or at any rate the needs that those who can't be named have stated to exist, and whose fulfilment would bring profit, to some at least. If you can't stand the heat, he was told. Of course, the future is never foreseeable. In the meantime, these were like the kitchens of Knowledge Management, where unremitting toil took place through the labyrinths of time leading towards that future reward. It had all been written in plain language, and then it had been translated, so that it could be understood. Who could not understand it? If such and such an uncle said it, then there must be something in it. As for the rest, they were people who moved in the shadows, and you must not even mention their names, not that one with his left eye full of blood, nor the other whose words all apparently alluded to wonderful secrets, even in the exile of these cold streets. It was all moment to moment, and apparently edgeless. Shaheed knew this; he knew by now to keep quiet. It was the best policy. He was invisible. I am very impressed with him.

## LIKE HITLER

WILL YOU be all right, love? inquires her mother Jo, looking into the bedroom before going off to work. Mimi merely grunts, and flicks a page of the magazine. Jo picks the teabag up off the carpet with a grimace and pops it in the waste paper basket. A map of a pink river remains on the back of the door. Jo says she has spoken to Gary. She has his side of the story. Gary said he said "Where's the daddy?" claiming it as a kind of joke, and Jo says she told him that was unkind and disrespectful. No response from Mimi to this. Jo says: You've got to take care of yourself, the condition you're in. There is a silence that follows this remark. He *was* a nice boy, says Jo, it's a shame. No response. Pale skin, pale eyes but with just the hint of a slant, dark straight hair asymmetric. I look like Hitler, she utters. Come on, for heaven's sake, says her mum. Can you do a stint in the restaurant this evening? I have a hospital appointment, says Mimi. I know you have, this afternoon; I mean after that. Your dad is on his own. No response. When she's gone, Mimi pulls a face and mimics: "The condition you're in." Then she feels bad about herself all over again.

In the mornings, Jo works for Richard and Annalisa. She arrives at their town house with the trim twin bay trees by the front door at nine o'clock. The first thing she has to do is take their four-year-old daughter Emma to play school. When she comes back, she will clear away the breakfast things and start the hoovering.

## SUZUKI METHOD

EMMA IS able to play "Twinkle Twinkle Little Star" on the violin (Suzuki method) and to vomit within twenty-three minutes of the start of any car journey. You must practise very hard, Jo tells her as they travel together, and you will be really good. My daughter Mimi, the one who was going to go to university, plays the cello, you know. That's like a very big violin. She practises every day. She plays *really* well. Emma receives this information with studied indifference, and eventually is delivered into the jurisdiction of the Happy Days nursery, where Jo's duty of care is transferred. Today, Emma's major issue is that the orange juice is not the correct brand. Look, Emma, suggests the teacher, Rosie, why don't you let Wayne play with you in the play house? But Emma hates Wayne; she once spat at him, which caused Rosie to have a serious discussion with Richard and Annalisa. Wayne may be a hideously ugly child with a peculiar smell, but he has a good heart. And a little bullet head that demands to be caressed. Where did she learn to spit? Rosie, privately, has had enough of her. She smiles and sings a song. Rosie, exhausted, is worried she is putting on too much weight. This is already becoming a recurring theme. A week ago, her best friend Lorraine, while doing her hair, reassured her that she was "a vision of loveliness". Rosie was half repelled by this extravagance, half intrigued and proud and wholly disbelieving.

Jo returns to her duties with Richard and Annalisa.

So at the end of the morning, the handyman, Geoff, comes in to have a cup of coffee with Rosie. Geoff's wife has thrown him out of the house and he is staying with friends. He has confided his problems to Rosie more than once.

Geoff: How's Rosie this morning, then?

Rosie (resentful of patronising tone, wary of sexual threat): As usual. And you?

Geoff: Got a bit of a hangover.

A pause.

Rosie: So what d'you think about Craig, then?

Geoff: Dunno, I didn't see it last night. Do you think he done it?

Rosie: They had a showdown, him and his mum. I don't really *believe* Craig.

Geoff: No, I know what you mean.


## WAS THE PROTOCOL FOLLOWED?

WEATHER FORECAST is decent until late afternoon, when wild speculation will replace cold hard climate facts. There will be a further inspection at 5.10pm. A Malaysian student, already injured, was attacked at knifepoint by young people and left with a broken jaw. Can you believe *that*? A woman jumped into the arms of a Romanian man called Adrian; she reported that it was a first for her. They say she is a celebrity now, and has even spent time in the jungle talking cobblers. Police say they have discovered "a couple of finds of some significance". She adds: "Well, when I say a first for me, I suppose I mean more like a thirst for me." Everyone laughs politely. There is a protocol. The protocol was previously agreed. At the weekend a child's skull was discovered on the premises. It doesn't appear from the face of it that that protocol was fully followed in this particular case. A man from Surbiton in the members' enclosure fumbles past a damp copy of The Daily Telegraph and retrieves his third scotch egg of the day. Replays show a very, very faint edge. Four men in the crowd are dressed as cowboys on horseback – clad in red and white gingham shirts, with fake blue jean legs worn over the horse bit like an inflatable skirt. If there's not some happy rowdiness there come tea-time then something will have gone badly wrong in the tented food village beyond. There are scorched patches where cars have been set alight. But this is not a time for nuance.


## IN REAL LIFE

IN "REAL LIFE" "Craig" and "his mother" are played by 27-year-old Michael and 52-year-old Maxine. Michael, contrary to stereotype, actually hates his mother, who abandoned him at the age of eight to a high-class prep school (his Estuary vowels and glottal stops are a late learned thing), where he was cold and unhappy, and which he now blames for his inability to form lasting emotional relationships. Michael's mother used to go off with her lover Serge, spending half the year in Biarritz.

Therefore the relations between him and Maxine on set are tense, as Michael projects his feelings towards his real mother onto the actress playing his screen mother... frankly, there are too many characters, and they're not believable either. How do they fit onto this small island? Where do they park? Some of them must always have to be on the move.

Maxine says: I think you're projecting your feelings towards your real mother onto me, Michael.

Michael: Maxine, you're full of shit.

The director: OK, settle down please, can we go to take 12, *please*.

Michael: Look, Mum, I know I've never said this, but ... I really love you.


## CROYDON (SHAHEED'S POEM)

IT'S SO nice that people change with the rain and dust. They are ephemera. And when some of them disappear, you can still see the shadows on the pavement and the silhouette of where they were and they are like ghosts. On the bus, said Shaheed, I could not get the ghost music out of my head. It was big music, but as if from very far away. Somebody was trying to tell me something. It was important. I couldn't understand. In the street outside, great piles of black plastic sacks lay on the pavement; some of them had been pecked open by large birds – I don't know the name, they are like cannibals – and their contents were laid out – broken baubles, dampened cardboard and fluid substances – while persons holding umbrellas and women with skins of pale velvet hurried by. I was hoping at one time they were real young to middle-aged dames who wished for obtainable males! It was at this time after all Spring, the most famous of all seasons of this United Kingdom, when the heart quickens, as the poets have said. On the bus, I amused myself and passed the time composing poetry in my head in English. And yet, I couldn't understand anything. It continued to rain, and there were men with long metal forks, but I couldn't figure what they were trying to do. The metal sign had a red circle with the number 27 in it. I need only one special individual to understand and then I can say. You could be that individual.

I don't know about that, I really don't, I'll have to think about it, said Mimi.

(Was there discontent here? I get the impression.)

When I get my papers, added Shaheed.

You have to go to Croydon for that.

Croydon?

That's where they deal with all the immigration stuff.

Ah, so I have heard, said Shaheed, remembering, or simulating memory. Is Croydon very far? Is it in London, or outside of London?

I think it's technically part of London.

I am astonished, marvelled Shaheed, London is so very huge and extensive that it's difficult to imagine in one's head. When I ride on the buses there is no end to it. You know what I do while I am riding to my work, I compose poetry in English in my head. Here is one that I can remember:

> *It is Spring! in the United*
> *Kingdom of Great Britain*
> *and Northern Ireland when the heart*
> *quickens*
> *of all the Spring*
> *chickens*

What do you think, it is maybe not very good, but I am learning fast? I think of this as my love poem, I am expressing what I feel, that is to say how I feel for you, my lovely Mimi, so that like sharing my work is how I channel my feelings, I think that by sharing my feelings I will prevent a build-up of emotions inside me. I am very open also easily to learn, so please ask me something if you don't understand. I hope to accomplish much more in any case.

Mimi: Mmm. Mmm.

She no longer knows what to say. Yes, there is a widening rift between them now.

Shaheed: I am not being told I am something I am not. I footstepped into your life I truly believe, but now I am not so sure.

They had their first row.

It was also their last.

On the bus later, amid the ghost music, Shaheed dreamt of the London Borough of Croydon. The destination seemed incredible, as unattainable as the tortoise is for the hare or the target for the arrow in Zeno's eternal paradox.


## WATCHING THE DETECTIVES

THE DETECTIVES are pretending to work, but in reality they are smoking round the back of the office, sheltering from the windswept pavement in front of rolled steel shutters and laughing about the football. Earlier, they watched their yellow-Post-it-stickered computer screens while their computer screens watched them. And all the women came and went. The word is that there will be a raid on the kitchens before the week is out. They are getting ready to come down hard on the miscreants. They are pictured on a mobile phone posing with items of goods seized in previous raids, including cereal packets and kitchen cleaning products; their faces are blacked out for security and legal reasons. They are on standby for action. They go into and out of the men's toilets, they stand at the urinals and pass badinage with the uniformed police; their working quarters are drab, their lives are empty, they crave a little excitement, who wouldn't?


## WALKING AND ROBBING

WHERE IS the daddy? demands Gary's friend, suddenly.

Fuck knows. Got deported or something.

So now you say she ain't going to uni?

What do *you* think?

Anyway, she got knocked up by this towel-head and now she's up the spout and she ain't going to uni?

Yeah, no, that's offensive, actually, he's not a towel-head.

Well, he's one of them, innit?

Innit? So why you talking black now?

I ain't.

OK. He Does Not Wear A Fucking Towel.

In hoods-up mode, they are walking about in the shopping centre (for no apparent reason). Because they have no money. Gary is bored. Why are we doing this? Gary's friend says, I rather go robbing. Where you been robbing? Well, my mate was working up the City, I was helping him, we went into this really swank flat, you know what I mean, like one of them warehouse apartments, and like we just walked in, you could take what you like, I'm not going to say nothing, am I? And they say it belongs to that bloke what's on the telly, you know the gay with the issues. Fucking brilliant.

So what did you nick?

I ain't saying. I ain't saying I nicked anything.

They walk around some more. Gary's fuckwit friend has retracted his confession – discretion, uncharacteristically, having got the better of ostentation. Now tight-lipped. The truth cannot be determined.

Gary's friend, who cannot be named for legal reasons, mutely contests all charges.

Gary says, I'm going home, mate. OK, cheers. He's finally given up, and decided to return to work on his novel about witchcraft, or wicca as he calls it, with Gothic and Christian imagery. That's about it. He has done 7,338 words so far. His mate would not understand in a million years. He gets on the bus. Floods of thoughts assail him through a marijuana haze. He has a plot idea, sexual in origin. He imagines multitudes. What happened to the cat? He's thinking about his mother. Now he's thinking about his sister, he feels guilty all of a sudden; he whips out his phone and texts: "Mimi sorry bout this am g x".

## DIMENSIONS OF A DREAM

IT'S NOT immediately clear what you are in. It's inside of a building that has had many lives as a factory. For one it's an atelier, for the other an archaeological site, entered through an atrium, but now it's home for both. They have the luxury of space: immense, floored with sheets of luminous hardwood; look how they gleam in pale sunlight that glances on them through the floor-to-ceiling industrial windows. And the two can rollerblade, they can play basketball indoors. Should they want to. The few pieces of furniture are on free-running rubber wheels so the space can be silently reconfigured in minutes. But Michael is discontented. I'd love to live in an ancient city, a magical spot, he often says, with that charming little laugh he has. This is all too new, he complains. For his partner, Christopher, however, rawness, demented industrial energy revealed by natural light, is of the essence: not necessarily of the essence of the new, indeed the knowing irony of vintage cast-iron radiators rather like the furnishings of a submarine has its place, as well as swivel chairs on castors, gleaming Macintosh computers, Dexion shelving and gunmetal office furniture. It's a bit too much try-hard urban cool and next to no charm, argues Michael, who longs for the garden he never had, just off-centre, the rose-red and the flesh-pink and the creamy-white geraniums peeping round pistachio stroke aquamarine corners of those awesome dimensions. And he longs for nothing more than to sit with his friend on the extended balcony overlooking the empires of finance, open a frosted bottle of Pino Grigio on a rare early evening when they can be together, and drink from twin sparkling slender-stemmed globes, the shadows gathering around them.

This is a conflict that can never be resolved.

The designer they hired, an architect by profession specialising in unusual buildings, decided he would have done better with relationship counselling skills. There are too many surprises here.

Four days a week, Michael puts on his Estuary vowels on the way to the studio from their shared home. While Christopher puts on a suit and striped shirt every morning and walks the few blocks to his job as a commodities trader, where he makes approximately a six-figure sum a year. He's only a bloody hedgie from the City, they say. And he does confess that he is making a lot of money from a downward market. But that doesn't excuse what happened. Nobody should have to take that shit. And I mean shit, like real faeces, in the middle of the hardwood floor. It happened while Christopher was trading and Michael was acting. What they came back to was horrendous, a violation. Somebody, some bodies, had been and gone. And the plasma screen TV, too, gone, the computers gone, the printer smashed, the books avalanched onto the floor in great heaps, tipped from their shelves, although of course none were missing, these kinds of people having no use for them. Amid this the flourish, the great human signature of human faeces. They clung, and wept. Well, it's not surprising that a regime of melancholy has by now begun to take hold, and we don't know how long it will persist – or if it will ever end. And this is closely accompanied by frustrated anger first aimed at the ghosts who have left, the burglar-ghosts that have returned to their unreachable realm of otherness. But because this otherness can never be breached, the bitterness of each turns on the other, in savage and exquisitely formed opera libretti they don't deserve. And beyond them, the viciousness starts in the social media. Of this there could be no end, because this is in the nature of the process in which they find themselves. Let's start cleaning up, says Christopher. Yes, says Michael. (They do not move.)

I am dreaming, thinks Michael, one day I will become a real boy.

And Christopher blames himself.

I am dreaming, thinks Michael in despair, that I am Craig, and to everyone Craig is someone who is nothing, or means nothing, that is to say, they don't *believe* him. (Or is it Craig dreaming forever he is Michael, an imaginary being?) And meanwhile Christopher relapses eventually into an awesome silence within which he can scarcely be found. And the detectives are never there when you need them.

But enough of these diversions.


## BIG MUSIC (MIMI'S POEM)

IT'S MIMI'S turn on the bus at last with the big music. She has left behind the rumpled bed, the delicate pink latticework of streams traced on the door, perhaps indelibly so. Whose trace? It's always someone's. She has put on her coat. She has gone down the narrow stairs. Now she is in the open air, she has closed the front door behind her, now she steps out into the neighbourhood, into the many-coloured street where the season is drawing to a close as people hurry past. Behind the milky-white translucence of the

shop window at the side the father will already be frying, antici-
pating lunchtime orders with his military precision, for he believes
the chips should always be done absolutely from fresh and not left
to chill and be re-heated, when they will become hard, unmal-
leable and of no use to any discerning punter. He is an hon-
ourable man. From an upper window a child is blowing bubbles
into the street; they drift languidly in a south-westerly direction.
That could have been Mimi once. But now, distracted only briefly,
once, by the pixellated image of a lost cat affixed to a passing
lamp-post (you need a cat, she thinks – a hound, however docile,
will not do), she hurries, arrives, waits and waits among a growing
gathering, finally sticks her arm out as the bus approaches, and
boards, finds a seat in the crush. All the world seems to be there.
They all suffer in silence, or at least, for some of them, in miniature private sound-worlds. The big musics in the small spaces.
And for herself she tries hard not to think, white buds embedded
in her little ears, especially not to picture the reported vastness of
London, which is not what she wants to imagine right now, the
huge buildings, the parks that drift by with swans in the water in
them that belong to the Queen, or maybe more likely shopping
trolleys that belong to Tesco. When she introspects, she feels she
has got some sort of blue-grey stuff inside. That she is no longer
human. She dreams in the air, setting a course across the offshore
wind, to places where agoraphobic frumps like herself need not
apply. She has made a tiny house out of her own skin, and she will
live in it for the rest of her days, she thinks and prefers. Maybe.
Secretly, she longs for new sounds and pictures to enter her brain,
and secretly suspects that none ever will. But not everything can
have been charted, surely, there must be more that will whisper to
her? Would that be poetry, then? lines that enter her brain, such as

> You need a cat, or music.
> Beauty is very brief.
> Food is like that, too.
> The dumpling is a forever food for me.

etc, words and cadences such as this. There is evidence of her
heritage there, obviously. For the first time in many weeks she

thinks of Shaheed, of where he might be now. She is only mild-ly curious. On the bus, Mimi almost sees things through Shaheed's eyes, but it doesn't last, it never does. How can it? What happened, clearly, is that a crevice opened up between them. The stories he told. Lies, really. Jo could never understand this, and was more troubled about it than anyone in the family. There was no further news. Ever. The detectives simply melted into the night, and you could no longer contact them. There is nothing but music. Beauty is very brief. Almost not there, really. For instance, what's this turning up on shuffle, Bach cello suite number one in G? She can't bear that stuff anymore, stabs at it, orders an onward movement, something else please. And when did a crevice become a crevasse? Oh, a pentatonic jingle now: it's her mother texting her, how u getting on; I haven't even got there yet, crossly she thinks, switching back. But no more music. With her forefinger, she pushes her glasses back up the bridge of her petite nose. Later, later. What happened to the uncles? The bus shudders to a stop, hums as the customers get on and off, shudders to start again. They'd have seen to it *they* were all right. Her stern father comes to mind, who sang songs of old Hong Kong under his breath as he dipped the cradle of battered fish pieces into boiling oil, and he is some kind of a survivor too. They are all bodies in thrall. A murmur of voices, real and electronic, comes and goes as the bus continues its trundle through those city streets on its long journey towards the hospital. It all started to go sour when marriage came up. Oh so you want to marry me so you can stay in this country? No, no, I love you Ling Valentine. Ling Valentine, female human expert. What the hell are you talking about? Oh I'm beginning to get the picture. It somehow took a worse turn from there, a turn that couldn't be undone.

Pentatonic ditty again interrupting persisting again, that's a text coming in from her brother now, fuck him. She can't be bothered. She deletes it unread.


FREQUENTLY ASKED QUESTIONS

IN THE HOT kitchens, mayhem rules. There are few if any famil-iar brands on view. Operatives hurry against the clock to carry out their duties within the harsh glare of arclights. It's like a factory farm. There are definitely business opportunities here. Fire leaps from the cast-iron pans with a roar. Customers come and go. In the folds of their garments, not to mention in their vocal folds, their identities are well hid. Simple things become impossible. The scent of heavy spices hangs in the steam that lingers. Music is monodic, heavily dependent on the incessant return of ostinati. There are shelves from floor to ceiling crammed with tins and plastic tubs full of substances. There are dead but clean animals. Shaheed has simple if repetitive tasks to perform. But something is about to change. Someone shouts, the angels are coming! (this might be a mishearing, or an imperfect translation). Up jump the uncles, all at once, they're out of here before you can blink. Pop, pop, pop. They are concerned about their families at home, after all. The oval window hums, and then finally pressure is released. Alarm bells ring. This is health & safety. Which is always paramount, of course. And here come the police in the hi-viz fluorescent jackets and accessories and the white decontamination suits that of course do make them resemble angels – followed at a discreet distance by the Metropolitan detectives. These are surprisingly short and sturdy; they strike poses incessantly; tough action is required. Everybody stop right there. OK. Rapid questions. What is in this [indicates giant paper sack, one of a number]? You say flour? Garam flour? Spell that, please. [Orders are given for the sacks to be taken away for analysis.] Those jars full of liquid, stacked upon yonder shelves? What are them golden sparks? Is there internet access from these machines? Are they refrigerators? Have they been checked? Can you line up against this wall, please? You, you and you. Yes, and you. We're going to need a bigger receptacle, one of the detectives remarks, which is followed by laughter. Shaheed is in the line of alleged miscreants, bewildered. They are forty thieves, no more. What's behind them doors? Those are the toilets. Search them. What is the English for that? There is severe deployment of personnel, there are logistical adjustments, within an environment of essential high temperature and confusion. A drone goes on. There are further developments; the night prolongs. A big dull cage, and another long period of travel in the dark. A long ride in the back of a short van. Dispersal and disposal, that is the next phase. Now Shaheed is no longer in the kitchens, he is in an underground room with fluorescent lighting, a formica-topped table, a plastic chair, another plastic chair whereon sits a detective who looks like a bureaucrat. What is your name? [He gives his name.] Your Christian name? With respect, sir, I am not a Christian. I beg your pardon, I mean your given name. [He gives it.] When did you enter this country? [Ambiguous reply.] How did you arrive? [Incoherent reply.] What do you mean when you say "shipwrecked"? Where is your passport? Do you have a visa or work permit? I intended to study, whether as a virtual or in-person presence, I craved for new experience. [Pause to sip water from a plastic cup.] Therefore I am intending to enroll in various learning programmes, for instance poetry and medicine, and I will be glad to have done so. Had I the means, I would have…. So you are saying you are a student? You have qualifications? You say medical qualifications? Where do you intend to enroll? No, I am intending first to claim asylum status, as one who is fleeing from oppression and danger, and also to become married. Are you aware that in order to claim asylum you would need to have presented yourself immediately or as soon as possible after your arrival in this country? As far as we can tell, you have not done so, is that correct? And is there any particular reason for this? I have not had the time, sir. As to the grounds for your claim, you say that your family have been killed in war in your country? That is correct, yes. Your father, your mother? Yes, sir. Your brothers and sisters? Yes, sir. And you fear for your own life if you are forced to return? Yes, sir. But we have no record of any war taking place in your country. It is not official war, it is not reported in the media, you see. [The detective writes in his notebook for some moments, then turns to rummage among catalogued belongings laid out on his desk.] So, soon I will ask you to read this statement to ascertain that it's correct, and to sign it. Do you understand? [Affirms understanding with a nod of the head.] Now, is this a photograph of your intended wife? No, that is Ling Valentine, Chinese Contract Hire female human expert, of whom I first became acquainted on internet, she is related. So this is not your wife, or intended wife? But you say she is related to this woman, who is the mother of your child? No, I did not mean that, she is related only in a manner of speaking, but my intended wife is expecting, yes. How, "in a manner of speaking"? [Pause.] I was talking of metaphor. That is irrelevant, can you stick to the facts please.


## THE HIGH POINT

BLUE-GREY STUFF, icons and legends, a moving digital tapestry generated by ultrasound. Some thing or probable entity represented by a shadow. It feels very whole, and sort of unreal. Just such a blur of possibilities.

Mimi is in the hospital, lying on a trolley bed.

Mimi is not fat, apart from her little belly, and does not resemble Hitler.

Behind her glasses, her eyelids are oval, then retract suddenly.

She views the monitor intently, as the radiographer points out various significant features. Blue-grey stuff. That flicker again: "She moved!" Again: "See?"

This, then, unexpectedly, while lying on a hospital trolley with her belly soaped with gloop to receive the travelling device, is the highest point of Mimi's life – how suddenly she shines with an unaccustomed delight that she will never quite feel again. It seems so strange how everything that has happened led up to this moment. That ghostly movement of pixels shall be named Miranda.


## A VISION

And there are various wet leaves descended from the plane trees that line the road, for by now it is Autumn ("season of mists and mellow fruitfulness"!) when such happens, which are flattened by the successive tyres of the London traffic that passes endlessly by here, and the same mists permeate our life, through which we can glimpse flashes of illumination that wink at us and are then no more. In the distance, for example, gleam suddenly the towers of the London Borough of Croydon.

There are too many characters, and few of them make any

sense. Which are real, and which imagined? Who cares about them? They strut their stuff for an instant, and are gone.

It is Friday in the United Kingdom, it's breezy with some sunshine, temperature 12°, wind WSW 10 m/s. But Miranda, such a mashed-up kid from the start, lives in amniotic fluid, inhabiting nimbly and without any knowledge of any of this, nor even of pleasure or pain, the space from which we characters all have to emerge. Eventually. Into the light for some brief time. She flickers. She is restless, glorious, doesn't know what's coming to her.

Miranda, a tiny scrap in the dark, a shadow, a mélange of incipient humanness, all her needs met for now, is grumbling: Is there anybody out there?

# The Homecoming

THE OLD train station building he remembered from his childhood, with its darkened brickwork and its dank overpass smelling mysteriously of male urine, had vanished. In its place was a thing of steel and blue-tinted glass that – combined with flesh tones – lent an on the whole greenish complexion to the few passengers wandering through that morning. Girders propped the glass up as an artificial sky. There was too much space here, and it was of the wrong kind. It seemed like a dream. It seemed as though what was outside was now what was called dreams, and only what was inside was real – but he still had no access to the inside.

The real shock, which should of course have been no shock to him at all, was that there was no one there to meet him, as there once had been when he used to return after term had finished at his boarding school. Nobody approached him smiling, or calling out his name. Of course he had known there was no one left – bar that one great-aunt, if she was still alive – that was the whole point. And even had there been, no one was expecting him to return. He had scarcely expected it himself. But it doesn't come home to you until you experience it, he reasoned. Faint and disgusting canned music was the underlying sound that cancelled out all others. A couple of blank-faced officials in fluorescent high-visibility jackets hung about doing not much. In fact, the first and only being to greet him had been a huge herring gull on the arrival platform, white and grey with a malevolent yellow eye that followed his movement in what seemed to be a paranoid fashion. It walked along the platform with little steps, in a fast and deliberate way, like Mrs Thatcher in the old news clips. Then it spread its wings and flew clumsily off.

IT WASN'T just because his car had been repossessed. He'd chosen to take the train for nostalgic reasons. But these trains were completely different from those of his childhood. They were brand new, and driven by computers – not like the old trembling diesels he remembered, with the slam doors. They whizzed from the capital through the pale English suburbs and the pale English countryside like ghosts. The air-conditioning was chilling. But that fleeting nostalgia he hoped he might have felt evidently gripped a couple of his fellow passengers.

The old ones – they was more solid, recalled a tubby grizzlehead in one of the seats across the aisle, whose forearms were blue with tattoos.

His female companion (bleached and bloated) replied: Oh god, yeah.

They was more solid, said grizzlehead.

They held the track better, agreed his companion.

The train hummed along, into a tunnel and out again. He looked out of the window, trying to concentrate. The countryside was grey and green.

After a few moments, the female companion contemplated the first class section at the end of the carriage, each seat back surmounted by a dainty antimacassar:

First Class, it's a joke. They've just got a piece of cloth, that's the only difference.

If I was a yuppy I wouldn't put up with that, said the grizzlehead primly.

No, you're right.

Mind you, I wouldn't want to be a yuppy. I'd rather kill myself than be a yuppy.

And then they relapsed once more into silence. At the next station, as though to confirm the truth of the interlocutors' assessment, the train refused to start. In fact, the doors also refused to open, so the handful of passengers were trapped. There were two crackly apologies during a delay of ten minutes. Finally, the whole system was shut down and rebooted; the hum returned, and they were on their way again. The incident provided a new topic of conversation.

Computers, it's all computers these days, innit? remarked the female companion. Your nephew, he's really into them?

Yeah. He had two laptops nicked. Nothing's safe these days. And that was in daylight.

Did he have insurance?

Oh yeah, I think he had insurance. But the problem is what's on the laptop.

Yeah.

The data what's on the laptop. You can't get that back.

No.

He's a cocky little shit, though. He can speak French. He speaks it all the time.

I could never get on with that.

Since he was fourteen he could speak French.

We learned it at school. But I could never get on with it.

I suppose if he moved to France, say he bought a house there, well, he could speak the language, he could speak to the local authorities and that.

Some people can pick it up. I could never get on with it, I gave it up.

At that, he'd had enough. He realised nothing had really changed. The ignorance, if nothing else, was unchanged from all those years ago. He'd got up and moved to the corridor connection between the carriages. Beyond the automatic sliding door, the undulating pathway over the speeding track was unstable. In the next carriage, there was only one passenger, a tanned man in his fifties wearing sunglasses and a small grey ponytail, speaking in the loud, confident voice that signifies use of a mobile phone. The man had a slight twang to his voice, and the demeanour of a retired police officer.

He was beginning to feel sick. This was not a good idea at all. It was a joke, say it was a joke. A sick joke. A woman's recorded voice had been intoning the dwindling names of the stations remaining. The woods sped by. They had been tidied up.

Grey ponytail remarked: Yeah, hoping to get in a bit of fishing.

Perhaps he was one who had deposited his clothes in a neat little bundle at the shoreline and disappeared into the sea to start a new life elsewhere, that is to say, here.

And now, as though responding to this cue, the train was curving round, offering passengers a brief sea glimpse ahead. The multitudinous sea. Flashes off the great school windows. Did he feel anything yet? He did not. There was always the possibility of abandoning the project, of getting straight onto the next train back as soon as he arrived.

Grey ponytail: No, this is sea angling.

[inaudible reply]

Grey ponytail: Yeah, that was my son. In Australia.

[inaudible]

Grey ponytail: He was skinning a mako shark, it was the biggest ever caught on the north coast, and we had shark on the menu for three months. But you have to soak it three times, because apparently they urinate inside when they're caught, so the aroma builds up.

[inaudible]

Grey ponytail: No, I didn't taste it. But he was doing Indian meals, he had a free hand, so he put kid on the menu.

They were arriving at their destination, where the train, as the conductor advised, would terminate.

SHE HAD said to him: You have no feelings. You don't know what it's like to have feelings. Except anger, that's the only feeling you know. That's what she said. But for fuck's sake, that was two years ago! Why was he brooding on it? It was over. Two years of "relationship", all over in five minutes. Just give me space, just give me some geography here, he said, I'm sinking here, the air is sinking all around me! But there were no voices talking back, nobody was talking to him. Mind you, it would be nice to have feelings. Just for once, you know, to experience emotion as it really is. He supposed. Never mind the talk, the talk didn't matter, it was mostly bollocks, just to feel the feeling, that would have been it. Anyway, that was all in the past. She'd packed up everything and gone, for the last time. He'd said: I didn't mean anything by it. And she went: You didn't mean anything? You didn't *mean* anything? The repeated, percussive sound of a coin being clattered on a table, the beats rapidly speeding up until they abruptly stopped. What was that feeling, was it incredulous disgust? Was that a feeling? It had lasted around two years, and then there were two years of nothing. Occasionally seeing mates. One by one they had left. He made them go. They weren't worth it. The Spanish guy was the last one who had tried to help him, took him out to the pub on a couple of occasions. Maybe not a good idea when he'd been trying to get off the drink. All he remembered was his face in his face: But *leesten* to me! In the end, he'd told him to fuck off as well. And that was the end of that.

CONSTRUCTION WAS happening even as he stepped out of the station into the warm sunshine: great travelling cranes in the sky remodelling the urban landscape. He scarcely recognised any of it. In terms of a homecoming, it was a disappointment. There was no coherence to it. A vintage fishing boat had – apparently recently – been dragged up here and tethered in the middle of a traffic island, in an effort to indicate to tourists something of the heritage of the town. The shops in the station road had been there since the ice age, but some were now vacated. Clearance sale, it said – everything must go. Plywood sheets covered the windows. A lorry reversed into a building site, white lights ablaze, a computerised voice repeatedly intoning its intention. A bus rumbled into a bay. From down the road, he imagined the faint scent of the sea being borne towards him on an intermittent breeze, and that did have a nostalgic shape to it.

The horror reached him. What if there *were* people still around who recognised him? What then? How would he cope? He glanced nervously from right to left. There were a few people visible. Some passengers off the train – he noted the sea angler, with his tackle, walking briskly down the road, and the ill-assorted couple already waiting in line to board the bus – and others arriving or mooching around with little evident purpose – a small giggling group of schoolgirls, a lardy gent with thick glasses – but nobody *he* recognised. Clearly he wouldn't – it had been too long – and by the same token, no one would by now be able to identify him.

And so he made up his mind, and set off on foot down to the seafront.

AT FIRST glance, they exhibited the bold body language of a young couple in love, walking arm locked in arm along the prom, the sea breeze moving their hair in unison, talking continuously to each other in a low tone. But on closer inspection, they clearly weren't that young; also, they wore matching black walking shoes, and in each case their trousers ended at the exact same point just below the knee, so that they exposed the same proportion of calf. Four white calves. So evidently they had converged some time ago. He felt the anger begin to well up again, and so had to steady himself, drop back behind them and let them walk on. He gripped the rail, pretending to gaze out to sea, until it passed.

The multitudinous sea. It was too early in the year, and the breeze too brisk, for anyone to be in it, though a group of two or three children were wandering over the shingle below. In the distance, a real fishing boat plied its trade. He remembered that he had painted a picture of the sea with crayons in infant school. He'd been proud of it, showed it to the teacher: a rough cross-hatching of blue across the top of the page to represent the sky, a yellow sun with spiky rays protruding from it, a scatter of Vs to represent seagulls flying, boats with inverted Vs or triangles for sails and a number of fish of unknown species disposed along the bottom. She was tall, her glasses glittered. She held the paper close. Very nice, she had said to him, but the sea isn't green, it's blue.

People were walking in a desultory way up and down the prom in the pale sunshine. An elderly woman in sunglasses motored past on a purring electric buggy, trailing behind her a small pack of dirty white Scotch terriers on individual, converging leads.

He had asserted that it *was* green, as he had represented it. He had in fact spent a great deal of mental energy scribbling and shading with two versions of green crayon to cover the entire portion of the page devoted to the sea. It *was* green.

She hadn't liked that. She'd clearly felt his insistence was out of order.

No, the sea is *blue*. Why don't you do another one, she'd said brightly.

It was around then that he had begun to understand. He hadn't quite given up then, but it was only a matter of time after that. Much later, he'd had several interesting conversations about this and other topics with the Spanish Buddhist, who'd tried to put him right. He had a moustache like Pancho Villa, but he talked like the Dalai Fucking Lama. He'd stressed the importance of detachment, but also of compassion. He counted off the two qualities, first touching his right index finger to his left index finger, and then to his left middle finger: detachment, compassion. And then he'd held his hand up in the air to emphasise the point, to let it sink in. He was originally a friend of hers, but he'd only really got to know him after she left. In answer to a question, this Spanish Buddhist said he did feel anger from time to time. In fact, once, talking about a prominent politician long gone, maybe it was Tony Blair, he'd said he really would like to kill him, and when he'd challenged him on this, him being a man of faith and all, he'd replied that it was OK to express such feelings honestly; after all, as a Buddhist, he had nothing to hide, and all he was doing was acknowledging that anger, but maintaining detachment from it. But I'd still like to kill the cunt, he said! Made a big joke of it, described with great precision the elaborate ways he would have tortured the offending politician. Weird guy. He'd liked him at one time.

But you've got to have just a leetle compassion, he used to say.

She said I have no insight, he told him.

Perhaps misunderstanding, he replied: There ees no inside and there ees no outside.

A shame he couldn't talk to him any more. It had been quite helpful having these conversations, especially in the year after she left him. Because a lot of things had happened, he hadn't actually just smashed his computer with all his poetry in it the minute she left, even though a narrative was already gathering, which he'd done nothing to deny, that this is what had occurred. No, that was a lot later, after a lot of conversation. What things had happened? Mostly a lot of drinking. And in fact, the computer's hard drive had already died, as they do, and he hadn't backed it up, so all the poems had gone anyway, except for the odd one that had been published in a pamphlet or a small magazine, or on someone's stupid website. Well, that was a liberation. And he'd only taken a hammer to the screen after that had happened, just to pretend he was the agent of his destiny, just to make himself feel better. In fact, that was only a week or two ago. And he hadn't seen the Buddhist for months. So much for a nice narrative arc.

RETREATING FROM the seafront, he ended up in one of the smart new pubs in the pedestrianised but still not quite smart enough town centre, because he decided he needed a drink – just one drink – before his next move. Did he feel at home yet? No, he did not. He sat at one of the tables outside with the smokers, a pint before him, gazing morosely at the people who came and went. The town had been partly tarted up, and partly deteriorated, and underneath all that strange memories and recognitions were happening, but at least he had got over his terror that someone he used to know might come up to him and hail him. No, he recognised nobody, and nobody recognised him.

Two girls marched by the tables, one with ash-blond hair gesticulating and shouting, the other silent. A man in shorts walked a boxer dog, its mouth crammed with a large bone. Sound of a baby incessantly crying. Another girl in a grey sweatshirt walked briskly towards the pub, her hands clasped under her chin, looking round her once or twice, furtively; she peered for some moments into the pub interior, then went away again. A child's voice sang out, querulously, on the verge of tears: "Will we *eat* people?" A short, square woman, her legs oedema-swollen, tottered slowly, hunched under the burden of a bulging carrier bag bearing the message I KNOW!

Pale sunshine. They were all, thankfully, strangers. Sound of a coin being clattered on a table, the beats rapidly speeding up until they approximated to chaos. Then abrupt silence.

From one side of the pedestrianised precinct an old, frail man appeared, pushing a walking frame; each step, or rather, shuffle, propelled him forward about four inches, after which he stopped momentarily to re-compose himself. Thus, a quick computation suggested that it would probably take him the rest of the morning to reach the other side of the square.

He couldn't bear to watch this, or even to think about it.

When the surface of the beer was exactly halfway down the glass, he took out his phone and keyed in the number.

It rang five times.

Who's that?

Her voice was still recognisable. A little more quavery perhaps; the voice of an ancient, now. A quality of suspicion, and of haunting.

He told her. It was her nephew. Her nephew. She didn't understand.

He made his voice into a laugh.

Is that Kenneth?

That is not my name, he said.

Kenneth, she said. After all these years. It must be ten years.

He said it was more like twenty.

You never kept in touch with your family.

He said he had been busy; he apologised. But, he added, he was in town now.

You're what?

In town, he repeated. He could come and visit her.

You're here, Kenneth?

That isn't my name.

What are you here for?

Just visiting, he explained. No special reason.

You never wanted to come home.

He couldn't think of a reply to this.

You can certainly come and visit me, Kenneth. I don't get many visits now.

He said he could drop by, if it wasn't too inconvenient.

You were a disappointment to us all, I'm bound to say. But there aren't many of us left, now.

Yes, he remembered the address. He found the conversation more than usually trying, but he tried scrupulously not to give any indication of this. Pleased it had concluded satisfactorily, he ended the call.

THE HOUSE was as he remembered it, though its paint had faded by a factor of twenty years. There was the same little steep gravel path up, and the front door actually around to the side.

He had walked all the way. It was twenty or twenty-five minutes from the centre of town. Clouds had brushed past overhead and were beginning to disperse again by the time he arrived. He pushed the rusty switch, and heard the bell sound within. And then an indistinct, shifting shape appeared within the bubble glass.

She was much smaller than he had expected. Did people really shrink with age? Her wizened face trembled visibly as she stared into his eyes. But what was weird: the family resemblance. It had never really struck him before. Suddenly, it seemed to him that he was looking into a mirror, but a mirror that revealed the future: his future. He had never expected, and had never had, a comparable experience. It terrified him.

Kenneth?

That is not my name.

Please do come in.

It occurred to him that he still had a chance to run. Just take off, run all the way back to the train station, board the next train to London.

But he thanked her, and entered.

By doing so, he gave implicit consent to the terms and conditions.

She shuffled down the corridor, using a black shiny stick. Would you like a cup of tea?

He said he would like that very much. What if things were otherwise? What if it could all be otherwise? How would we live? What if I were you, and you were me? The terror of it! Distance is what makes it bearable.

He was in the little, stuffy living room, sitting on the overstuffed sofa, with all the same little objects dotted around, and he went dizzy; it seemed as though the room was the only world there was, and it was spinning round him. Time passed. The smell of stale sweat and rose-petals. He accepted a china teacup and saucer that clattered in his hands. You were always a nervous boy, she told him. He looked for a place to put down the cup and saucer, but could see none. She laid her stick on the side. Here, she said, was a photograph of so-and-so, and here a photograph of such-and-such. He nodded. They were all dead. Human remains had been swept into the margins. Ah, yes, he grinned, he nodded. He was taking part in a ceremonial, he fancied, he was intoning a liturgy. Everything had collapsed. She sat in the opposite, high-backed chair, and indeed she seemed very tiny. His parents were dead. The air was dead. His brain was dead. Loyalty was important. Loyalty was collapsing.

You were very talented, I remember, she said. You did some lovely drawings. Do you still do drawing?

He told her that he had not done any since he was about fifteen years old. He told her that he had written poetry since. And had it published. She gave no evidence of understanding this. Lovely drawings, she repeated. You never did anything with that.

He was still doing his poetry, he told her; no, he remembered now, he wasn't doing his poetry any more. That was all in the past. He was going to start a new job sometime. He told her that. Everything wanted soothing. He wanted nothing so much as to lay his head down and go to sleep. For a long time.

Her teeth were very white. Of course, they were dentures. And her glasses glittered. He didn't like that. He didn't like that at all. But she had invited him in, and in doing so agreed to the terms and conditions.

I'm only human, is the gist of what he tried to point out during the conversation, but she talked over him.

In the room were: a china shepherd boy simpering; a black sculpted Scotch terrier; thirteen (he counted them) gilt-framed photographs; several heavy candlesticks without candles; a bullfight poster from Torremolinos; a French ormolu clock in a glass dome; a small tray with a picture of the Blackpool tower; a framed picture of a hunting scene; a framed reproduction of *The Haywain*; a pink teddy bear.

You were a great disappointment to your parents, Kenneth.

I'm only fucking human, is what he meant to say, but it came out as "I'm sorry that is the way you feel."

Why did you come back?

He floundered for an answer.

Why did you come?

He said that it was to see her.

That's not true, is it, dear? You haven't been in touch for years.

He failed to reply.

Not for years. But there's no reason to visit this town. There's nothing here now; it's gone to the dogs. This was a nice town once. You remember it, Kenneth? You remember when you were a child? You used to love the beach! The pier! Do you remember the pier?

No reply.

It was a lovely town then. Not any more. Yobs rule the roost now. No parental control, that's all out of the window. And the blacks. Used to be all English here, we were all one happy family. I don't go to the corner shop now. It was taken over by Indians, or Pakistanis, or whatever they call themselves. They call it a mini-supermarket now. They're all smiley-smiley, pretend to be friendly, but they're out to do you, they just want your money, you know, they want to diddle you out of your money, and me a pensioner, I can't make ends meet, what with the council tax and this that and the other, it doesn't feel like my country any more, do you know what I mean, Kenneth, it's not our country, we might as well be living in a foreign country, all you hear is foreign languages in the street, can't understand a blessed word, everyone's rude, no consideration at all, especially for old people, it's terrible, I can't understand what's going to come of it all.

He opened and closed his mouth.

Another cup of tea? she enquired solicitously.

He tried to mouth something. He had only drunk half his tea, and the rest lay cooling in his cup. A spasm struck his hands and the cup and saucer went tumbling onto the patterned carpet.

Oh dear. Oh dear, oh dear.

He mumbled an apology, gathering up the china, which had not broken.

Would you go in the kitchen, dear, and fetch a rag from under the sink?

He dutifully made to obey.

That was always you all over, Kenneth.

THAT IS NOT MY NAME THAT IS NOT MY NAME
THAT IS NOT MY NAME THAT IS NOT MY NAME.

He threw the cup and saucer at her. The saucer hit her right on the forehead, sending her glasses flying across the room.

The sea isn't green, Kenneth, it's blue.

She had fallen to the floor without a sound. Like a scrap of paper.

He grabbed her stick and began beating. He finished off the job with one of the candlesticks. The skull cracked like an egg. There wasn't much sound from start to finish, except his own heavy breathing, which he was startled to become aware of. There was, though, quite a bit of blood, beginning to seep into the pile. Ugly. He went into the kitchen to look for that rag, before realising this was futile. He went upstairs. Damn, he'd left bloody footprints on the carpet all the way up. The bathroom was tiny, and all a sort of horrible pink. He tried to clean himself up as best he could. There was blood all over his hands. He kept the water flowing. But the hot water was too hot and the cold water was too cold. He solved the problem by squeezing the stopper in the plughole and filling the bowl. Then the water turned dark pink, to match the décor. He urinated in the pink toilet – god, he was dying for that – and pulled the chain. Oh fuck, he said, oh fuck. What *is* my name, he giggled, what was my name before I was born?

Downstairs, the body lay still, like a tiny doll, where it had fallen. Carefully, he collected the cup and saucer, and stacked them neatly by the kitchen sink. Everything had collapsed now. It shouldn't have happened this way, it was regrettable. But here wasn't a great deal more he could usefully do.


HE WAS on the front again, before the ebbing tide. It was a bit chilly now that the sun was sinking feebly from cloud to cloud and the afternoon was drawing on into evening; and there were fewer people about. Off to his right, the pier sprawled into the sea. Happy memories? He began to saunter towards it, humming a low melody to himself, bouncing his left hand on the railing.

It looked a gaunt ruin; no sign of life. The structure was held up by a forest of rusting cast iron pillars and girders. To some of the columns had been fixed notices with bold white lettering out of a scarlet background:

## Danger of Falling Debris –
## KEEP OUT

Waves lapped in the dark forest below. A mysterious eco-system, flutterings within, waves washing its floor, penetrated eternally by debris. The tide was receding remorselessly now, and on the glassy, flat sand beside the ruined pier, before the shingle began, a flock of around a dozen pigeons were rooting around for scraps. He stood for some moments on the paving; the constant hum of traffic behind him. A couple came slowly past with a glum child in a buggy. He turned round to appeal to the man, who was skinny and, despite the fresh breeze, wore a sleeveless vest, a tattoo on his dark bicep imitating a metal band.

Don't you know, mate? Pier's been closed for 'bout a year. Been condemned. Danger to the public.

Pink fat of the baby's arm waving randomly from its buggy. The woman, pasty-faced, holding the buggy handles, stared at him vacantly while chewing gum, as though there was something wrong with him. After a while, he realised it was he who had been staring at them, perhaps wildly; he just couldn't think of anything to say. It was embarrassing. The couple glanced at each other briefly, and by common consent ended the encounter by pushing the buggy on.

It's a disgrace, he thought. A fucking shame. The gates at the entrance to the pier were padlocked shut, and barbed wire decorated the railings. A faded banner hung, torn in two, the halves flapping listlessly. It was not possible to discern what the message had been. The orange crumple of a plastic bag moved over grey shadowy ground. The copper of the twin cupolas at the entrance had turned a dirty grey-green, and one of the flagpoles surmounting them was bent at an angle of forty-five degrees.

All of this was telling him to keep out. He was being shut out of his childhood. It was a shame. He walked up and down several times.

But now, this was something. Over on the right, he observed, the railings were bent; clearly, someone had successfully attempted entry. Looking over his shoulder, he followed suit. It was a tight squeeze, but he was in.

It was very sad. The notices proclaiming the delights of the pier, DELUXE AMUSEMENTS and SHOPS, were still there, much faded, but the central gallery of buildings was tight shut, and there were off-white curtains masking the dead windows. He moved onto the decking at the side; his footsteps echoed. The ironwork trailed streaks of rust.

He walked the length of the structure, his footsteps echoing on the decking, making him feel self-conscious. The wood, the cast iron, all were badly spattered with whitish seagull droppings. There was an unpleasant stench everywhere, and faint, zoo-like sounds on the breeze. The pale sun, now low in the sky, gleamed on the tips of the waves below that rolled in lazily, but already clouds were beginning to bank up on the horizon, preparing to obscure it.

The last building on the pier, the great ballroom, was equally mute, patently abandoned long ago. He remembered being told that the Rolling Stones and Jimi Hendrix had once played here. But that was before his time. He tried to peer in through a window, pulling himself up with his hands, but it was hard to make out anything in the gloom within. He fancied that the deserted ballroom had been given over to the birds, which entered and exited via broken glass panels, which had made of its guano-encrusted interior a wild and echoing home. Once, he thought he heard the explosion of flapping wings. He gave up attempting to look inside, and tried to skirt the building. It was hard. The smell was getting worse. Behind it, the structure of the pier itself abruptly came to an end; but rusty vertical pillars continued to protrude from the sea beyond.

Giving up the attempt to go any further, sitting on the very last bench left intact, facing out to sea, he saw that the shoreline was now a long way off. That was some comfort. He needed the space. He took out his phone and keyed 999. He asked for the police.

In response to the girl's question, he gave his location.

You mean you're actually *on* the pier? she said.

He confirmed this.

There was then some confusion in the conversation.

No, no, he laughed gently, the incident had not taken place here. Politely, he gave the full name and address.

And you say you think you've killed this lady, sir?

He said that he believed he had.

At that address?

At that very address.

OK, please stay where you are, sir, and an officer will be with you very shortly.

He ended the call. That had gone well.

It was peaceful here, halfway out to sea on a breezy day. On the railing, to his right, two herring gulls sat side by side, evidently a pair, although it was impossible to distinguish male from female. Over to his left, the sky was mirrored in the flat wet sand at the edge of the tide. Shingle banked up against a new groyne, and from here he could see a tiny sea angler cast his line towards the rolling wavelets. Below, if he stood up, he could observe deep green water swirling and eddying. He practised what he would say to the police when they arrived. This my hand, this my hand.

One of the gulls stood up. It threw its head back, opened its beak and uttered a harsh series of shrieks at the sky. The other gull also stood, its pink feet shifting uneasily. Then the first spread its wings and launched itself off the pier and over the waves. It glided around in a great arc out to sea and then back leftward towards land, occasionally propelling itself with a powerful movement of its wings, then floating on the wind. And was that the sound of a siren on the wind? No, it couldn't be, not just yet. Presently, the other also took off, in a complementary trajectory, rather lower over the water. The souls of dead sailors, or some shit like that, that's what they were supposed to be. He'd read that in a novel.

This my hand will rather the multitudinous seas incarnadine.

That was it. Still traces of dark pink in the crevices around his fingernails. That's what he would say. Of course, Plod wouldn't understand him. It would be hilarious. Would you come along with us, sir, is all they would respond. Then, he supposed, he would be interviewed at the station. They would take a statement. They would take his poetic language and turn it into Plod language.

Making the green one red.

So even fucking Shakespeare agreed it was green!

He watched the two gulls flying around, tracking their movements as far as he could, until he lost them in the general flux of things.

They were poor, helpless creatures like himself. He felt compassion for them!

Did he?

Immediately, he was not so sure. What was compassion, anyway? There was a definite feeling there, but was that what he was feeling?

He laughed out loud. Come along with us, sir, they would say. Yes, he would, yes, officer. At any rate, he no longer felt either at home or the need to feel at home, and that, for starters, was an immense relief.

# Free Improvisation

## SCENE ONE: THE LOCAL

JACK WENT into a local pub he didn't normally frequent. At the bar, he saw Lynton, a musician he recognised, talking to another man that he did not, in a pork-pie hat; but being shy by nature, he didn't go up to him; in fact, he subconsciously averted his face as he ordered his half-pint. However, Lynton spied him, and, at the first opportunity for eye-contact, nodded and smiled.

All right, Jack? he called.

Jack smiled to indicate that he was all right, though he wasn't that evening, if the truth be known. He raised his glass in salutation.

What is there to fear today for Jack? Apart from the rain drizzling down incessantly outside?

The other man went to the toilet, and Lynton moved over to stand next to Jack.

Hi, how you doing?

This and that.

What about that business with your kids?

My wife is still not allowing access, Jack confessed.

That's very poor. Very poor. I'm sorry to hear that, Jack.

Jack said that he was going for a job, of which he was quite hopeful. He described how he had been alerted to it by a mutual friend, briefly summed up the opportunities and threats entailed, the mental dilemmas posed for him. Lynton listened thoughtfully, nodding from time to time. That's good … that's good, he said. Jack mentioned he had an interview. That's very good, said Lynton.

Just then, Lynton's friend returned from the toilet. Lynton said: This is Jack … Bob. The two shook hands.

Lynton said: His name's not really Bob, that's what we all call him, that right, Bob? Because of Bob Marley.

Bob nodded glumly.

Ah, I see, the locks, smiled Jack. Under the pork-pie hat, Bob showed very neat, short dreadlocks, not in fact bearing much of a resemblance to those of Bob Marley.

Lynton said to Bob: Jack's a musician too.

Ah, disclaimed Jack modestly, not really.

You not still playing your horn? Haven't seen you for a while.

Haven't touched it for weeks, confessed Jack.

That's a shame, said Lynton, you got a good tone.

What kind of music you play? asked Bob.

Jack said that when he did play, he tried to play jazz. He went to a jazz workshop, that's how he knew Lynton, but he hadn't been going recently. Too busy, he said, with this and that. Alto saxophone. He played mainly standards, but he was interested in all sorts of music.

Lynton interjected that Bob was into weird stuff.

What kind of stuff do you play, then, Bob? inquired Jack, his attention awakened.

It's not that weird, said Bob with a brief smile. I'm doing a lot of free improv at the moment. I got bored with the changes.

Yeah, I get bored with the changes sometimes, said Jack, brightening. Is it like, Ornette Coleman, that kind of thing?

Yeah, kind of thing. Even broader, maybe. We got a bloke plays accordion, and even a woman plays cello.

No charts?

No charts, no tunes.

That's cool, said Jack.

Well, you should join us, man, said Bob. I lead a workshop every week.

How do you workshop on free improvisation?

Well, we have one rule, said Bob.

(Get this! interjected Lynton, beaming.)

One rule, which is, as soon as you turn up, you start improvising.

As soon as you turn up?

Yeah, don't matter if there's no one else there yet, you get out your instrument and start playing. Whatever you feel like, whatever moves you, you know? Then as each person turns up they join in.

That's intriguing, commented Jack.

Man, that's just too weird for me, said Lynton, draining his pint.

You fancy that, then, Jack?

Jack said that it might be just the thing to get him going again.

Well, you're welcome, said Bob. He named the day and the hour of the next session.

And where does this take place?

The Queen Victoria, said Bob. You know it?

It's that big old pub, that big hotel, right on the corner of … yeah, I know it.

In the ballroom, said Bob.

In the ballroom? Blimey.

Just bring your horn, said Bob.

He's got an excellent tone, Lynton assured Bob.


## SCENE TWO: THE BALLROOM

IT'S ON a drizzly early evening in autumn that this guy (Jack) goes into a pub (the Queen Victoria, a huge, drab building that has seen better days). He goes up to the girl behind the bar and asks where the ballroom is.

There is not much action. Two or three men are gathered, drinking, beneath a large TV screen showing a rugby match, but they don't appear to be paying much attention to it. No soundtrack. A faint smell of disinfectant from somewhere. The beginning of mildew in a corner of the plum-coloured carpet. Tarnished brass hooks under the counter for your coats. Traces of a vanished menu, scrubbed out on a chalkboard. A glimpse of green baize in an adjoining bar.

Vigorously drying a glass, the barmaid pauses to indicate with her free hand a door to the left of the bar.

Behind the door is a steep, narrow wooden staircase, winding upwards into the dark. Jack hitches his saxophone case on his back and ascends, arriving soon at a landing. Reverberation quality and a musty-air feel tell him he is entering a large enclosed space, but he can't find a light switch. Obviously he is quite early; nobody else has arrived yet. It is impossibly dim. As he makes his way forward, he trips on a bunch of tangled cable. Shit, he mutters. His eyes are beginning to get used to the darkness. Faint illumination from somewhere, an ambient grey. Slowly, his initial panic that there may not be enough oxygen in the room for him to take in begins to be allayed. Now he can discern speaker cabinets, or mixers, or their bulked up ghosts or something. His eyes are perched on the end of their stalks. Switches, please. There has got to be one near the door. He lays his case down carefully on the floor, which is made of wood, and slowly retraces his steps. Near where he came in, he pats the wall all the way up and down. A bank of switches is finally discovered; one by one he trips them: nothing: nothing; nothing; then finally lights flare at the far end of the room, red, green, blue. It's all set up for a disco party. A huge fresco is dimly revealed on the wall, sea-green, maybe a Caribbean beach. A beach party. There are fake palm fronds, glued shells. Is that a painted fish, or a sea-monster arising from the middle of the dusky water? It reveals only a single eye, as baleful as anything. This could be a beach on an alien planet, actually, light years from anywhere known. Glitter effects could be dying stars at the outer fringes of the galaxy. At one end is a simulated beach-side bar, with a thatched roof, but it is all closed up; there will be no rum cocktails tonight. What if a ghost barman were suddenly to appear, though? There are painted huts, in which anything could lurk. Give him the willies.

Jack returns to his instrument case, which happens to be in the exact centre of the space, this time stepping carefully around the tangle of cables and extension sockets. He takes off his coat and lays that on the floor. Kneeling, he opens the case, takes out the body of his alto saxophone. He hitches the strap on it, and around himself. He adjusts the crook and fits the mouthpiece. He selects a reed from his little tin box, fits it carefully into the mouthpiece and tightens the ligature. Still no-one else has turned up. But he is early. Standing, he puts the instrument to his lips and tries a long concert A, *mezzo-forte*: when the note dies, a beautiful reverberation is revealed in the stillness. It sounds wonderful, and is probably in tune; he's not sure. Not much point in tuning anyway, no-one to tune against, and he can always adjust later when the others arrive and join in. He starts at the bottom of the range, upward on a blues scale, but gets distracted by an interval he needs to repeat, nudging at it, bending the upper note in a plaintive attempt to meet the lower. Is it, in fact, meant to be a whale, that one-eyed creature? There are countless nuances, and the possibility of nuances, in a single note, Jack has discovered, the sound opening and closing, lurking in the shade and then emerging into the full light of day. He rocks slightly on his heels, back and forth, blowing gently, loving the reverb. And then listening to the silence that ensues. What's he going to play? He hasn't decided, but then he realises he's playing it anyway. He's already playing it. So keep going, Jack, he tells himself. A glance at the illuminated watch reveals that it's now seven-forty-five. What time did Bob say? Was the start seven-thirty or eight? But, whatever, he did definitely stipulate: just play when you get there, just start playing, until you are joined by the others. So he begins now to weave a skein of lovely notes, reaching tentatively into the upper register. Now this is a new place to play, somewhere he hasn't been before, somewhere to tiptoe, to explore, a web-like environment he is creating for himself, made out of scales, in which he may navigate or dance. He is beginning to enjoy himself, a lonely figure in the middle of a half-dark ballroom where gilt and cobwebs adorn the top corners. He weaves into the domain of the spider. He leaves spaces, then weaves again, and again pauses. Is that a response? Did someone just reply to the phrase he played? Stops to listen. No, he must have been mistaken. Still nobody. No humans, that is.

It's now well past eight o'clock. Any time now, the others will be turning up. One by one, they will enter through the door at the top of the stairs, each clutching their instrument case. Perhaps they will pause on the sidelines to listen to what he is doing; then each will in turn advance, settle themselves down, extract their instrument from the case, play a few quiet notes to warm up, then join in gradually. The experiment has been under way for some time. But still those others don't show. Meanwhile, boffin Jack is advancing in his experimental procedure. It's a kind of applied mathematics, which gives him great satisfaction, solving musical puzzles as he goes, that is to say, providing his own solutions to self-imposed, ever-changing musical questions. There is a dynamic equilibrium that is possible to achieve after a while: the music becomes a self-sustaining system. He hits a high note, stays on it. Thankfully, the technical problem he's had recently with the saxophone, with unwanted squeaking, has not returned tonight; everything is very smooth. Shadows seem to move, right above him; his own body casts overlapping shadows in the red-green-blue light on the wooden floorboards. When he turns, he is shocked for a moment to discover he is not, after all, alone; there is a twin saxophonist accompanying him, the dome of his head shining softly in that luminosity as he plays. The second shock is that this is, of course, no more than an image of himself: high in the north-east corner, angled towards him, is a mirror in which he is pictured. For some while, he watches himself as he plays. The empty ballroom watches him. Everything is suspended. But in reality there is no such emptiness. Spiders skitter. Mice stop in their tracks, ears pricked, whiskers trembling, listening. Painted salamanders and barracudas come to life. There's a lot of breath in his sound. It's suffused with the rhythm and sonority of respiration. Somebody is breathing in the quantum void. Everything is reflected. Every sound that is born soon dies. Who's playing, is it Jack or his mirror image? Is it the mirror playing, and is Jack merely copying what emerges? His phrases become longer; they merge together into sentences. The sentences appear to make sense at first, and then they don't. He is starting to gibber, to gulp at the air in the room. Air forms into unknown shapes. There are unknown geometries involved. He plays more than one sound at the same time: something he was previously unaware he could do. Notes get into formation as a troupe of scissor-like beings, jabbing, jabbing. The rests become shorter; start to vanish. Jack is in a frenzy now; he shakes as he plays, the notes pouring out crazily from his horn. Painted life-forms hide in their painted huts, and the blue moon comes out over the alien, teeming, painted ocean, shining on Jack's pate, which is beaded with sweat now, and on his silvery horn. Jack is nimble; Jack is quick. Time starts to speed up; it's now eight-thirty, and still there's nobody home, Bob must be really late. Where is he? Where are they all? Jack's slowly forgetting them, though, he's teetering from one extreme to the other, all registers of his sax in play simultaneously, no resolution in sight, rolling in an ocean of sound like some kind of brain surfer, bellowing here, screeching there, wailing in some other place, never staying in one aural location for long, buffeted and buffeting, breath coming in fast and vacating his body even faster; sometimes the horn sounds as though it's sobbing uncontrollably with unnamed grief, at other times guffawing with full-bodied merriment, the blues scale left far behind, indeed, all scales abandoned for the time being, in an area of tonality that has no formal designation; and every so often he seems to pose another question, with a rising intonation, but by now, inevitably, there is no satisfactory reply, for there is no-one there to reply, so onward he goes, on and on, without rest, without further reflection, into areas of pleasure that morph into pain and back again, almost bursting his sides in a show of abandon, for minutes, hours, centuries, epochs, until at last his energy levels show signs of beginning to flag, he becomes aware of himself again, and of his surroundings, in this bizarre ballroom that it seems no-one will ever enter, as if it were all an immense joke of which he was the intended butt, except that he has turned the tables, he's given more than he got, he's given everything and still he's got more.

Jack has come to the end; he has no sound left. He stands still for a long time, taking breaths, trembling slightly. The ballroom appeared to have become vast in the time that elapsed, like a universe that expanded, but it's now regaining its shape and proper size. No human, no being above the level of a spider or small rodent, has witnessed his performance, his greatest ever, nor will any ever witness it. Essentially unrepeatable, it's gone, finished, done – lost to humanity for all time. He glances at his luminous watch again: past nine-thirty. A tidal wave of anger envelops him: fucking Bob, must have cancelled the session, never told him. He's just been forgotten about. Fuck him! Bach said all his music was composed "for the glory of God", but that's no use to Jack, who has no deity in his scope to act as witness, as the repository of such a musical experience. Useless, useless! But there is no solution; after all, most of everything is soon lost, like the information that disappears into a black hole, and finally everything is lost forever.

Somewhere, in an abandoned world beyond the great, awesome silence, he can now hear very faint sounds coming up from below, of conversation perhaps, clinking of glasses, a TV soundtrack, the click of snooker balls. He begins to entertain the faint hope that the others were waiting in the wings, too awe-struck to interrupt his performance, and will now emerge to congratulate him. But nobody enters the ballroom. Not Bob, nor the man with the accordion, nor the lady with the cello, nor any others. Nobody will be turning up now. Perhaps it was his fault after all; perhaps he got the day wrong. What a waste of time and effort it all was. Jack unhitches his saxophone, drops to his knees, disassembles it and puts it back in its case. A shame they haven't come; he would like to have met them.

## SCENE THREE: THE LOCAL

LYNTON AND JACK sat at opposite sides of the stained wooden table, Lynton with the dregs of a pint of Guinness, Jack with a Diet Coke, their elbows leaning on the table, their eyes looking away from each other, each in their own universe. Jack finally broke the silence, and said: Yeah, I'm getting to see my kids at the weekend.

That's great, Jack.

God knows what I'm going to do with them. Especially as I'm skint. You got any ideas?

Winter had returned.

The door banged open suddenly, a gust of air rushing in, together with street noise. You would think anything could enter thereby; another story could begin.

Lynton said: Oh, by the way, how did you get on with Bob's free improvisation class?

Yeah, I nearly forgot. That was brilliant. It was totally fucking amazing. Greatest experience I ever had in my life.

Someone left the bar, went over to the door and shut it gently, so that harshness ceased.

D'you want another of the same, Jack enquired.

I don't mind, said Lynton, yeah, thanks.

# The Edge

WELCOME TO The Edge.

The Edge is suitable for all the family. There is almost a freefall here, and beauty can be enjoyed at its very best.

The Edge is like nowhere you can imagine. From the timeless tranquillity of the desert to the lively bustle of the market, The Edge does not only boast the best contemporary sightings but has also preserved some of the most intriguing historical attractions. The major attraction is of course the Event Horizon, tantalising glimpses of which can be obtained between the narrow streets of the Old Town. The complex boasts remarkable skyscrapers, and is also in the process of developing one of the most technologically advanced buildings in the world: a residential tower is set to be embedded with the latest gadgets that will have the power to change interior design and window views to almost anything imaginable.

Golden beaches have been built, with unrivalled views of the Event Horizon. Its sands are covered with the fastest cars.

You can see everything from the Sky Bar. Artefacts from excavated graves can be viewed. There are camels: little ones and enormous ones. A white prancing horse adorns a hill (a room has been built in its stomach). Deadly weapons also form the major part of the attractions, such as swords, spears, bows, arrows, shields, pistols and axes. Visitors to the farm are greeted by a cannon. Buildings are still growing. The Heritage Village offers a great example of how life was in The Edge before its modernisation, with its traditional fort, mud houses and stone buildings. In this village you can visit the famous homes that were designed just a couple of decades ago. Where is the zoo? It is ideally located in the lush green suburbs. Probably, it is the greenest spot in this area, covered with a variety of trees. There is a random selection of Malls. The street-front stores side alleys of smaller shops with glittering show windows.

There are all nationalities at The Edge: French, Germans, Slovakians from the Danube, many Norwegians, South Africans, US citizens including from the African American community, Italian Americans, Hispanics, also British subjects from the United Kingdom… for this is one of the most multicultural places on Earth. So, what are you waiting for?

Nowhere is like The Edge.


## A CITY SEEMED TO FALL FROM THE SKY

IMMERSE YOURSELF in our new interactive portal, even before you arrive here, to avail yourself of previews of all our many attractions. You will see all the colours in full resolution: white, pale pink, peach, mauve, pale yellow, sky blue, mustard, lime green, sand. The updated information will enable you to find the best facilities and venues to meet your accessibility requirements and will assist you in making an informed choice when planning a trip to The Edge either for a holiday, short trip or for business. You will see many buildings of the finest concrete with traditional cast iron balconies, glass, and chain-link fencing for your protection.

Visitors will be delighted beyond their expectations. As one of the safest and most relaxed environments on earth – The Edge is truly distinctive. The Edge is a holiday paradise – white beaches on which to relax and enjoy the sun, the best hotels in the world and an absolute shopper's delight offering a unique and richly exotic experience that is both modern and traditional. View the Event Horizon from numerous comfortably equipped vantage points within the complex. "It's like a melody appearing out of white noise." It is safe to swim here. Naked children romp in the shallows. Once within the Protected Zone, you will experience a Global Village indeed, and a Huge Cultural Entertainment Centre. Apartments for sale or rent are available throughout the complex at competitive prices.

A city seemed to fall from the sky, and this is The Edge. These are the Last Days of Everything, and so no expense has been spared. There are islands shaped like poems. It's hot from one end of the year to the next, and there is no taxation.

The city is designed in a modern style, combining both architectural and natural designs, recreational facilities, Cable Car, Restaurants etc. Discerning visitors will find that it offers the perfect blend of luxury and leisure, shopping and culture, in an environment that is hospitable, safe and virtually crime free. *Please key in your PIN.* The Event Horizon shopping centre is open daily from 10am-10pm (12 midnight Thursday-Saturday). Stores teem with the latest electronics, silks from India, top fragrances, watches, cameras and other international items. Brands include Marella, DKNY, Phillippe Charrioll, Burberry, Movado, Benetton, Tiffany & Co, Givenchy. It has Starbucks and Dunkin' Donuts and the Gucci styles that are highly enjoyed all round the World. Enjoy a drink at Paddy's Irish Pub or Murphy's Irish Pub, or meals and light refreshment at Snack Bar O Sole Mio, Golden Curry Indian Restaurant, Funky Fish, or even Restaurant Indonesia. For your everyday needs, try Minimarket, or Lidl is coming to this neighbourhood soon. Amid the traditional rows of orange trees lining the streets are Citroen, Mercedes or Audi dealers, or Rent a Car from numerous outlets. *This choice is currently unavailable.*

There is no specific food at The Edge. Therefore you are invited to put your fork into a range of tempting dishes. If your idea of romance is to gaze into the mirror of water with your partner amidst luxurious surroundings, then it's time to check out.

There is a wide range of hotels and furnished apartments. For example, The Excelsior is a 5-Star Hotel in the heart of the city, 231 rooms including 2 ambassador suites and 2 suites for physically challenged guests. Numerous nightclubs offer hip-hop, house and salsa music until the early hours of the morning, within metres of the Event Horizon. *This choice is currently unavailable.* Elsewhere, talented acts from all over the world provide lively international shows at many venues. The Edge increasingly attracts top names from the world of entertainment. These include popular singers and entertainers from both West and East.

By night, The Edge is neon-lit and fantastic, an urban temple that will take your breath away. There are fireworks displays nightly that can be seen from the moon. Lions roam the streets. Max Cineplex will have you on the edge of your seat. "There is nothing there". Shopping is Just the Beginning. Security patrols the perimeter 24 hours a day for your protection.

Exchange money? No problem! *Please key in your PIN.* You can change money at any one of a thousand exchange points around the complex.

We don't want you to fall ill, but if the worst happens there is a private hospital within the complex fully equipped with state-of-the-art facilities. *Please wear your green wristband at all times.*

Feel free to leave a comment in the Guest Book. We are always interested in hearing your comments and views about The Edge. It is The Edge Corporation's Policy to listen and respond to the views of our customers and stakeholders, and in particular respond positively to complaints, and put our mistakes right.

There are frequent buses to and from the airport, which is 30km outside the Protected Zone. The road to the airport is convenient and safe.


## AN EXCLUSIVE PARADISE FOR EVERYBODY

THE EDGE Corporation provides unrivalled opportunities for investors from all over the World. The Edge's economic performance has been remarkable, with double-digit real growth and a relatively high per capita income. You will be able to purchase debt at low prices, ensuring a guaranteed return (subject to legal and physical laws). A variety of assets and bonds have demonstrated remarkable performance over an astonishing period of time. Economic performance at the sectoral level has also been impressive, led by trade, construction and real estate sectors, with good signs of successful diversification. Workforce planning is designed to provide the maximum return for investors. (Issues of sewage contamination have been exaggerated in the media, and have largely been eliminated.)

The Edge Investments achieved immense growth and witnessed a great number of positive developments in the past year. Our total consolidated income for the period until December 31 was $3.72 billion – 82 percent increase on last year. We posted a net profit of $1.5 billion for the year, a growth of over 52 percent compared to last year. We have put in motion plans that will ensure continued success for the group and each of its arms and subsidiaries, witness the launch of many diverse projects and companies. These new developments will help us to cement ourselves as an integral part of high growth-potential establishments in the private equity field. Its momentous achievements in past years have strengthened our belief that it is meant for big things. From the onset, The Edge Investments has always pursued an uncompromising policy in creating a team of world-class professionals. We believe that it is this core unit that has made the company the success it is today and together we will continue to make the next the best and most memorable year.

Time doesn't seem to pass in the malls, where turnover increases rapidly year on year. And investment doesn't stand still! The Universe is a development of private and commercial islands, an exclusive paradise for everybody. This is your chance to own a part of the future. It's not too late. The future, of course, is an unmatchable option. *Please key in your PIN.* The Edge Corporation has announced that it expects to achieve a production capacity of over 75,000 metric tonnes annually following completion of its factory expansion. Extruded polystyrene has been a success story. ÔÈÈÔ?Ô'·Ò??Ò *I'm sorry, that number has not been recognised. Please try again.* Harvesting of stem cells will become an important resource. There has been significant investment also in 12-lane freeways packed with Mercedes, Lexus and other vehicles. Private equity is the thrust, and a hot topic regionally. Real estate, switchgear, structured cabling and fibre optics, logistics, culture industries: whatever the field, our focus has always been on acquiring profitable entities, investing in them and assisting to take them to the next level of growth. Once we believe that the company has attained its objective we initiate an "exit strategy" and offer our shares up for sale. *For technical reasons, this offer is not open to citizens of Bangladesh, Pakistan, or a number of countries of Sub Saharan Africa (with the exception of South Africa).*

You are advised that the terrorist problem has largely been eliminated.

The journey has just begun. The destinations are diverse. What's not possible here?

## THE EVENT HORIZON

OF COURSE, the most impressive feature of The Edge, which all visitors are agog to see, is the Event Horizon. "It's like nowhere!" says Barry, a visitor from the United Kingdom. And Lisa May, from Tucson, Arizona, USA, comments: "I have never seen anything like it. You think you have seen water in the distance, but you get close and you only get a mouthful of sand."

But what is the Event Horizon?

The Universe is undergoing Massive Condensation. Its huge investment of matter has to go somewhere, and some experts call its final destination the Great Offshore Attractor, situated right at The Edge. Material is constantly being absorbed by the Attractor. As The Universe shrinks, its assets are continuously being re-absorbed. They go through layers of processes, like holding companies, to get to the Ultimate Asset. The gravity of the operation starts to take hold. At this point, the laws of physics begin to break down. The sight of this is truly magnificent. The ubiquitous travelling cranes have paused on the skyline, as if stuck in time, the limits of material credit having been achieved. And then things begin to spill over into a series of issues as the ripple effect takes hold. Experts believe that this has been happening since Time Immemorial.

It is difficult to explain, but let us try. We are all present. But beyond The Edge, presence is no longer possible. Suppose that within the zone of presence, you look out over in the direction of the Event Horizon, well then, you will witness absence. That is the meaning of absence: it is what presence points to. It only points one way (this is sometimes called the Arrow of Time). The Event Horizon is the limit beyond which no return is possible. Once past the Event Horizon, matter cannot be retrieved.

Its structure breaks down at that point, and all investment of energy fails, that is to say we do not expect a return, within any significant time. Speech fails, and with it metaphor of all kind, and images as well as structured sound. There is white noise (the sound of an untuned TV set). Where matter has existed, for example, water, the individual molecules break down into constituent atoms, and the atoms then into protons and electrons, and finally into particles called quarks and gluons.

The dream is alive! A splendid view of the Event Horizon can be obtained from any of the observation platforms. You can imagine anything beyond the Event Horizon, and you will. It is also considered to be a captivating phenomenon that offers both extremes: a traditional past interlinked with modern day. "It just gets better and better," comment many of our guests. "The air smells of ozone."

When you go to view the Event Horizon, you will see that everything has already happened.

Be warned that the periphery is decreasing by the year, and therefore cannot be depended upon. But this poses no threat to visitors, provided safety procedures are adhered to; please follow your tour guide's instructions, and hold onto the handrails in the observation platforms. Your guide will ensure you remain at a safe distance. *Please wear your green wristband at all times.*

"What happens if I fall off?" many visitors ask. Well, this is not possible except in the rare event of an anomaly in the rate of condensation. Millions of visitors enjoy the Event Horizon Experience every year, without ill effects.

The Universe has become a metaphor, almost religious, for any type of mysterious bottomless pit, and the Event Horizon is where^*æμ ßø®®¥ †?? ~ ¨μ ? ´® ?åß ~ø† ?´´~ ® ´çø©~^ß´ ∂?□ ¬ ´ åß´ †®¥ å ©å^~*. A splendid view of the Event Horizon can be obtained from any of the observation platforms. *Please do not venture beyond the boundaries of the Protected Zone.* "I can see wisps of haze appearing to creep over flat countryside." But the Ultimate Asset itself cannot be observed directly. It can be said that this is an imaginary endpoint.

*Normal service will be resumed very shortly.* The second annual football championship conducted by The Edge Corporation has concluded with Permits Department Team being declared champions. The Ladies Masters Golf Tournament will take place next February. The Global Film Festival will introduce major celebrity guests. These events are organised by The Edge Corporation, with sponsorship from our major stakeholder partners. Events outside the Protected Zone cannot be guaranteed. *The Edge Corporation can accept no liability for anomalies that may occur.*

Please ensure that Enjoy a traditional night of entertainment at Britannia Pub & Dylan's Irish Bar or Pub O'Brien. We have the red telephone box, and London bus-stop signs. *Please key in your PIN.* Beware of unauthorised vendors. Please report any such activities to Administration. *Thank you for your co-operation. I'm sorry, that number has not been recognised. Please try again.*

Security staff are there to protect you from ^~†®¨∂´®ß ÏÂØ? ØËÊÍÈÎ‰ †?´ ?®ø†´ç†´∂ Ûø~The people who built the complex can be seen in long chain-gangs by the side of the road, or working all day at the top of the tallest buildings in the world. They are identifiable by their smart blue overalls. *The road to the airport is currently unavailable.* Enjoy your visit†Hiß ç?ø^ç´IS ç¨®®´~†¬¥ Ë?Â?ÍÈÒÂ`Ò‰. A splendid view of the Event Horizon

Max Cineplex *This choice is currently unavailable.* a very interesting documentary

white, pale pink, peach, mauve, pale yellow, sky blue, mustard, lime green, sand.


## YOUR SAFETY IS IMPORTANT

SECURITY STAFF patrol the perimeter at all times; you can identify them by their smart blue uniforms. If a member of our security staff requires you to produce evidence of your identity, please do not be offended; thank you for your co-operation in this. Your safety is important to us. The terrorist problem has largely been eliminated. Beware of unauthorised vendors of sunglasses, DVDs and other merchandise – they are often intruders from outside the Protected Zone.

In the event of an anomaly, †Hiß ç?ø^ç´IS ç¨®®´~†¬¥

Ë?Á?ÍÈÒÀ⅃Ò‰. safety procedures will come into operation immediately (Approximate cost to be determined.) *Please key in your PIN.* "no, it smells of shit" *I'm sorry, that number has not been recognised.*

Like nowhere! The Edge is nowhere. "Things have got to stop somewhere, haven't they?" remarks Heike from Hamburg. *I'm SORRY< THAT ?Ë?›‰Á ?ØÊ ›‰Á? ® ´ƒø©~^ß´∂. PÒ‰ÁÍ‰ †®¥ ÁÌÀÈ?.* "We have a problem."

crisis is a symptom of a broader malaise. He said it was raising credibility concerns. All over the complex, there are people sleeping secretly in the sand-dunes or the airport or in their cars. MALICIOUS MEDIA REPORTS HAVE NO FOUNDATION STATES THE EDGE CORPORATION TODAY ∑?^†´?ÅÒ‰ ?È?? □ ´åç? ?ÅË?? ?ÅÒ‰ ¥´¬¬ø Í?Á ›ÒË‰ µ¨ß†å®∂ ¬^µ´©®´´~ÍÅ?Î

Investors need to stay calm. There is no cause for concern. There is no cause for concern. There is no cause for concern. There is no cause for concern. *I'm sorry, that number has not been recognised. Please try again.*

In a statement today
the white molecules of water
*This choice is currently unavailable.*

sky blue, mustard, lime green, sand sand sand sand sand sand sand sand sand sand sand sand sand sand sand sand Brands include Armani, Gucci and Jimmy Choo sand sand sand sand sand sand sand sand *I'm SORRY< THAT ?Ë?‰Á ?ØÊ ›‰Á? ® ´ƒø©~^ß´∂. PÒ‰ÁÍ‰ †®¥ ÁÌÀÈ?.* sand sand sand sand sand sand sand sand such as Dolce & Gabbana, Cartier, Calvin Klein and Tiffany sand sand sand sand Please do not drink the water. Animals are wounded, and refuse to speak. "You've got to draw the line somewhere." "She just disappeared into the haze." "I love you, Mummy." *†Hiß ƒ?ø^ƒ´IS ƒ¨®® ´~†¬¥ Ë?Á?ÍÈÒÀ⅃Ò‰.*

*The road to the airport is currently unavailable.*
*The road to the airport is currently unavailable.*

«««««««««««««†he ´∂©e È~√´ß†µ´~†ß åç?^´√´ ^µµ´~ß´ ©®ø∑†? å~∂ ∑^†~´ßß´∂ å ©®´å† ~¨µ?´® ø? □ øß^†^√´ ∂´√´¬ø□µ´~†ß ^~†?´¿¿¿¿¿¿¿¿□ åß† ¥´å®. Ø¨® †ø†å¬ çø~ßø¬^∂´†´∂

^~çøµ´?ø® †?´□ ´®^ø∂ ¨~†^¬ Î∂´ç´µ?´® #¡ ∑åß ¢#?¶?
?^¬¬^ø~– •?□ ´®ç´~† ^~ç®´åß´ø~¬åß† ¥´å®?//////////
"mummy, mummy" ÎÈÎ ÁØË ?Ø„ „´□øß†´∂ å ~´†□®ø?^† ø?
›¡?? ?^¬¬^ø~ ?ø® †?´¥´å®, å ©®ø∑†? ø? ø√´® ??
□´¿¿¿¿¿¿¿//////////®ç´~† çøµ□ å®´∂ †ø ¬åß† ¥´å®.
Ê?´‰∂©´È~√´ß†µ´~†ß "I try not to see," she says.ÓÅÍ
ÅÒ„ÅÁÍ ?ËÂÍË‰Î Å? Ë?ÇØ??ÂØ?ÈÍÈ?Î ?ØÒÈÇÁ È?
ÇÂ‰ÅÊÈ?Ì Å Ê‰Å? ØÏ „ØÂÒÎ—ÇÒÅÍÍ ?ÂØÏ‰ÍÍÈ?ÅÒÍ
/////////////There are many stunning items such as pearl
necklaces, diamond rings and gold bangles to choose
from.„´?´¬^´√´ÊÓÅÊ „´?´¬^´√´ÊÓÅÊ .„´?´¬^´√´ÊÓÅÊ
¿¿¿¿¿¿¿ «««««««¿¿¿¿¿¿ /////////////¿¿¿¿¿¿¿¿¿¿ ¿¿¿¿¿¿¿¿¿¿ ¿¿¿¿¿¿¿
¿¿¿¿¿¿¿¿¿¿¿¿ ««««««««¿¿¿¿¿¿¿¿¿¿¿¿¿¿¿ ¿¿¿¿¿¿¿ ¿¿¿¿¿¿¿
¿¿¿¿¿¿¿¿¿¿//////// //// /////// anomaly ////////
//////////>>>>>> »»»»»»»»»»» »» ¿¿¿¿¿¿¿¿¿¿ ¿¿¿¿¿¿¿
¿¿¿¿¿¿¿¿¿¿ ««««««««¿¿¿¿¿¿ ¿¿¿¿¿¿¿¿¿ ¿¿¿¿¿¿ sky blue, ¿¿¿¿¿¿¿
¿¿¿¿¿¿¿¿¿//////// //// /////// ////////
//////////>>>>>> »»»»»sand¿¿¿ ¿¿¿¿¿¿¿¿ ¿¿¿¿¿¿¿¿ ¿¿¿¿¿¿¿
««««««««¿¿¿¿¿¿ ¿¿¿¿¿¿¿¿¿¿ ¿¿¿¿¿¿¿ ¿¿¿¿¿¿¿¿ ¿¿¿¿¿¿¿¿¿¿////// ////
/////// //////// //////////>>>>>> »»»»».............. ... .
.…... .. . .. …. ... ….. .. . ….. .. .. ….. .. .. »»»»».............… ... .. .
.. . . . . .. .. …....... .. .. …. ... .. .. .. . .….... . . .… .... ... . ..
.…... . . . . …... .. ….. …. … ... ... . ... . .
.…... .. ....... ... .. .. .. »»»»».............… .. . .. . ... ... . ... .. .
.…......... . .. ........ .. ...........….. . . .. . ... ... . ... . . . ...
. . . . .. . . . . . . . .. . . . .
. . . . .

*You cannot leave The Edge at this time. Please remain calm.*

# Nothing doing

SOMEBODY:
There's nothing.

NOBODY:
Where?

SOMEBODY:
Here. Everywhere. Nowhere.

[silence]

NOBODY:
This is some kind of place, isn't it?

SOMEBODY:
Well, I can't see anything. There is nothing left.

[silence]

NOBODY:
I think there must have been people living here once.

SOMEBODY:
Where?

NOBODY:
I don't know. I believe there were people.

SOMEBODY:
Well, they've all gone, then. There's nobody left.

NOBODY:
Where did they live? Where are their houses? They must have had houses?

SOMEBODY:
All vanished.

NOBODY:
Extraordinary.

SOMEBODY:
Absolutely nothing to be seen.

NOBODY:
Houses can't just vanish!

[silence]

SOMEBODY:
They must have destroyed them.

NOBODY:
That must be it, I guess. They must have destroyed all their own houses. That's terrible!

SOMEBODY:
They must have destroyed everything. Everything has disappeared.

NOBODY:
Are you sure?

SOMEBODY:
Can you see anything?

NOBODY:
No, I must admit I can't.

SOMEBODY:
Nothing moving.

NOBODY:
Not even a stone skipping across a lake.

SOMEBODY:
No lake!

NOBODY:
Not even a sound, the plop as the stone hits the water for the last time and sinks, not even that.

SOMEBODY:
There's not a single sound. Not even the wind. Just silence everywhere. The people have vanished. And their animals, and all their belongings. The houses have vanished. The lake has entirely vanished.

NOBODY:
It's uncanny.

[silence]

SOMEBODY:
The people must have destroyed their houses. Then they destroyed the lake. And the mountains all around, which might have been heavily forested, for all we know, and all the creatures that dwelt there, if there were creatures, they destroyed those too. [pause] Then they destroyed themselves.

NOBODY:
Why would they want to do that?

SOMEBODY:
Who knows?

NOBODY:
Perhaps they didn't.

SOMEBODY:
What?

NOBODY:
Perhaps they didn't destroy themselves. Perhaps they got away.

SOMEBODY:
Where to? There isn't anywhere else!

NOBODY:
I guess not.

SOMEBODY:
There's nowhere for them to go.

NOBODY:
We don't know that.

SOMEBODY:
And how? How could they get away?

NOBODY:
By road?

SOMEBODY:
There are no roads!

NOBODY:
I have to admit you're right. There's no sign of a road.

SOMEBODY:
I suppose they could have destroyed the roads behind them as

they went. You know, they could have covered their traces.

NOBODY:
But surely there would be some evidence of this? There'd be, I don't know, rubble.

SOMEBODY:
Rubble?

NOBODY:
But there is no rubble. I would expect to see rubble and detritus, that kind of thing, I would expect to see it and smell it, but there's not a sign of it anywhere. So even the rubble has vanished!

SOMEBODY:
They could have had some very powerful weapons. They could have had extremely advanced technology, capable of vapourising even the rubble they created when they destroyed their roads and houses. The technology might even have vapourised the lake, how about that?

NOBODY:
That would be awe-inspiring.

SOMEBODY:
Such technology would have taken years and years to develop. Millennia, even. It's almost inconceivable. Generation upon generation, these people would have worked patiently on their technology, perfecting it bit by bit. They would have tested it from time to time, let's say on a cowshed, or an enemy, tried to see if they could destroy that with any success. Then back to the drawing board. Passing on what they had learned in their lifetime to their children. Can you imagine? The men with their strength and obduracy, the women with their brains, and their breasts bursting with milk. They must have had a huge capacity for application and selfless endeavour, without expectation of an ultimate reward.

NOBODY:
Yes, that's right, generations would have been born and lived and died without knowing whether they were going to succeed in the end.

SOMEBODY:
Without even knowing what success might look like.

NOBODY:
They weren't to know.

SOMEBODY:
Weren't to know what?

NOBODY:
That it would look like [pause] nothing.

SOMEBODY:
I tell you what, it looks exactly like nothing. There's nothing there!

NOBODY:
100% success!

SOMEBODY:
Who would have thought it?

NOBODY:
They could've...

SOMEBODY:
They could've created a beautiful environment.

NOBODY:
I don't know. These people ... you've got to hand it to them. They weren't stupid. They must have perceived, I don't know: a need, a ... threat. Yes, a threat perhaps, that's what they would have been responding to, working hard to eliminate the threat.

SOMEBODY:
A threat from where? As we've seen, there isn't anywhere else.

NOBODY:
It could've been a threat from within. An existential threat, if you like. What they created might have been too much for them, they would've needed to deal with it, and if they couldn't deal with it, they would've needed to eliminate it. To make it, you know … vanish. [pause] I'm not putting it very well.

SOMEBODY:
Go on.

NOBODY:
You have to create, how can I say, the means to cope with this, to cope with this sense of threat. It's not enough to make things, to make things that are beautiful, things that delight, let's just say, for the sake of argument; that's not enough, you have to have the capability to make things *vanish*, be gone and not come back, because, what am I trying to say, there's a terror in existence, a finality to it, even beauty is dreadful, especially beauty, beauty is a threat, it's the end of everything, I mean – bear with me – I mean, it's a full stop, it has to be destroyed, otherwise no movement is possible. [pause] Do you see? [pause] You need a culture of vanishing. In order to continue. Do you see what I mean?

[silence]

SOMEBODY:
You're not making any sense.

NOBODY:
No, I suppose not.

SOMEBODY:
Are you talking about … progress?

NOBODY:

I'm talking about movement. It's impossible. Beauty makes movement impossible, because of its finality. But then destroying it...

SOMEBODY:

Perhaps there never were any people.

NOBODY:

You're kidding!

SOMEBODY:

Perhaps there never were.

NOBODY:

It's a moot point.

SOMEBODY:

Perhaps none of this ever happened. That's a possibility, isn't it? There were no people, there was no town or city, there were no animals to be domesticated and husbanded, no mountains or forests, there was no lake, no sky, no fresh-smelling earth or grass. Perhaps there was never a murmur of insects, or the calling of birds from one tree to the next, or the thrum of machinery or even the hum of human conversation and music playing in a distant bar. Perhaps...

NOBODY:

Did we invent all this, then?

SOMEBODY:

Somebody did.

NOBODY:

But there's nobody!

SOMEBODY:

Good point.

NOBODY:
So it's impossible.

SOMEBODY:
Either all of this existed, and it completely vanished, or…

NOBODY:
…it never existed at all.

SOMEBODY:
It's impossible to tell the difference.

NOBODY:
Yes.

[silence]

SOMEBODY:
So where are we, anyway?

NOBODY:
Who knows? We're here. That's all I know.

SOMEBODY:
Where's that?

NOBODY:
[silence]

SOMEBODY:
Where's here?

NOBODY:
[silence]

SOMEBODY:
Why are we here?

NOBODY:
I don't know. There's nothing for either of us to do here. There's nothing for us here.

[silence]

SOMEBODY:
Who are you?

NOBODY:
Nobody.

# In Gondwanaland

THERE WAS not, so far as I can recall, such an evening: we never again went for a walk in the park, we didn't sit on a bench, never watched the young Asian men play cricket on the common. I certainly can't remember them wearing brightly coloured polo shirts, nor whether any wore a turban. I can't imagine them showing the tremendous application that would have been evident. Nor their heartfelt appeals. Shouting would have an echo to it that would be evocative. It would have become a kind of liquid. Liquid would never condense on skin like that, sticky with it, wicked. There was no such park, and no such young men had ever been born. It was said there were two great coloured balloons in the sky above the park, if it had ever existed, representing mind and matter, but I don't remember them either, nor a large kite representing a footballer's lower torso that was said to have been observed. People hadn't set out their stalls. Had they done so, you can imagine how a Chinese couple in charge of one of them might have created calligraphed idiograms for their customers, a black couple, representing their names: his could have been Noir, rendered as the word Black, hers Bobbie, rendered as two equivalent syllables. A strange fancy. Cakes and beer were never offered. There was no mingle of scents. Days and days may have gone by, or not. Drifting over from a window of one of the houses overlooking the common it was not possible to recognise a melody, played on an out-of-tune piano; high over the ox-bow lakes of the Flood, whose water might have produced a matt sheen in the remaining late afternoon light, no distant hang-glider did ever float; tonight would not be a night of 100 violins. No lone cormorant, vigilant on a bank; no grebes; no heron. Some said a local group produced a poem-essay about 50 yards long, on a sort of parchment or bedsheet that was dragged along the pavement, but I never saw it. This "artwork" could never have been sold or bartered for other artefacts or opportunities, as some asserted. Which was in any event not at all interesting, or urban fox-like. A lamb did not land by parachute (and her name was not Larry); in the blue-grey dusk below, there was no distant scimitar of brightness, the kind that would have seemed as though reflected off a dome, but was actually a curving line of separate lights. You might have heard a storm circling far away, but the trestle tables were never restored and the party never took place as planned in the open. Tennis was not promised either. We didn't help carry the trestles, tabletops and benches back down the road whence they had come. Neither did we go on an hour's circular walk down country lanes that we never imagined existing in the heart of this city, picking windfall plums. Among the disused factories and abandoned office blocks, there was no strange attractor. The great bowl of the sky: vanished as though it had never been. On the various billboards situated on bridges and the sides of buildings above the high street, texts could not, as had been predicted, be observed to move and trans-form subtly, so that now they were Chinese or Hebrew and then English, yet seeming hardly to have changed. In any case, I wouldn't have been able discern what their messages were. That would have come in time, I was told, but I have my doubts. During the proceedings, I didn't encounter a fox rummaging in the dustbins and general garbage in the place where the fruit and vegetable stalls set up, just next to the Quality Butcher. If such an animal had been observed, its size and state of health could-n't have been ascertained; it could not have watched me warily with bright steady eyes but without fear had I stopped still to look at it. Were the houses clearly derelict? Was there a rusting hulk of a van? I can't say. But it got no lighter, wind did not arise, weather failed to break up, there was no thunder in the air. Life did not start all over again. It was hardly as though we were at the beginning of the era wherein everyone knew their place. Unknowing thus became the theme.

I had never noticed how very wide the floorboards were in the living room. Weirdly shaped rooms failed to open off one another unexpectedly. I was no "stranger in paradise". Gold sun on the horizon didn't blind me. Crows weren't flying to roost. I never spoke words of wisdom to you, and if I did, I can't now recall them, or their import. There was never a day of torrential thunderstorms, interspersed with weirdly bright sunshine. You don't remember them either. No drink, no piece of pie, no soup outside the Old Father Time, where there were no lightweight metal tables or chairs. No ancient dog lay near us. Cool, grey-blue? I couldn't discern any citrus fruit on dense, trellised branches. No twitter of sparrows, no hum of voices. Was there a beautiful and very intense young Egyptian student called Easter sitting next to us, who was interested in breaking up words into coloured fragments? Even if she had been there, she couldn't have told us about her brother who was re-inventing extended vocal techniques even though he'd never learned music formally and had not previously been known to sing; nor would we have learnt about her mother, 75 years old at the last count, who recently smoked a spliff for the very first time. Would she have enjoyed it? I think not. Remember how everything faded into history and was lost? And how we got used to the fact that eventually everything that had once loomed large and exciting would be forgotten? This was not so fantastically great and truly out of time. I didn't know whether I was coming, going or standing still. We couldn't just walk back home in five minutes at the end of the day. We failed to observe the icy dew on the surfaces and the moon through gaps, nor the block ahead of us, all lit up like an ocean liner (unless it was the Titanic). We could never again both work separately and together in the same space, and then meet up once more. You didn't acquire a set of pastels nor a new miniature wall of books. We didn't stir-fry giant prawns. In the early hours of the morning you could not have pulled me to you in bed, almost asleep, saying I was your music and I was getting away from you, a dream state I couldn't have understood. Because you weren't there. You were never there. During that walk in the woods, no sexual itch coincided with a fox crossing the path we had just traversed. Spent bluebells, and blue dragon-

144

flies stationary in the air – no trace of them. You never disported yourself, eyes shining, in a shirt of muslin and a floppy hat. You never bounced with excitement as we slipped back for sex in the afternoon while the Titanic sank all over again. I must have invented your unnerving and moving gratitude. No sulky warmth settled into the streets. You didn't wake me with kisses in the middle of the night. I don't recall asking "Where am I?" nor my lack of disturbance. (If I did, you didn't answer.) You didn't excite the molecules of my body in unforeseen ways. What were the limits or boundaries? what did "unforeseen" actually mean? We couldn't have pretended to be on a package holiday in our own back yard, could we? How could we? That week we could have planned to turn our attention to the bathroom, to clean and paint to the sounds of African music coming over from the pub garden, but this didn't happen, nor were there children from many ethnic backgrounds playing in the back yard in sunshine, following each other in a conga line that snaked all up and down the fire escapes. No, nothing could ever become human again. At the end, there was no sparkling, seaside-themed bathroom, with conch shell, pebbles and flourishing plants on the gleaming window shelf. You weren't kissing and cuddling me nor telling me how attractive I had become.

8.00 am: Did not make love. "Lightness & drift."

10.00 am: Did not move books from shelf to shelf.

The flat failed to glow in the early evening light. There was no trace of your rug on the living-room floor, the dusky red throw over the sofa, the flowers, the rearranged books, your pink lampshade, the view from the bay – all were gone. It was no pleasure to contemplate where the bookshelves and wooden music stand had been. No kids were playing or screaming outside. Not tapping on metal. The wind-chimes didn't move at the fire-escape door outside the kitchen. There was no feeding frenzy of tits in the early morning light outside our bedroom window. We failed to go for another walk when the rain clouds lifted, giving us brief sunshine once more. I don't remember waiting for you to get out of the bath so I could use your water. Observing cumulo-nimbus beginning to cover the sky over the park at the end of a very hot and humid day, I believe you would have predicted another thunderstorm, one that would arrive just after midnight, crashing dramatically for just a few minutes almost overhead, flashing golden-white light through the blinds and bringing with it sudden torrential rain. But this didn't occur. Because there was no you. Because you had not been born. No, there was no thunder, nor sheeting water, nor lights passing away. And we didn't awake or hug. Didn't drift from room to room. You didn't compare me to an ant in industry and resilience, nor to a rock in fortitude. I had no occasion to be flattered thereby. Beech did not gleam. We didn't clean the flat, nor install busy lizzies in the window-box. I didn't plant a herb garden on the fire escape: neither oregano, marjoram, thyme, rosemary, nor basil. If there was ever yellow blossom in the back yard it had now faded, and none of the young trees lining the diagonal path across the common to the Flood carried such a heavy freight of white or pink blossom as they might have done. I can't say whether the mature plane trees across the road from us were beginning to sport their full complement of young leaves, nor whether the growth started very conspicuously from the lower branches, and only reached the upper parts later. There were no buds on the biggest tree, and the tall spindly one to our right, bare last week, had not acquired greenery; while behind it, bronze leafery, deepening to copper, had not appeared. No gardeners were at work, I never found my way to the secret room with the aspidistra and the view onto the imaginary garden, I never played the piano, I didn't experience a single note reiterated, the warped reverberations of heavy bass chords

The music was not broken

Because it was not loved

and I could have played for hours in the darkening ambience which had become a new theatre, a note becoming a chord and a chord's multiple possibilities dying and dying, getting further and further dispersed on an impossible trajectory that had no end, as the lights went on and off in the buildings outside and distant figures moved – yes, it's all possible, but again, I have no recollection of this. There was no pleasure, there was not even scary rolling thunder and screeching bits. There was never one music, manifesting to us in different ways, depending on the methods we used to perceive it: either introspection, or observation through the senses, that is to say, hearing. No – you never existed. Therefore you never told me that Freud said consciousness was a perception of what was going on in the mind, but that the mind itself was unconscious. I didn't discover that we could only perceive evidence of "the soul" but never the soul itself. That consciousness created the illusion that mind and matter were two different things, but that they were the same, just as lightning and thunder are different aspects of the same phenomenon.

## Epilogue: In the House of Exile

THE DANCER:
Something happened.

THE SCIENTIST:
That's a fact.

THE DANCER:
It could have been ... I felt it moving ... it could have been a composition of some kind. But I hear no music. Possibly vibrations, as of molecules, or elementary particles. Where are we?

THE SCIENTIST:
They move through us: vibrating, oscillating, dancing filaments. It is the dance that defines the space; and so, by definition, the space we inhabit trembles, always on that cusp between formation and annihilation. We name it at our peril.

THE DANCER:
It seems to me as though we're in a house. Or a flat in an apartment block, somewhere in a city. A city we have moved to, from some other country, for reasons that have been forgotten. At the back, it overlooks a quiet garden. Perhaps the season is early spring. And in front, a road; some people move briskly by in dark coats, one carrying a ladder on his shoulder. There's a park where dogs are walked, disappearing into some distance. The distance maybe has grey buildings in it. Some are for sale. Inside the flat, the sound of a refrigerator ceases, releasing silence into the air.

THE SCIENTIST:
We move through this space. Or does it move through us?

THE DANCER:
These are the forms of its presence. I hear the sound of distant traffic. And of men who move on the decaying fire-escape, emptying bins of things we no longer want. They call to each other. And a bird falls silent in the garden. I hear a thump, a cry of pain. I hear the radio or TV playing noise softly, perhaps in another part of the building. A hum of power, as it travels through cables entering the building, to set machines to work. Someone is playing the piano.

THE SCIENTIST:
That can't be right.

THE DANCER:
Listen: they are crushed chords, gorgeous with promise of inner life. A beam of sunlight aslant on them.

THE SCIENTIST:
You wouldn't expect image capture to be that precise. And yet extra resolution is available at a cost premium. Recall that the intuitive physics and technical intelligence within the human mind facilitate rapid and efficient learning about the world of objects.

THE DANCER:
But who is it playing? It can't be either of us. Therefore there must be someone else in this apartment.

SOMEONE ELSE:
I don't know how I came to be here. I sit at the bay window, playing the piano. Chords and arpeggios emerge spontaneously from the hardware of my fingers, stamping themselves deeply into the matter that we are. I'm overlooking a quiet garden. There's a ruined hut where nobody goes. A paper bag drifts slowly across the path. New leaves on the shrubs. Vanishing happens.

THE SCIENTIST:
The existence of such an agent can be predicted with a high percentage probability of accuracy.

THE DANCER:
Mistakes can happen.

SOMEONE ELSE:
Yellow blossom is very bright on some trees. Almost everything is a vessel. Birds arrive. The keyboard shares my inner life. A mistake happens.

THE SCIENTIST:
In "mistake" lurks the sense of "self-knowledge". In "vanishing" lurks the sense of "progression". In "light" lurks the sense of "memory".

THE DANCER:
It's hard to let it be. But what is this "inner life"?

SOMEONE ELSE:
I gaze out of the window as I play, letting my gaze itself play on the forms of presence that arise, an irresistible scrutiny at work on substance, on earth, on leaf and air, on broken chord and ravishment, slipping from interior into distance. The mistake happens: a wrong note, an unexpected note. My mistake opens up a whole world. Lemons rot in the ground, sparrows vanish, a bag inflates with breeze. There are innumerable covenants, and then those covenants are broken. A postage stamp, a sycamore, a field of corn. A boy kicks a ball, and a man shouts out to him from across the field. A Grand Unified Theory is slowly constructed; it resembles a vast railway terminus permeated with the scent of scorched sugar.

THE SCIENTIST:
There is no inner life.

THE DANCER:
We only have each other. Talk to me! It may be that.... Did some-one else say window? I shall open the window. I believe there's a window.

SOMEONE ELSE:
And in the middle is the garden, where chords hang, where nobody goes.

NOBODY:
I am in a garden, approaching a building, the object of my long search.

THE SCIENTIST:
There is no certainty that there is a window. How, in that case, can it be opened?

THE DANCER:
There's the door, then. I shall open it, to find the outside.

SOMEONE ELSE:
My fingers stamp all this, peacefully yet passionately, into invisi-bility. All these things become, and even as they become, they become invisible.

NOBODY:
I have always been approaching the house, sweating, thirsty, with my rucksack on my back. I think I have come a long way. The sun has emerged, and vanished many times. And now the shad-ow comes once more. The doorway is dark; I can't see whether the years have brought any changes. The smells are the same. There is an inner space; I enter the well of it. A flight of stairs, shabby walls hung with dirt. Somehow, the sounds of outside begin to fade. It costs all the energy I have to mount the stairs. No-one has swept them for years. Now I have reached the land-ing, where I remember I sat as a child, on the bottom step of the next flight up, waiting for my mother after school. A door. Time, the heaviest of the dimensions, is traversed. My mother doesn't

arrive. A heavy, dark brown door. But I have a key in my hand. Will it fit the lock?

THE SCIENTIST:
There is no certainty that there is an outside. However, evolution will continue after our demise. This era will persist for billions of years. Once the universe has given birth to the last star, the stelliferous era must come to an end. The degenerate era continues while the galaxies remain intact, but everything must die and they too will end when the dwarfs evaporate and are ejected into galactic space. After that, the dark era, for now there is nothing left but atomic particles – positrons, electrons, neutrinos and the odd bit of cosmological radiation.

THE DANCER:
Suppose we were not really here?

SOMEONE ELSE:
Nobody is in the house.

NOBODY:
What if I were to...?

# NOSTALGIA FOR
# UNKNOWN CITIES

# Preface

THE PROTAGONIST, charged with an unwelcome task, remembers the city of his birth, but the memories are no longer reliable. A considerable time later, he wakes from a dream which he recalls only dimly as having something to do with this. There's no clear reason why this should be so: in the dream, which was located in the realm of dreams that bears no obvious resemblance to any actual city that may exist or might have existed, there were large computer screens (perhaps mounted on the sides of buildings) on which endless texts scrolled, changing too fast to permit deciphering; also, land reclamation and underground passages figured, but exact topographical references were not obtainable. The unwelcome task, should it have existed (and there is some doubt about this too), involved taking the ashes of his recently deceased father on a plane journey to be buried in that city, which is also his father's birthplace: the plastic urn provided by the funeral directors, carried as cabin baggage and stowed in the overhead compartment of the aircraft, a source, naturally, of anxiety for the duration of the journey. It isn't the origin of this project, but auto-confirms it.

The starting point is the first person, that arbitrary signifier for the whole concatenation of processes and functions that we call the self: the pandemonium, the "heap or collection of different perceptions, unified together by certain relations" (Hume). And in the unfolding of these accounts very soon the first drifts into the second and then the third, in a semi-rigorous pursuit of objectivity. But if there is some scientific pretension about the accounts, just what is being claimed here? It may be a proposition of these texts that cities dissolve the myriad fleeting selves of which they are composed, that, paradoxically, in so doing they counter also the individual terror of annihilation and lead perhaps to new models of consciousness.

Starting from a different origin, then, the protagonist is returned to contemplation of the unknowable complexities of the city in which he has spent the greater part of his life by far. But the memories of this are no more substantial than those of that other city (that of his birth), and he fears he has already started to lose them. From his new vantage point, out-side of it and them, he recognises them for what they are, aspects of that oh so familiar collective dream in which we all partake, which must too soon utterly vanish.

This leads him, then, into considering all the cities in which he has ever spent time – whether it be a day, three weeks or more than half a life – and indeed those in which he has never set foot but whose hidden corners and by-ways he has fanta-sised about, cities which may no longer exist or may never have existed – and to attempt to catalogue the experiences within some kind of implicit framework.

Much of his effort goes into forestalling the premature nar-ratives that arise, unwanted and unsought, and yet this quickly reveals itself as an impossible task, as impossible as the original task that gave rise to the project, because try as he may, rear-ranging the sentences in whatever arbitrary form or order, whether just as they fall in chronological sequence, or in alpha-betical sequence, or by length, or other taxonomy, a narrative reimposes itself as a by-product of the experiment, as inex-orably as the time that passes. But a narrative whose end is uncertain and unpredictable, where nothing is resolved because everything already is.

# 1 City of Reclamation

ABOUT 3AM I awoke from a dream of the city in which I was born; and I recalled that I had actually revisited the city, though not for many years after I had first exiled myself from it; but the dream seemed more real than the visit. Above the space created by the dream, a mediaeval tower loomed, overlooking the prison yard, where occasionally you could see prisoners performing sweeping-up chores, and volumes of white sheets on a washing line. A cock began to crow in that early hour. All afternoon, my parents would lean side by side, arms folded and touching each other at the window, gazing down through the slanting shutters at teeming street life below: tradespeople following the dictates of commerce, families promenading, soldiers and sailors, cars, vans and bicycles, stray dogs and idlers – an unwitting precursor of reality television, perhaps. An irrevocable event occurred around that time, which meant that I could never return to the city; or to put it another way, if I were to return I would be so changed that it would not be the same I; or alternatively, had I remained I, then the city would have turned out to be a different city entirely. And so back up the hill, leaving the town area, I passed the house in which we once lived, the one we moved to later, now shuttered (but the same yellow stucco, and riotous bougainvillaea overtumbling the wall from the mysterious garden next door where a hierarchy of cats would play out their opera in the depth of the night). Animals, eroticism, food and artefacts all played a role in my dream of the city. As I review these sentences, it becomes increasingly difficult to separate the dream accounts from "real memories".

And so back up the hill, leaving the town area, I passed the house in which we once lived.

As LAND had been reclaimed from the sea within the port area in recent years, the urban zone had spread westward (much later, I was to write, addressing the evanescent self: "But you my beauty who find yourself in a place / vastly crammed with incident and resource, and see / no way out of it, you do not know it. / You venture onto 'reclaimed land' but it's dark to you: // ahead, huge buildings with screens on which luminous text / scrolls & forever transforms, yet seems hardly to change."). As we were conducting the argument, at a street corner, a man passed by with a lion cub on a lead (but this may have happened in a different city entirely). At night, the hills across the bay were dotted with faint electric glows, but the dark sea barely returned the starlight. At the yacht club, people sat talking, reminiscing for hours, drinking and eating kebabs until it was dark. At this point, I had been absent from the city for some thirty years; and so I was astonished at the number of people who appeared still to know me. At weekends, the city was almost deserted as people took to their cars and drove out to picnic in the hinterland that had once been wild, either fishing coast or oak forest, but now, with its endless golf courses and hotels, increasingly resembled the environment they may have wished, consciously or not, to escape. Bastions remained proud. Bathing took place in a familiar atmosphere; cheap goods were available. (Before long, we shall be back on the aircraft and all of this will be forgotten.) Below ground, however, it was said an anti-city existed of paved tunnels, circuses, embrasures, vaults, futuristic hospitals for avant-garde surgery, endless kitchens, tubular structures, ducts of all kinds, locked cabinets, vast and echoing garages, all long since abandoned to the night, its reality denied by day-to-day pedestrians. Beside the swimming-pool, the ghost of an iguana. Beyond these intervals, lemon and olive groves might cover summer-browned slopes, out of present vision. Big buildings – some gargoyled. Bless me father, for I have seen. Border controls were unusually relaxed, so that we were allowed to proceed through the narrow streets to the fair, where people dressed up in "national costume" and the usual strange rituals were played out and strange aromas lingered in the air. Both sides of the street were lined with attractive colonial style buildings with beautiful forged iron balconies on which families might assemble to greet the parade. Breakfast was exceedingly colourful. Bright sunshine and warmth all day, I could weep with relief. But in any case there wasn't a single I: for the city contained, as well as an I that was the standard referent for the self, a fictionalised I who could be made to do anything necessary for the purpose of the narrative, and a transcendent I who could only be inferred. By day, trees shaded green benches; by night, the lamps were lit and the fountain played. By the lighthouse on a Sunday afternoon, the wind blew and men were playing cricket on the hot clay in front of the new white mosque that had been built with "oil money". Climbing the hill once again, making quite good sense of all the bits, we hoped that eventually all would come together and make some kind of a picture. Coloured lights, projections of the neon signage above the ice-cream parlour on the opposite side of the street, played on the bedroom ceiling, while the early hits of Del Shannon, Buddy Holly and the Everly Brothers made their flourishes as they slowly entered the mythic dimension. Daily encounters with buildings, which hour by hour became invisible, buildings that erased themselves even as they dizzied us with the glint of their windows. Derricks on the wharf, corroded, not in use. Dogs roamed free. Dolphins in schools and small family groups, both common and bottle-nosed, would skip through the waters way beyond the harbour, unheeding our merely human life. Elegant, wide boulevards were scarcely a feature; rather, public spaces were compressed in such a way as to give comfort to the citizens. Engines were blanketed by cloud. Esoteric musics from another continent, featuring plucked, bowed and blown instruments and the persistent, spine-chilling wail of humans, hung on the short-wave band, drifting periodically. Even now, the bay was dense with shipping. Every time I stayed over, my grandfather would offer to take me for a walk down to the wharf, and sometimes, my hand in his, he would detour through the old market, where turkeys gobbled in a makeshift pen and hens and ducks lay listlessly in stacked cages, and one of the stallholders, taking a shine to me, might offer me an orange or a banana, before, finally, the water-light flooded in, and there before us would be the two ancient tenders, rusting and bobbing gently at their moorings. Everybody had grown portly in the intervening years. Everybody loves you here, they said, except those that don't. Everyone tried to avoid a tiresome Englishman in the bar. Exotic variants of familiar games were played. Flags hung from every window and embrasure. For nearly an hour, we stared over the runway at the frontier, the newly built sports stadium and the distant mountains. Free association was discouraged. From the east, the wind blew, striking the edge from a clear sky to form a great dark cloud that streamed away and blotted out the sun. Ghost workers had once been lodged in the now deserted army barracks. Great commotion one morning, as one of the monkeys, a large male, had come down into the city, scattering sparrows, and now sat on a parapet, glaring balefully at passers by while picking at a piece of tinfoil. He showed us where a balcony had been abandoned to the seagulls, which were now a protected species, the wrought iron-work encrusted with guano. Here, we're all first person plural, he said, or intimated as much. Hi, we are your friends, they all said, and sometimes your relations, and we will do anything for you if you will only understand us, and this gave me great comfort and longing, though the feelings later changed, I don't know why. Horror at the sight of a one-legged man coming up the street below, observed by me and my mother from the window of the flat; my first intimation of mortality. I felt a sense of melancholy, not just because the warmth and light had been left behind, but at the thought of not belonging, of floating free. I had attributed this to the explosion, while I was still a baby, of a barge laden with ammunition in the harbour, which had caused glass to fly, woodwork to splinter, ceilings to fall and buildings to shudder, while the sky was temporarily darkened by a great mushroom cloud of smoke. Iron and steel clanged throughout the working day, cranes shuddered, men cried warnings, coaling stages loomed overhead, great vessels were removed from the sea, buoys rang out, mud was exposed, a dirty submarine leaked at the end of a detached mole, businesses flourished and expired as the years elapsed. I stumbled through the strangely familiar streets, wanting an exit, fearing that I would come face to face with myself in a different guise. In the botanical gardens, among the old cannons, we strolled in peace. In the cathedral yard, the same blue and white picture tiles, the same palm tree, now several years older and several metres taller. In the museum were fragments of neolithic and bronze age pots, Greek pots (one with a fat hairy man doing an ungainly dance on it), sarcophagi, the cargo of wrecked ships, models and miniature masks of theatrical characters. In the triumphal last room of the museum, a complete scale model of the city in which we actually stood, plus its environs and borders (the paradoxes entailed by this). In the remote distance a railway, of broad gauge, the rusted iron rails reaching beyond the distance, trembling in anticipation of a freight train from the forest. In this city, there were endless possibilities of bad faith, and to select none of them was to push one's luck. In those days a horse racing course occupied the central area of flat ground. It had once been a small, fan-shaped city completely enclosed by thick stone walls and built on three distinct levels, following natural contours. It was the end of voyaging, some said, and the entrance to Hades. It was the forlorn hope that I could bring the lost part of my life into renewed focus that kept me following the narrative whichever way it might lead. It was to be my father's final resting place. Keys played a crucial if obscure role in this narrative. Language was the only subject that was never spoken about by the citizens. Many of them were Genoese traders escaping from Napoleon, British soldiers and sailors, Jews whose ancestors had been driven from their homeland, Maltese merchants, Minorcans and French royalists. Men from the electricity station were playing dominoes in the bar. Military aircraft flew overhead. My father's ashes in a plastic box, carried as hand luggage. My grandmother used to lower a basket on a string from her apartment window, to be loaded with bread or other goods by an itinerant tradesman. My mother fell off her bicycle at the racecourse, injured her leg, and was punished for this. My uncle conducted the orchestra in a great, gloomy cave illuminated by coloured lights. Narrow passages with steps cut their way between buildings, and I recalled narrow streets where geraniums were beginning to wilt and the scent of horse droppings still lingered; a mule waiting patiently, tethered to its cart, but with an enormous erection; shops shuttered for the holy days and feast days; the novelty and excitement of football on television in blizzardy monochrome; longing for the beach white-out. On Sundays, after we'd walked in the gardens among the tall pines and dragon trees, we would meet my uncle for lunch down by the marina – he was slow and distant as he stopped by our table. On the beach, only the encroaching shadow of the great rock towards the waning of the afternoon gave any clue that time would not continue to stand still. Once, a magnificent ur-city had been built within the confines of the present city, containing mosques and palaces; and elaborate water channels had been constructed to provide a natural water supply for the habitations and the numerous gardens below. Origin this is not; for discontinuity is a feature. Overlooking the lagoon was the "jungle", about which the less said the better. People talked freely in the streets about what was happening. Persistent, damp mist hid the family names that my father was destined to join. Portliness was a quality shared by the school chums who turned up to the afternoon event. Reclaimed land provided the location, the sea having given up its mystery to quotidian human affairs. Resemble nobody, I had tried to tell myself; but that wouldn't work here. Resisting the imperative to use the city as metaphor, an opportunity offering too perfect a fit between "proper" and "figurative" meaning, leaving no space to wander, sailors, arm in arm, wove a complex path up the main street as they returned to their ships, roaring in rough harmony. Salt was removed from the sea. Seas were frightening to all city folk when they asserted their terrible dignity. Shaping took place inside as well as outside. Shining and sweet smelling in the bright, warm sunlight lay our most lovely decoration: thousands upon thousands of white narcissi. Six great piers, standing in their own solid shadow, framed the sluice-gates. Slow, rhythmic sound of breathing of thirty thousand inhabitants. So we bought rolls, sat by the pool, swam, slept. Soldiers marched, stood at attention, men came in on bicycles, cultures jigsawed, languages melted, fused or self-destructed, women came in on foot and left by bus, economies mutated, flags fluttered or went down. Some nervous folk dived into their cars and drove at full speed to the border. Somehow, and for no reason that I can easily explain, I had left this city many years ago, and now came back as a ghost (guest). Streets and passageways became an "archipelagic zigzag". Surfaces were plastered over with a smooth layer of mortar and finished with a thin wash of exceedingly hard but finer plaster. Terrible presence dwelt in these streets, never to be recognised. The building had been undergoing recent refurbishment, as evidenced by ladders and neat piles of aggregate and brick, but in other respects was still the building in my dream. The entrance was exactly as gloomy, the tiling intact, as I remembered it from my dream and from my memory. The faces of the tower were scarred with the wounds of many bombardments. The narrow main street began to fill with excited people, and then distantly we heard the first faint strains of the approaching military band. The nearby beach resort, which had been the cause of much eager anticipation, proved to be sadly run-down and depressing. The resemblance became apparent to a great human corpse laid out on its back and covered with a winding sheet, its head to the north, its feet pointing at Africa. The sun began to shine fiercely. The town drunk marched solemnly in front of the band master, using a rolled-up newspaper, or perhaps a stick, to mimic his complicated twirls and thrusts, until he was led away gently by police. The town tramp, often observed squatting with a beer bottle in various locations throughout my childhood, was known by a single nickname, which I associated with "shit", because other children had made me look at the occasional deposit he left; but when many years later he was finally taken into hospital and died, the local newspaper report, which gave his hitherto unknown full name, seemed to be about someone else entirely. The weather was perfect for the cable car. There was no hinterland to speak of. They crept down the wall from the garden next door, clinging on suckered feet, and I now believe they were geckos, but my father used to call them salamanders. They took refuge in the cliffs above the city. This is pre-linguistic, unrepresentable memory. This narrator isn't and is in the story, or it

The entrance was exactly as gloomy, the tiling intact, as I
remembered it

could be my mother, I don't know, I'm tired and I want to go to sleep. This, the steepling alleyway with the centre railing, midway on my journey to school, was the place where I first heard Lorca's voice; and where a girl from the high school, whom I'd observed with longing for days, stopped me to ask me my name, and I was unable to answer. To reinvent this space would pose a terrifying problem. Traders would arrive every day, it was recalled, crossing the frontier (the point at which cobbles gave way to tarmac); one wore a flat hat, on which he balanced his comestibles as he slow-marched proudly around the city, proclaiming; another hauled a wagon laden with water-barrels; and a herd of goats preceded a third, who would stop as required to milk one for the convenience of a customer, unless I have this wrong. Two tribes inhabited the city, each of a separate persuasion; but chance alone determined which of the two any individual citizen might fall under, and so it was impossible to be certain of avoiding offence. "Uncle Arthur" was a common name for a single man living in the apartment upstairs, possibly homosexual or possibly not, though this was not a subject for debate, who might have a room dedicated entirely to an aviary of finches, or else would possess a gramophone capable of putting out stereophonic sound, years before such a novelty became commonplace. Unsure of what I was doing, I carried the casket to its resting place. Unwittingly, we were stepping on an ancient sea-bed. Up by the long abandoned military battery, swirling in cloud, the gulls screamed in panic as a griffon vulture glided past, the bolder among them harrying the big dark bird from their skies. Voices were placed at precise locations, and, to our amazement, a military band marched slowly and purposefully from the left-hand speaker to the right. Walking back to the Continental Hotel, we talked about what had been lost and gained. We heard about the bombs. We heard, but did not see, the fireworks. We used to play in the ruins of what had once been the Grand Stores, bombed during "the war". We went to a gate in the side of the rock, which when unlocked revealed a long, narrow passage, at the end of which was a trapdoor let into the floor, and one by one we descended a flight of wooden steps about twelve feet long, at the bottom of which we saw a

This, the steepling alleyway with the centre railing.

large hall or cave that resembled somewhat a huge rabbit warren; its floor appeared to be very wet and the light illuminating it made it look very dangerous to walk on, but to my surprise it was quite easy to move about and not near so dangerous as it first seemed; and so after passing through this cave we descended slightly, rounding a bend in so doing, where we were told that here it would be necessary for us to slide down a knotted rope about eight feet long, which required effort but which we managed quite well; and once again gaining a foothold we found we were standing in another cave or hall, the walls of which looked as if they had been carved by some primitive sculptor, some of the carvings resembling faces, some flowers and foliage, and I looked round for a second exit but there seemed to be none. We were led by an Irish Christian Brother round another bend, necessitating a crawl on our hands and knees through a small gap between two rocks, coming out on a high rock and between this and a rock on the other side where it was necessary for us to cross, some kind engineer had fixed and fastened a rope, so in single file we passed hand over hand along this rope to the other side, taking a foothold whenever and wherever possible, till we reached another large cave, the most beautiful we had so far seen, with objects like pipes and icicles in white, cream, grey and brownish-red, and there were other objects that resembled elephants' ears, and clusters of pipe-like objects close together which when tapped gave all different sounds; and there were other creations of nature that resembled very closely a pulpit, spears and knives and many other weird instruments, but there were also occasional pools of water which were said to be very deep and dangerous if one had the ill luck to fall into one, and in every dark spot everything seemed so deathly quiet that it seemed there was no coming back from this. When television was first introduced, I became frightened at the first strains of the music for "The Invisible Man", even though (or especially because) a storm of interference scarcely permitted any clear view of the protagonist as he removed his bandages to reveal his nothingness. When the plane landed at the airport late Thursday afternoon I felt an unexpected welling of emotion. Why I left in the first place is because I wanted to blur the distinction between objects that were situated in space and those that were not. Wild birds passed this way. With regard to my return, it appears to be a case of denying my presence in the act of affirming it. Years later, I was to write a poem called "El Hombre Invisible", which tried to locate that fear. You could say I'm trying to get to the point where I'm able to begin.

# 2 City Break

ACROSS THE river and via the island lots of people milling around watching street performances a blues band a weird mime show which reminded you of the lodger and his Japanese girlfriend and there they were being exceptionally good monkeys in front of a seemingly appreciative crowd then at the top there was a terrific view the gentle swell of the river a scary glass of wine a detour through the space-age hall where two models were laughing and being photographed and now the sun had almost set leaving behind a beautiful pink and mauve sky the buskers and more street performers body poets creatures eating fire and a jazz band a man in tails irritating people with takeaway food you forgot to mention the woman with the haunting voice and the bells on her calf who sang about the distant mountains in front of a statue amid disasters and other fun like this the station the liberation monument the menagerie you wanted to kidnap a baby lion with enormous paws all of which interfered with the schedule the bank was closed so you had to go to the garden and drink and eat and put yourself in a better mood but a queue had formed and they wouldn't reopen the bank because they couldn't find the keys and not only that the train reservation computer had broken down and anyway the international tickets happened somewhere else so cheques could only be cashed in a funny bank where the customers took the ladies behind the counter out for coffee and then everything became very late the metro station the river again the bank was still shut but the reservation machine was working again but you collapsed into a bus before suppertime found the

Irish pub which was much like all Irish pubs in all the cities of the world having little Irish about it apart from serving Guinness and had to play games in trying circumstances accompanied by three chattering nuns who didn't seem very pleased to see you and were standing outside in the passage waiting a bit of a contrast it took seven and a half hours checking into the hotel a tiny dark room and a shower down the corridor hunting for food with anxiety about money and time spilling brandy on the carpet impossible it's impossible to continue it's the last straw an invasion by two young men in addition to the nuns frenetic shopping your dreams were realised in a wonderful blue and silver train as dusk fell again a little Down's syndrome girl insisted on giving you many kisses quite impossible and finally a bit of a letdown a big wooden bed much recovery and unpacking taking to the streets the heat making an interesting circular walk including the cathedral beautiful though slightly seedier than the photos had led you to believe the royal palace guarded by bus-conductors with machine guns a beautifully fitted together set of buildings in the bright sunshine that faded to haze the square the irregular façades on which pigeons perched the majesty of the Renaissance some unidentified "sights" an unsuccessful diversion very hot into the palisaded and pedestrianised zones containing all the fashionable boutiques where you re-emerged into the street it was dark but quite hectic nowadays there is a large immigrant population attached but not attached kind of opposite and free-floating on the river-bank two young men in leather jackets fishing with their dog an oily scum under the steel bridge the soup was itself followed by another soup course which was a big mistake and due to another error an over-large egg salad to finish this was not the restaurant you had been recommended where you would have expected grilled pike-perch fillet with a small dollop of raspberry sauce Thai steamed rice and pineapple and where your companion could have had red mullet fillets with basil sauce no that was a different one it had a website or perhaps that was in a different city there was a canary singing just near the room in a cage on a window ledge very upset the episode of the lion cub may have occurred at this point the station again

Some unidentified "sights".

the metro steaming hot a bullet without air-conditioning over-crowded until people changed seats confusing the ticket inspector a lady in a green dress a large monument on a hill which was the geographical centre the building was public and gloomy yellow flattish and with hardly any signs of life the organs bronze the ground grey and purple night fell on the terrace all chattering with great excitement a new bench on cobblestones you shouting in your dreams a lawn of curiously fleshy grass bordered by beds of roses shrubs evergreen trees and strange succulent type plants and many other plants in pots and vines trailed over the top though the geraniums had stopped flowering a grey cat called Lucy many flies and ants there was a swimming pool in the shade of the terrace where you sat while people appeared and disappeared in the endless process of preparing for departure disappearing completely at last a replica of the BBC World Service hanging in the air running and conscious cars and bikes rushing up the road hurried coffee sun brightening the sky a never-ending amount of traffic nobody stopped and it soon became clear it was too late bridges crammed full of people by balancing on flowerpots you could see over their heads but you gave up after a while and walked around the adjoining church grounds where there was a spectacular if misty view through a coin-in-the-slot telescope the winding streets a long march would be forthcoming but sadly it was completely unsuccessful having covered the central area two or three times in the process watching all the preparations in the sanctuary the bus the long conversations with people who wanted to find out what you thought of "the world" and what you had been and what you had done and what you would be doing with your life and then once more to the bank and to the post office a delightful re-creation of the Franciscan monastery that had once stood on the site but to your surprise it was closed somebody said there were regional elections all the little people on little wooden beds packed together and shops and restaurants selling hamburgers only too late spotting a plate of mixed fish which had everything you'd ever wanted on it whereupon cloud and humidity gave way to sunshine two cats on a flat roof so you hung around until the supermarket opened bought some miniature bottles and went back to the station a young man with a naked stump for one leg and crutches laid by slumped motionless in the subway next to a small polystyrene container with a few coins in it rows of gypsies holding out embroidered rugs and shawls for sale set off once again just missed the bus in the bar were sailors from the Spanish Armada watching football on TV you could do this now cloud descended the sky repeatedly darkened and yellowed part of the road was missing and this caused the bus some delay a very nice promenade behind the hotel coffee and Coke and big juicy raisins most places were closed but were much prettier at night the fountain that changed colours purple and pink and found a dressing gown in blue silk with embroidered flowers to walk down in it the pitch blackness just inside drunk with 12° pilsner beer at 11.30 pm in the hotel over which Venus shines next to the moon as Leonard Cohen's "Suzanne" plays on the radio a choice of films either *Emmanuelle, die Nackte von Sados* or *Pussy in the Bathhouse* walk all the way till morning each morning the church-bells chime without melody or rhythm little sweet biscuits plain toast didn't sleep very well for mopeds screaming down the alleyway streetcleaners and loud altercations what a chore going on and on without paradigm shift all the way to change some money fail to make contact whether to or not whether to meet tonight or not whether or not you phoned the hotel but failed bought provisions and little brown bowls which were your treasure but did not get brandy all this took three hours organising and pottering making you hot and bothered had seen the sunrise the station cafeteria the shop (closed) thought a suitcase was a bomb bought magazines went through narrow footpaths with tiny people on them a bag belonging to a fat man with a fat cigar fell on the woman next to him air-conditioning cold hit all your carefully laid plans a bar round the corner just closing for the night a long walk then to the celebrated art gallery with one of the most important collections in the region where imagination's purely wrecked and everything is remarkable and back again a fountain again a statue of a lady being pulled along by lions beautiful wide avenues soft and wooded and the houses all changed their style to rough multi-grey stone with muted roofs all the clever money had moved here confronted with millions of noisy people and nobody to help queued for some money then along the avenue with all the smart shops but couldn't go any further because the workers were on strike feeling decidedly sore needed some wine joined an enormous queue outside an ice-cream shop to compensate and you could see the very cannon-balls embedded in the walls in and around the ramparts in the cathedral and out to the old town you have to see the old town but first there's early 20th century architecture including a cubist lamp-post neo-renaissance and art nouveau buildings and an example of early modernism severe plate-glass all the way round but beyond the runes of power the municipal piles the balcony from where the crowds were greeted in those terrible days but you can't leave the city without a visit to the old town terribly cramped and quaint the walls crumbling subject to restoration donations gratefully received the celebrated "mediaeval core" a community known to have existed here since the Bronze and Iron ages and the Jewish quarter a labyrinth of alleyways and such but there are no Jews any more not since the great charter and the wool merchants passed through here time running out there haven't been any for some time an epoch even the Jewish quarter without Jews or the Arab quarter no Arabs they have all been banished to the "outlying districts" and you peered into the cemetery from the gate near the bridge below the other bridge near the national theatre (a "Mecca for culture lovers") the poor people names carved from memory were rounded up here were walled in were driven out were slaughtered in their hundreds and thousands the terrible days terrible years glass shattered blood in the runnels breasts hacked off eviscerations performed in the classical fashion by the approved method children terrified belongings scattered names misplaced businesses ransacked all tidied up now names and bones and names and bones and artefacts with little labels to remember them by little labels arranged methodically in the museum in the old town so quaint with the evocative street names the street of the revolution the winding stair of tears the avenue of despair boulevard of dreadful transgres-

You peered into the cemetery from the gate near the bridge.

sion square of hideous metastasis and gloom the old cemetery yes you must see the old cemetery and here you are this is the place this must be the place to which all data trails tend the place where all income streams flow here you are the very place a famous composer is here and you are here at the end of all narratives the place sanctified by history upon which still stands the old opera house definitely worth a visit meet your friends there for a coffee as people used to do in the old days but nobody showed up so you had to get out of here there's nowhere to go you consulted the map so conveniently provided by the tourist board in association with the chamber of commerce here's Konrad Adenauer street there's Winston Churchill boulevard and General Charles de Gaulle place which is not called that any more but in any case none of this was marked on the map not at any rate the place from where you headed for the hills after lunch in a restaurant where the menu was completely incomprehensible soon after which you found yourself at the periphery the city limits the ring road or peripheral highway where the traffic fled flashing by on the overpass pedestrians this way on the underpass there was a drive-in or drive-through where you were so nearly assailed by two dogs one of them a giant very nearly left your bag behind on a miserable journey through the underpass and therefore under the overpass which was a boulevard that had been driven through the amazing labyrinth and beyond hot and stuffy bumpy with poor street lighting in that world outside beyond the periphery the old suburbs the outskirts the "outlying districts" where the riot police patrol as dusk falls protecting the centre in their vehicles dilapidated furniture on the street distressed concrete drainage sumps inscrutable graffiti none of this shown on the map very probably recent developments usual scatter of tower blocks railway lines flat wagons bearing armoured personnel carriers patches of greenery giving way to gravel warehouses the celebrated powder mill had evidently vanished too and now pylons and stadiums terribly wet and glistening platforms placards hoardings a distant vista of supermarkets and hypermarkets in the even more distant Eurozone the new citadel of commerce since the millennium soon to be connected on all

The street of the revolution the winding stair of tears
the avenue of despair boulevard of dreadful
transgression.

sides reached by floodlit ribbon development chain-link fencing cycle tracks storm drains all within the larger metropolitan area where programmes of cultural activity are promised but it is your "delight to set out towards a horizon"....

# 3 City of Grain Elevators

HOW BEAUTIFUL the distant, wispy clouds were in an otherwise clear cerulean sky. Early Sunday morning, and little traffic on the roads. The bag had begun to split at the sides. Coffee was taken, one capuccino and one filter, and a Danish pastry shared. Perpendicular architecture. Waiting to be called. The various aircraft moved slowly into and out of their positions at the boarding gates. In a field that raced by, chickens ran to be fed. A book had been forgotten – fortunately, little damage was done. The feeling, once all the arrangements had been made and the requirements of safety and bureaucracy complied with, that matters were out of their hands and that therefore there was no alternative but to sit back and let events take their course – and the comfort in this. Water in a glass, the small ice cubes swiftly disappearing. Shoes were removed. Hunger. The slow movement of metal in wind. On an impulse, they took a taxi, possible outcomes having become evident. These things would live on in their memories, or if not in their memories then in the record, on paper or laptop computer, as an aid to or substitute for memory. Whether in fact a city existed was as yet unknown – the photographs had been removed.

THE GREEN of the suburbs took them by surprise. They were driven along the side of the cemetery for some minutes, then turned into a tree-lined avenue. The woman with the key was not at home. Houses of every design, colour and size lined the avenue; some sported notices in their porches inviting blessings on the nation. There was a choice of beer. A table wobbled. Some time later, they were admitted to the place they had imagined, which was somewhat bigger than they had anticipated. At 3am, distant birdsong was heard, its repetitive nature leading to the suggestion that it was produced in captivity. Clanging of a hammer echoed in the avenue. The rain came down; it looked as though it would settle for the day. They would never forget this. A magnifying glass and some coasters on a low table. The length of the corridor surprised and delighted them. Voile veiled the windows. Chilled white wine was poured. Books, postcards and other items were propped on the ledge of the wood panelling that ran all the way round the room. In half the attic, chairs had been drawn up, as though for an event that would never now happen. Cleaning fluids of all kinds produced milky stains in the black lacquer. Dumpsters were positioned next door. The same black youth, his head tightly bandaged, racing endlessly up and down the escalator in the subway station, from morning until late afternoon. Another branch in the path. Slipping on mud, twice. Unseasonable rain, and an absence of population. Flimsy rain jackets were hurriedly unrolled, but they produced more moisture inside than they repelled outside. Evidence of wealth, but none of its production. Wings were invented here. The way the suicide of the defence ministry adviser was reported was interesting. They would always remember how footsore they were. A purple house, and the picture in a newspaper of a purple polar bear, its colour the inadvertent side-effect of medication. Flags.


ON MONDAY morning, senior citizens sheltering from the rain played cards in a coffee-shop. When the lights indicated, they crossed the road behind the old lady, but on the other side she made to turn right while they turned left; confusion ensued, resolved with smiles and polite formulations. Several of the houses appeared to be uninhabited, or offered for sale or rent; others may have been left empty by their inhabitants for the summer season. It was uncertain which was the correct way in. The new owner indicated that he intended to pay an official visit

The length of the corridor surprised and delighted them.

on Tuesday. But that was when he was naïve and lacking in experience. The kettle whistled, and would not yield. The time and the ambient temperature were projected. As daylight approached , it faded and was finally invisible. "I can't think of a wine shop, but there is a liquor store three blocks away where you can get wine." Sandwiches and soft drinks were consumed. Shoes were examined, including the soles. In the art gallery, giggling housewives and silent teenagers were shepherded quickly past the modern art. Flash photography was not permitted. The road led undeviatingly through neighbourhoods of different ethnicities, social classes and economic brackets. Once again, the clouds came over and it turned humid. A sofas-on-the-street kind of neighbourhood. Italian delicacies and fresh produce were offered for sale. After some discussion, a box of bin-liners was produced. The outline, against a grey sky, of the psychiatric institution, extensive and grim as a castle. A glimpse of the park and lake, impossibly enticing. Inside the apartment, John Coltrane played "My Favorite Things"; outside, the builders shouted at one another. Three pear-shaped wax candles in the disused fireplace: one milky yellow, one raspberry coloured, the third lime green. The phone rang four times, the answering machine was triggered, but after a series of clicks and whirrs no message was left. After several years, the memories would still be strong, if inevitably selective.

WHAT HAD once been a show tune was transformed into something hinting at eastern modes, full of melancholy and yearning. The big blue refuse truck moved slowly up the residential street. Its roar receded slowly, until eventually it was heard no more. Evidence of the length of time since the last inhabitants left: the calendar's leaves torn off only up to May 7. You could say they got their fingers burnt. Distant siren. Rubble and a rectangular trench in the back yard – the back of the house, which would otherwise have been exposed, temporarily covered with plywood boarding, the only evidence of the builders who had worked through the evening in a thunderstorm. "The news" was presented in a way that brooked no argument. Presently, the sky

Inside the apartment, John Coltrane played "My Favorite Things"; outside, the builders shouted at one another.

cleared, and the streets, vast runnels only an hour previously, were dry once more. Information was presented as entertainment, and vice versa. An ambulance charged. It was terrifying in its symmetry. Rye bread, ham and salami were unpacked. Books were consumed. A clockwork monster and a furry hedgehog on top of a clock. Swarms of sparrows, boldly pecking. Although there was a candle in every window, there was very little information outside the building. Part of the mound of rubble had been sheared off by the force of the rain during the night, leaving an unstable cliff edge, and had fallen into the trench – the remainder of which had filled with milky water. The smell of coffee, the quiet sound of the rain. A china rabbit on a small chest. The further they went downtown, the more bizarre the architecture appeared. A man with bare arms and a snake round his neck inquired how they were doing. Japanese lamps, kites, leather belts, T-shirts and novelty crockery were offered for sale. Wandering in ever increasing circles, coming across the same streets again and again. A franchise corner store, limited and high-priced – that was where you got the phone cards. A breakfast wrap was ordered. Breeze-blocks were delivered. The waitress was extremely friendly, but then disappeared for half an hour. Passing the outdoor tables of the bar, the man suddenly turned and barked, "You know, alcohol is a *drug*!" then continued calmly on his way. Thousands of gravestones in the sunshine. Golfers had taken over the entire space. A man examining a blue wheelie bin at the verge turned round and smiled: "I'm going through my own garbage!" A burly man led two huge black dogs that walked as he jogged. The animals, visible between the slats, moved only minimally – all visitors having departed. This would live on in their imagination for a long time, or if not in their imagination at least in their memory. From the number of people congregated on benches round the tennis courts, it was clear this was serious stuff. Ice cream was not available because the ice cream machine was frozen. The girl was leafing through what could have been a poetry magazine or a book of recipes; her companion was reading *Moby-Dick*.

THE WEATHER front moved on, and the day cleared. It became so much more interesting. Budget cuts were discussed. A hummus wrap or a breakfast wrap? One species had the curiosity to want to make a spectacle of all the others, and the intelligence to be able to round them up and keep them in the one place in order to do so. They were sitting around disconsolately; it wasn't unreasonable. It was a major source of buzz. The gorillas spent most of their time avoiding the gaze of the humans who had come to view them. The bison moved slightly in the sun. "That's half-pig, half-monkey" was one remark. Glittering water at the edge of the promenade. Extremely slow food. Bubbles of cloud welled ominously at the horizon, but it seemed the weather front was receding again. She wore blond dreadlocks tucked into a voluminous woollen hat. Bungalows lined the edge of pleasant woodland. The bandanna came off. It was the second time in two days, at exactly the same spot, that someone had called from a passing car, asking for directions that they could not provide. There was too much of a frantic quality, you got edgy here. A couple had appeared to quit their café table, but returned quickly to reclaim it. "Your mother never liked Herbie's mother," said the woman. Whole cakes were displayed under glass. As evening came on, people started to bring their own chairs for an open-air gathering. A sudden influx of about a hundred young cyclists riding up the avenue. The night had been the warmest yet, and even the sheet felt oppressive. A tiny caterpillar truck backed into the alley delivering its pallet. Timber planks were brought; they were to be used for the framework. They looked as though they were moving house by bus. Everything was used up before appearing again in different guises. The woman uttered a piercing shriek from the back of the bus, but the man at the front went on patiently searching through his pockets for change with which to pay the driver. Ice creams were worth two tickets, but you had to walk a block for the tickets. First a drum, then a bass guitar, then a whole band, but the audience hadn't even turned up yet. Sharp winds blew in from the lake, and napkins and paper cups were scattered. To their left, the golden dome and the clock they had surveyed so often, recorded by the webcam on the website, was revealed in "real life". It was designated a national historic landmark in 1986. To make it safer and more aesthetically pleasing, the entire deck and support systems had been replaced. They needed to watch their food, lest the birds help themselves. The prognosis was mixed. Birds of paradise appeared over the "vast reaches of his domain". Down the stairs to the cellar, the place of cleansing and therefore of fear. The possibilities of trips up tall buildings, round lakes and into entirely other regions were idly discussed. Two bridges, and getting them mixed up. The voice of a radio celebrity on your answering machine, offered as a prize. The only guided missile cruiser open to the public. Shearing bricks in two on a Sunday morning. It was a liquidity event that validated the moment. They were laying the foundations. Long notes were initiated. They had built a considerable extent of wall. She appeared at just the wrong moment, that of the arrival of the owner. Both machines worked perfectly well, in fact the phrase "like a dream" came to mind. Ambient temperatures were all over the place. Ants in the pantry were disposed of. Hot and bone dry at last. He dreamt that he was locked out of his computer, having deliberately committed a violation. They were to talk about it for days, and even years, ahead. Jewels and clams were offered for sale. The barman, on hearing where he was from, shook his hand effusively, and a woman customer at the bar wondered aloud why he'd chosen to come here. The walk wasn't worth the outcome. Lights came on in the passageway.

AT THE end of the ornamental lake, a faint aroma of sewage. It was glorious to watch the swallows skimming low over the lake and the surrounding grassy banks. A vast range of sandwiches was listed, though upon closer inspection they all seemed virtually identical. The lake, olive with light blue rippling highlights as the sun came out. Brightly coloured banners hanging between the Ionian columns. Boys sketching on the promenade. She rummaged in the bag for her dark glasses. A sandwich fit for a king *and* a queen. The potato chips tasted particularly lovely. A distant view of trucks moving on the highway past the historical museum. As each jogger approached, they had to make a decision whether to acknowledge them or not. A black pug had done its business. The sky seemed to drain colour from the park and the surrounding buildings whenever the sun went in. Yellow was the colour of the bus. A shopping district in hell. Tattoo parlours abounded. Many of the shops were for sale or rent. The area beneath the railway bridge was plentifully supplied with guano. They were beginning to figure out how the park-ways intersected with the system of avenues and streets, but even so it was still a mild shock to come out from a new angle at the familiar corner with the bookshop and café. A baby rabbit emerged from under a parked car. It led its owner back home. Hot air from the tropics was met by a cold front moving in from the lakes. A sparrow dipped its beak in a stainless steel bowl of water on the pavement. A little girl lay with her head on one dog and her feet on another. The melancholy of the jazz singer on late night radio, negotiating the angles and by-ways of a melody that sounded as though it had been abandoned on the farthest coast.

THEY FELT obliged to participate in the practices of visitors, although really they would have preferred their usual routines. The arrangements in the bus station, remembered from over 25 years ago. A huge slam on the back of the bus from a surly would-be passenger. Photographing the statue of a founder of the nation in the main square. The bus driver was an elderly woman in sunglasses; it was clearly her first time driving a bus on this route; once, she went astray at an intersection, ending up on the freeway and having to be guided back onto the regular route by one of the passengers, and later she drove over deep ruts, causing the vehicle almost to shake apart. The tallest build-ing lorded it over the rest. A flag flew at half-mast; possibly because a favourite comedian had died the day before. Mist in the distance shrouded part of a science fiction skyline. Another country lay opposite, but with familiar furniture. The spray came off the fall in concentric clouds. Industrial tubes and domes, rust and disused railway tracks: such were the first impressions on crossing the bridge. Mildew in the marina; gas cylinders; container trucks in a vast parking lot. At least one other person had a map. Pylons strode across the estuary, the great cables dipping above the waves. They were entering a deaf child area. Purple and yellow flowers on the waste ground of an island between cities. Suddenly, the neighbourhood changed. A squirrel skittered across a red roof. Dogs nosed their grocery bags. Local people showed pride in their neighbourhood. The band consisted of Senegalese, African-Americans and Americans. A woman's voice that had previously been heard on an answering machine was now aired on the radio. She was told she looked like Paul McCartney. A hat signified African origins, but most of the audience was white. Beer was not available for taking out. Motorised pedal scooters, very noisy, were ridden on the sidewalk with impunity. A boy repeatedly leapt to try and touch the road sign. Running while clutching weights; running while clutching a bottle of water; running while clutching nothing. Floating scum. A jet airliner flying below the clouds. In the distance, classical statuary; the museum; the pedestrians' and cyclists' bridge. Sparrows were abundant in every location. A wheelie bin was chained to a lamp-post. The workmen hacked away relentlessly at the roof tiles from morning till late afternoon; the following day a man, perhaps the owner, appeared on the balcony to contemplate the result. A resident of the 100 block of O__ reports an unknown black man, 5'8" all dressed in black, who did enter the residence and did steal 3 credit cards. The thrice attempted delivery of a computer was documented by stickers affixed to the door. Two men in beards, dark glasses, khaki shorts, sandals, each carrying a guitar case. The college clock struck the quarter-hour. Odd to see a white man in one of those gaudily coloured loose suits with half-mast pants and matching hat. A thick-spectacled black man with a grizzled beard, in shorts, bare-chested, wheeled his bicycle up to the bin, parked it, opened the bin to inspect the contents, removed a transparent plastic glove from his bicycle bag, put it on one hand, leant into the bin propelling his feet off the ground and, reaching within, withdrew a bottle which he first placed on the ground, then, after closing the lid, removed it to the bicycle bag and moved on to the next bin – talking to himself the whole while. A fluorescent yellow tennis ball was thrown into the lake for the black retriever to fetch, concentric ripples widening from the plunge of its heavy form. Water, here calm, was elsewhere impelled by titanic forces in opposition, such that they cancelled each other, and thus produced the semblance of calm. They remembered the distant cloud in front of the distant buildings that turned out to be vapour from the falls. She often felt nostalgia for an experience even before it had ended. A famous architect had designed the house on the corner, described as "like a boat", though length was possibly the only resemblance. Large ants occasionally wandered into the apartment and circled aimlessly until either they somehow found their way out or were exterminated. Cool haze came as a balm and contrast to the hot sunshine of the previous two days. A model of the city when it was a village – rather dusty. At the side of the church, the Loaves & Fishes Restaurant. Silent attendants staffed the Great Wall Chinese restaurant. They bought ice creams in glasses one could take home. Courteously, the cyclist pinged his bell as he came up behind, and thanked them for making way as he rode past. A Japanese garden tucked into the curve of the ring-road. Grey-white was the colour of the sky – the sun a brighter white patch in it. A grand piano with electric lamps built in, when that was the latest technology. Cars converted into works of art and mounted at various points in the city. Small children were wheeled round in brightly painted four-wheel hand trolleys. They read the story of how the city had been burned to the ground even before it was born, and of its rise to power within 50 years, and its subsequent industrial decline in the last half of the 20th century. They agreed they would never forget this.


THE RADIO station was hard to find, in either sense. It was now too hot to work. She had had to learn all the new technology at once. They were supposed to be looking for a building fronted by a parking lot; but parking lots fronted all the buildings. They searched for another copy of the book that had been left in the toilet. Symmetry underlay the design of the railings. Styrofoam cups were offered, to be filled with water ad lib. They heard a fly

The metaphysical abyss, filled by work.

buzz in the recording studio. All the trains were inbound, meaning the outbound limit had been reached. The building felt like a school, and was a school. A resident reports, while at the foot of F__ at 5. 20am she sat in a friend's vehicle with a Hispanic male called "Aida" or "Chico", 5'3" medium build with a buzz cut and hoop earring in the left ear. Railway lines had once ringed the city, but all were gone now. Pot luck was expected on Sunday. The reason many of the houses were divided in two was economics, as the model showed. The way vowel and consonant sounds could interfere with the timbre. They had not even entered the municipal building, and that the lighting in the corridor could be fixed at all was a major surprise. In the early hours of the morning there was a spat outside the house between a swearing man (or woman) and an unknown opponent – with unknown result. The foundation blocks had finally been laid, and the site filled in with dirt. The noise of the digger was quite insupportable. The dewpoint temperature just went up and up. Pushing as hard as possible and for as long as possible in a particular direction appeared to be the best way to achieve a result. If the window was open, the flute could not be heard above the din from the building site; but if the window was closed, it became too hot unless the fan was switched on – again rendering the flute inaudible. Notebooks were filled, one after another. Her interview technique was gentle, and elicited the right result. Water had left their bodies copiously during the night. The waiters were probably students at the city's university on their vacation jobs; at any rate, the service was eager but erratic. All quiet on the bookstore front. The houses in the avenue simply refused to be photographed. A second visit brought everything into much clearer focus. High-priced and very fragile. The waiter said he had been made to sleep in a room above the restaurant – it wasn't clear if he was joking. They decided that if they were still feeling guilty by Monday morning there was still time to do something about it. A spot of detective work, and contact was made. As the weeks wore on, the same people could be recognised walking up and down the avenue or patronising the numerous bars and restaurants that lined it. An arrangement in cast iron, ceramic and wood. Architecture was always more

Deer had repeatedly stripped the branches, so that they had been permanently laid bare and the tree was killed.

attractive when it was lived in. Wooden flutes were very cheap. Singing was heard from the bathroom. The metaphysical abyss, filled by work. Two muffins, some milk and the paper. Customs of another city, another country, maintained here for comfort. A schedule was thrown out of kilter by the change in the weather. Clamminess reached far beyond the confines of the city. The pain in their ankles throughout the night would always live on as a memory. "Will you switch off the air?" asked a woman in the shop. Wing glasses made her look like a madwoman. The wind-screen had suffered an extensive crack and looked as though it might shatter at any moment. They headed north, far beyond the boundaries they had already explored. Everybody brought a contribution. Furniture was built out of scrap steel, or was inflatable. There was always another T-shirt to be bought. They had repeatedly been told that the way they talked was lovable, but the effect produced was that of alienation. Food and drink was offered from all directions. The evening darkened over the gathering on the balcony. Nothing was certain: what the next job would be, where they would be living, who their friends would be. A disavowal of content did not bear much close examination. Gravel had been shovelled into the extension: that was new.

ELSEWHERE, MEANWHILE, the war continued unabated.

THE GLUTINOUS scent of a breakfast cereal hung over the plant. An extremely rusty building appeared. A cruise ship, out of condition, or commission. They were taken south of the city, where deer, rabbits, wild turkey, herons, hawks (engaged in mid-air courtship), nuthatches, chickadees, frogs, snakes and muskrats were observed, and once a beaver followed them briefly down the woodland path. Cool breeze from the shoreline. The print of a deer on the muddy path. The rumble of a freight train passing unseen behind the trees at the far side of the marshes. Deer had repeatedly stripped the branches, so that they had been permanently laid bare and the tree was killed. Disused grain elevators

The sun going down behind the abandoned plants.

and factories amid the tracks. The sun going down behind the abandoned plants. He described how he had spent a year of his life living under canvas 14,000ft in the mountains, next to a dying cannabis farm, reading poetry and fetching his own water from a stream every day. In the woods, the closeness of the city was quickly forgotten. Beer, wings, fries, conversation and a yellow half-moon. The mysterious, decaying industrial structures at the horizon.

# 4 Drowned City

A CITY convinces by the form it creates, not by argument. But when its time comes, the end can be swift. Grey outlines of churches, offices, warehouses, girders, etc. Brownish, clay-like stuff was used extensively. Cold Chinese food. A black man, whimpering, had been cornered by police like an animal in the garden. Flashback. He freaked out, went on a binge, spent $25 on a "relief massage" and lost his sweatshirt. He had insisted on picking up a discarded cable drum for use as a table, which was a big mistake. He was uptight because his woman was leaving him. She spoke of voices in the wind. She said that Krishnamurti said the followers of Zen were "doomed". She asked why people liked the city, and was told "Because it's full of crazy people doing meaningless things." Four homeless social workers crowded into the office, phoning round for stopgaps. It was a huge green psycho-bubble filled with water in which people swam. For more than 250 years excavators found no human remains.

ON THE radio JC Bach followed CPE; then John Lee Hooker singing "Tupelo": the poor people, they had no place to go. Once there was order, but now there is disorder, they claimed, and the answer is faith: that is, if we believe, never mind in what, we shall be saved; this is called existentialism. Their bodies radiated like beacons. The preacher went around in sky-blue vestments, chanting or mumbling (his wife or female personal assistant in tow, singing harmony), and was once observed standing outside the hotel lobby, his hands outstretched to the sky. The radio, Coltrane, "Africa Brass", faded into the midnight air. There was incense, frying food and a ten-year-old kid playing drums. There were rows of shops, bars, houses, an amphitheatre, a small theatre, a lovely house with terracotta and black plastering patterned with fleur-de-lys like on Florentine leatherwork, and a gym, and among all these, dead bodies in various postures. They remembered the smell of cats, they recalled flea-ridden rooms, electric bar firelight bouncing off dusty Melanex wallpaper. They were in sight of land at last. Through a synthesis of A (that which remains constant) and B (feelings/emotions) we arrive at C, which is actually a departure point. Colours: muted oranges, yellows, greens, blues. Indifferent saxophone mingled with a police siren. Oily pools in the gutters. One of them was offered a joint and some strange, fruity-flavoured rosé wine. On late-night TV, Bo Diddley playing classical violin. Reconstituted rooms featured furniture, lamps, sculpture and daily implements for living, tools, cookware, plates, cups, eating utensils, cosmetics. The TV worked if you bashed it on the side. Various items of clothing, confectionery and a suitcase, a bottle of green peppermint cordial, a French phrase-book, a bar of chocolate and a candle, all waiting for an advertised festival which never happened, which would never now happen again.

THEY WERE rounded up into work camps and held by armed guards. They were prevented from leaving as the waters rose. There was an alternative. A steamer played "Bye Bye Blackbird" as it sailed away. The violence that followed the floods helped persuade many to move north. And when they did decide to leave, they took people with them that otherwise had no means of getting out of the city, even though they were piled on top of each other in the van and they had to drill holes in abandoned cars' gas tanks to get enough fuel to leave. "All our people had evacuated and we locked the city down," said the chief of police. Before they were close enough to speak, they began firing their weapons over the group's heads. But even as they were closing the bridge, the authorities were telling people that it was the only way out of the city. In addition to security concerns, an unmoored vessel on the river raised the threat level. It was not a question of if but when. It was only a matter of time. Police from surrounding jurisdictions shut down several access points to one of the only ways out, effectively trapping victims in the devastated city. The bridge was the major artery heading west. The city would have been overwhelmed by the influx, it was said. These were code words.

AROUND NOON, the military finally reached the convention centre and began feeding people. While the mood at the centre improved, many people didn't want to eat. A man screamed at a woman to look at the body of a person who died while waiting for buses to rescue them. Dozens of old people, obviously from a nursing home, were dumped in the middle of the street and were dying in the blistering sun. Couple that with the fact that it was very hot, there was dirty water and mosquitoes everywhere. Every day they would say the buses were coming, but they didn't come, everything was sitting in that house and slowly drowning, it now began to pour down rain, but it didn't dampen their enthusiasm, for, miraculously, they had internet, though no phones, no electricity, and no running water, and the future was murky, but, one of them said, my son will now witness it, the same rebuilding I did as a child, as a child enjoys sitting in the park across from the convention centre, likes to feel the sun on her face and escape the frigid air inside the temporary shelter. With two other people, he was set adrift on a raft. Water snakes coiled themselves among the crushed palisades. While the ground seemed to be swaying all morning, he felt weak and thought incessantly and with longing of steak and fries. Some of them had cell phone contact with family and friends outside. The aquarium suffered significant loss of animal life when the facility's emergency generator failed and made conditions unlivable for most of its animals. The building got a few bumps and bruises, but it held up. The tradition is something which we truly need to imagine that we can remain connected with or even immersed in. And when the worst of the storm had passed, there were corpses all over the city, the stores were being looted, nurses took over on mechanical ventilators and spent many hours on end manually forcing air into the lungs of unconscious patients to keep them alive, there was smoke in the dome, you didn't know if you were going to burn up or if the building was going to fall down around you, there were numerous frightening moments and strange sounds coming from the cement roof; these, in sum, were code words for: if you are poor and black, you are not crossing the river. Two days after the event, the store at the corner remained locked. The dairy display case was clearly visible through the windows, food in it slowly decaying. Through the cracks in the floors rose the stench of the greasy water swirling through the windows below. They designated a storm drain as the bathroom, and the kids built an elaborate enclosure for privacy out of plastic, broken umbrellas and other scraps; the officials responded that they were going to take care of them, and some of them got a sinking feeling. Strangers on the street offered them money and toiletries with words of welcome. They waited for 48 hours for the buses. While wealthy residents fled the city in SUVs, racial politics continued to permeate the social fabric.

A REPRESENTATIVE for a business located in the 2000 block of N__ reports a known 38-40 year old black man who did enter the business via a back door and took a bag of dry cleaned shirts and fled on a bicycle. In the city centre he spent some time trying to find a phone box; when he found an empty one, the receiver was lying on the floor, the wires torn out of their socket. With his eyes closed, he was overcome by a strange inability to visualise anything. A resident of the 200 block of B__ reports a known suspect residing in the 600 block of L__, who did make threatening phone calls to her home to harass, threaten and annoy her in violation of an Order of Protection. And he said that they had made a universal extermination camp the ideal terminus of this whole civilisation. The very structure of the city itself, with the stone container dominating the magnet, may in the past have been in no small degree responsible for this resistance. She reported that he had said to her: "Thou art my glory, and the lifter up of mine head." Flirtation and courtship created those moments of suspense and uncertainty, of blandishment and withdrawal, that serve as safeguards against satiety: a counterpoise to the regimentation of habit. Accordingly, two cities have been formed by two loves, in relatively self-contained and balanced communities, with a sound industrial base. In the one, the princes and the nations it subdues are ruled by the love of ruling; in the other, the princes and the subjects serve one another in love, the latter obeying, while the former take thought for all. Every Human Vegetated Form is in its inward recesses. Though the ruin was widespread, large patches of healthy tissue fortunately remained. Armies, governments, capitalistic enterprises took the characteristic animus and form of this order, in all its inflated dimensions. They became vain in their imaginations, and their foolish heart was darkened; professing themselves to be wise, that is, glorying in their own wisdom, and being possessed by pride. Thus absolute power would become in fact absolute nihilism. Morality would become police. Explosives would reach cosmic violence. Disintegration would overcome integration. But the earthly city, which shall not be everlasting (for it will no longer be a city when it has been committed to the extreme penalty), has its good in this world, and rejoices in it with such joy as such things can afford. You could see a man combing his hair with his fingers, you could see girls moving backwards as they danced, you could see men standing up and buttoning their coats, you could hear the noise the cards made as they were shuffled, but you did not have to dwell on it any more. But as this is not a good which can discharge its devotees of all distresses, this city is often divided against itself by litigations, wars, quarrels, and such victories as are either life-destroying or short-lived. All this had a direct effect upon both old structures and new. For each part of it that arms against another part of it seeks to triumph over the nations though itself in bondage to vice. If, when it has conquered, it is inflated with pride, its victory is life-destroying; but if it turns its thoughts upon the common casualties of our mortal condition, and is rather anxious concerning the disasters that may befall it than elated with the successes already achieved, this victory, though of a higher kind, is still only short-lived; for it cannot abidingly rule over those whom it has victoriously subjugated. A D__ resident reports hearing a loud boom while driving north on G__ Street between B__ and P__ as her rear window exploded into the vehicle. But the things which this city desires cannot justly be said to be evil, for it is itself, in its own kind, better than all other human good. For it desires earthly peace for the sake of enjoying earthly goods, and it makes war in order to attain to this peace; since, if it has conquered, and there remains no one to resist it, it enjoys a peace which it had not while there were opposing parties who contested for the enjoyment of those things which were too small to satisfy both. A resident of the 500 block of N__ reports an unknown person did cut the lock off a garage door to access it and take a lawnmower worth $28. A resident of O__ L__ Road reports, while at F__ L__ Cemetery, an unknown person did enter the chapel and take his leather strapped satchel containing 3 checkbooks, cash and personal papers, purchased by toilsome wars, obtained by what they style a glorious victory. Now, when victory remains with the party which had the juster cause, who hesitates to congratulate the victor, and style it a desirable peace? These things, then, are good things. But if they neglect the better things of the heavenly city, which are secured by eternal victory and peace never-ending, and so inordinately covet these present good things that they believe them to be the only desirable things, or love them better than those things which are believed to be better – if this be so, then it is necessary that misery follow and ever increase. A D__ resident reports, while at A__ and D__ an unknown black male, 20s, 5'8" and of thin build, who did approach her and say, "How you doing" while running his hand over his head. "When we shall have reached that peace," she said, "this mortal life shall give place to one that is eternal, and our body shall be no more this animal body which by its corruption weighs down the soul, but a spiritual body feeling no want, and in all its members subjected to the will." In its pilgrim state, where the shadow of the helicopter raced across the mottled green surface of the water, the heavenly city possesses this peace by faith; and by this faith it lives righteously when it refers to the attainment of that peace every good action towards God and man; for the life of the city is a social life.


SHE WALKED out of the city, with her cats and luggage in a grocery cart. I'm sure we'll hear from her very soon with more details once she can communicate. She said she was interviewed for Dateline for tonight, so I'll watch and tape if she is. I'm so devastated and happy. This morning I woke up on James' sofa with a cat curled up on my head. I sat up and walked into James' room and we talked. Then, I went and sat outside to watch the antics of three little hummingbirds and a big blue jay. The grass is green. The weather is beautiful. I don't feel so alone. We are drowned, and we know that we shall never die.

# 5 Bruised Rationals
## (City of Angels)

YOU GOT it. You got what you paid for (it). You want it, for what, you got the money paid. What for, what they want? What you got, blue screen, she'd break the fiscal, money? It's paid for. Blue you want? Floats on a curve of money that they paid for up on the screen. It's what got the break, the fiscal weather she brought, peaking volumes into a narcotic maul. You want blue? Break in the weather? Fiscal burning? They want that peaking curve she brought to the screen. Up on what do those volumes of money float? Narcotic patterns? Then go into a perfect mall, you paid for it, you got it. They want that peaking curve on the blue screen, or to imagine a lightbulb burning, floating on perfect water, breaking volumes of narcotic patterns. The money you paid is brought to you. Then what? The intention of the weather is … to destroy intention. For glass descended, unable to go into.… she breaks up. She got fiscal in a mall? You want to go fiscal? To destroy intention, to float? To imagine money peaking, breaking, curving on a glass screen? It's perfect blue water, moving into the realms of the future. It's weather patterns breaking up, or volumes of narcotics in the blood now flowing backwards, descending into heat; not the heat of a lightbulb burning, but sexual in the mall, paid for with what she's got. Unstable or unable? A bird of unknown provenance. Then what? She'd break behind the darkness? Brought to the real, falling out in the perfect city, falling through blue glass, falling through real estate, they know that. Not the heat, not intention, money on glass not moving, not descending, water moving, not breaking, flowing, not to want imagine or destroy, not to imagine perfect blue, no volumes descending, no sexual burning. To go, to float into what the future brought, out and through, not falling in the fiscal dark, they behind, then, or in the weather patterns, that real blue glass, not in the realms of, nor the provenance, not paid for with money or narcotics. An unstable screen breaking up. What blood, what lightbulb? What mall in what perfect city? Unable to what? The estate of the real? But where? Got up where? It's here! It's what you want, in the realms of then, and not brought, not falling to or unable to fall. Not falling, she not falling, not now, not the unknown bird, not peaking, curving backwards, not you.

IT IS whose flows of what may mean not even there was different were in dreams a rush all peaking to incorporate a curve a blue who fail when loved to imagine on screen burning glass through morning something opened and spoke density through the future without regard on water of peaceful conversations like what you got the certain patterns folds you turn you walk you're in the structure meanwhile people don't have dumbly sonorous openings into the conjunction close down the light below the dog but all is love guns have money intention to destroy as happens when a bullet has the heat viewed through and being evidence place spiced blue-screen wisdom brightening he wished that's how blinds turned and he a bird is rich he came they ate the sound there were the women remembered light whole being for all to create don't look

IT IS, after all, what you want, a crisis of the self whose blood now flows backwards. It's a signifier of what? It may not mean, not even…. There were chimes of all sizes and there was information, all tuned to different needs: computers, dolphins and dreams. A cohort of young lesbians were in attendance. They say we dream 40 dreams a night. Narcotics rush into the brain, peaking volumes. Why should they want to incorporate such reluctance? A curve, a perfect blue, don't move. Who can fail to appreciate limbs when they are loved or curved, or to imagine snakes? The fog soon lifted to reveal the cormorants on the rocks below. He had it up on screen but, the reading lamp burning his left hand, she brought a glass of water through an incipient maze of morning glory and crustacea. So of course it was something completely different. He opened the lid and spoke into it softly, as though attempting to wake a child. A kind of density through time moves into the realms of the future without regard to perspective, floats on the wrong water like a diagram of a peaceful voyage, and the conversations vanished like that foam. So after all you got what you paid for. You got your break in the uncertain fiscal weather. You are at certain patterns, a whole city white and red, the luminous folds of the fog before a stuffed bulletin board at an unventilated table. You turn into a mall, you walk a few blocks and suddenly you're in Korea. It seems to be clean but the structure has collapsed. A Zen priest floats in a tweed jacket aspiring to laconicity, the others meanwhile approach a "where are they now" situation, and the young people don't have a "thing". Well there's a whole regime of fills, dumbly sonorous, but those openings into openings "traced for the conjunction of worlds" show the darkness never far away. Behind the lightbulb strings – the smell of dust burning on a lightbulb close to Haiti. So he drives down the coast past the real estate, the tables dappled with light and the seabirds on the flat, nothing below the bridge. He loves his dog Suzie dearly but all he's really interested in is death and money; love guns and anti-tank grenades – just so long as they have the right money. The intention of shooting at short range is to destroy the vital centres of the medulla, as happens when a captive bolt is used for slaughtering cattle; a bullet produces a cavity which has a volume several hundred times that of the bullet. Cavitation is probably due to the heat dissipated when the impact of the bullet boils the water and volatile fats in the tissue which it strikes. Lifeguard towers are viewed through blue glasses. He discovered he was gay *and* being sued for sexual harassment. Nowhere is there evidence that these conversations actually took place. When he remembered it, it was like a dream, but when he forgot, it wasn't – it was to do with patterns of blood flow in the

Those openings into openings "traced for the conjunction of worlds".

Lifeguard towers are viewed through blue glasses.

brain. What is it? cooked spiced minced beef with just a hint of sewage? Canalised, a filthy trickle behind a blue-screen power-book – a jerk; worse than a jerk. Wisdom crieth, brightening, solemnly celebrated – she'd break if not, utters. Exactly how the tables turned he didn't know, she did it and he wished she had-n't. That's how it breaks: the curved, painted horses going round and round, a national monument. Blinds turned, screen blank, everybody falling to, falling out today – not in terms of tech-nique but of information. And he was quoting directly, it's insane! A bird in a blanket, a blue bird of unknown provenance. The soil is rich, and supports an abundance of flowering plants and fruit trees: several kinds of peach, apricot, oranges, lemons and others. He came initially to study for a year, and ended up staying permanently, in a city where permanence is unknown, whose capacity to render void or at least unstable any sense of identity or of comfort is well documented, where the FedEx man passes up and down the street bearing jiffy bags. They wan-dered around, ate hamburger, bought socks and CDs, then headed up to the hills to see the world all spread out beneath, framed softly by light smog. Indy rock on the sound system, a shabby assorted collection, mustard, leather, terrible coffee, duct, fan. And lo, the library descended onto the hilltop and there perched, a thing of glass and steel. And there were zebra striped walls and violet strip lightning strobing at 50 Hz, mirrors and black beer, limes, chili dip and grey meat. The women were too beautiful and they didn't go to work. He had a feeling he remembered great white spaces, big light. It's part of your whole being. For all of our sakes. Unable to create file. Go quickly, don't look back....

# 6 City on the Marshes

WATER. SAND. Clay. Time. Vernacular brick. They remembered. Some remains. Overhead creaks. At night. Dark rain. Beech gleamed. It was. A circling helicopter. The Tigris supermarket. The waiting area. It was time. The hysterical girls. They remembered this. Did it exist? Had it existed? Water streaming down. It was sand. Bumps and scrapes. They recalled sand. The deserted ballroom. A discarded mattress. The building disappeared. The thresholds cracked. Tapping on metal. Many dismal events. It was gold. Aqueous grey sky. Even the birds. A doner kebab. Conditions were extremely localised. Chimes in the wind. The whole building rumbled. Did they dream it? Diabolical liberties were took. They cracked the sink. Hints of anti-capitalist activity. It was all sand. Humps for 700 yards. Big trucks clanking slowly. Industrial sounds all night. Humps for 300 yards. Ghosts on the common. They had imagined it. Acres of high teak. It was only matter. A sheen on windscreens. Dreaming of the Peloponnese. Everything they touched became transparent. A rising star, light pollution. Boom of the bass upstairs. Obdurate clay at the bottom. Water running down the walls. A small, dark animal, quivering. Water pouring down the walls. How they all got soaked. They had imagined the city. Signal failures in all directions. A strong smell of burning. They saw the police cordons. Smoke hung in the air. They recalled loud, quick African voices. Waking to central heating and Elgar. A man screaming in the street. Morning fog that never entirely cleared. Passengers waiting in line without ambition. An ancient dog lay near them. Unseemly scrambles for vacant bus seats. Buildings being constructed for unknown purposes. A vast pool of undrained water. There was a defective train ahead. The basement was packed, stuffy, glaring. Flawlessly polished readings in the gallery. The stadium resplendent as twilight gathered. The springy turf at the conclusion. Bird, traffic and aircraft sounds, intermittent. They especially liked the exploded church. The Kingdom Hall of Jehovah's Witnesses. Of course, there was no signposting.


IT WAS only a matter of time. A vista of dismal interiors, harshly lit. Here was a picture of Russian dolls. A fine smog made their eyes water. One city, one zone from 4 January. The wreck of the next door garden. The supply of used mattresses seemed inexhaustible. Wind chimes banging against the bedroom window. He was spied lurking with a bird. Poor air quality, liquid condensed on skin. Indifferent pub lunch by the crowded river. Someone talked at length about cash flow. It was rather lost in the acoustics. Text in saline, in a dense mash. Part of the park had been flooded. Ducks, dogs and footballers were the principal inhabitants. The city spoke in noise clusters, lingered thunderously. Vernacular yellow brick stained by generations of salts. Yellow was the colour of the CCTV cameras. A car-park of a different colour, blistering fast. A woman changed her socks on the train. The new library with its proud iconic sign. Monteverdi, Radiohead and John Coltrane at the workstation. The place had been thoroughly cleaned and degreased. Newly appointed as librarian, he suddenly acquired gravitic mass. A dense forest of scaffolding obscured the turning. Speckled with snow, and dust from the works. A slick of biriani clinging to the pavement. The damp smell created by sparse fat raindrops. They saw the comet in the north-west sky. Already the heating was on for short periods. They "flew through the day with sugar-free wings". They were pitching chilling microtones and sweet harmonies. The war was not going nearly so well. Sunshine in the basin, and shadow in the crypt. Some of those glassy buildings had never been occupied. Chainlink fencing had been erected around the never-ending works. Blocks of air to breathe in between the bricks. They could find nowhere to buy a humble lightbulb. They reassembled the Dexion shelving in the mysterious corridor. Silently, the giant wheel stood in the evening light. They remembered it as laden with objects and status. Thunder, and sheeting rain, then a lighted bus passed. A monk, or possibly a madman, boarded the bus. One of the water tanks fell through the roof. The park had turned fresh once more following rain. The dog walkers and bird feeders were out again. Three serious joggers followed each other at long intervals. The viola player said: "You've had you ears lowered." After a while, they no longer took any notice. Rubbish began to pile by the pub wall again. Many yellow, brown and gold leaves on the ground. A pie and mash lunch before Monteverdi's *Return of Ulysses*. They settled in the front row before the ludicrous proscenium. They were incredibly casual, operating in a sort of half-kitchen. This heat drives people to kill, asserted the picture editor. He hung in his plexiglas box, persecuted by drunken sceptics. About 40 people clustered into three-quarters of a small bare-boarded room. The woman's performing voice sounded like a tape being played backwards. They started off with "analogue sources", but could have ended earlier. Their hands empty of maps, they had returned from the shops. Delays were attributed to a defective train earlier at this station. Waiting around most of the week in the L-shaped assembly area. They heard that it was "not a question of *if* but *when*". How leaning against the doors again prevented the "train from motoring". A man in a white coat climbed into a wheelie bin. The area was now of course crawling with fluorescent jacketed police. Water was pouring through the bathroom ceiling via the light fittings. They experienced disappointment as another mattress was deposited on the greensward. The moon stood in the day's afterglow above the furniture warehouse. They remembered, but the memory itself then became a forgotten thing. Three taps on the window, but nobody on the fire escape. The tidal rhythms of refrigerators in every flat in the block. A sudden gust of wind outside, flinging hailstones against the glass. One of them shattered and was displayed afterwards in bloody pieces. Having to use upward of two night buses to get home. How amber light from the blazing car made the shadows wobble violently. The huge branches of

Delays were attributed to a defective train earlier at this station.

The tidal rhythms of refrigerators in every flat in the block.

the roadside plane tree swinging in the wind. Being trapped in docklands among property, lacking a workstation or any direction. Stomach queasy and hot, morale very low as the regions were abolished. Conversations of besuited persons of both sexes at lunchtime, empty and amusing. One said "That's a matter of conjecture" quite loudly in the garden. Another said: "If they're helping Africans, they might as well help me." They pretended to be on a package holiday in their own neighbourhood. It was a "bring a work of art, take one away" do. Radio people with their tall mikes were waiting to do the interviews. They particularly delighted in the body language of the artist known as "Wobble". It was very Scandinavian, blond and chrome, but the lifts were being deconstructed. Artworks projected onto a suspended sheet, striated by light from the venetian blind. One performer showed everybody his penis, flickering briefly against a "no-signal" video screen. The food was good, if expensive, the outlook over the glittering river magical. The wine was kept in a plastic rubbish bin, packed with ice cubes. But all too soon, it was cold outside, and birdsong could be heard. Dark shadows, yellow light seeping, but a pale sky prepared to precipitate rain. Fear of widespread rail disruption following an incident at a major railway terminus. Fear of plunging into the rush hour once again, mowing down homecoming schoolchildren. There was an industrial tang to the air, a diesel aroma that lingered. Most of the damage was done in a swift spell when the shape collapsed. Below the surface was a narrow, damp-smelling tube faced with white ceramic tiles. Water streamed down the walls; years later, the yellow streaks remained as testimony. Surfaces were built up, then partially removed, destroyed, burnt through, leaving evidence, tracings, traces. A tour behind the scenes revealed distinctly industrial looking ducts, stores and floodgates underground. Up above there were continuous rumbling noises as of bodies being endlessly wheeled around. A sheen on windscreens, a shabby teddy bear affixed to the top of scaffolding. Corrections, negotiations, a trip to the copy shop as the temperature dipped once more. In the bank, the two-year-old's mother snarled: "Close your legs, you're a girl child!" It was only a matter of time before things would come to a head. That day, every-

Fear of widespread rail disruption following an incident at a major railway terminus.

body tried to log onto news websites, which slowed to a standstill. The orange-back-lit dummy fireman in the first-storey window endlessly gestured to the passing traffic. A flock of seagulls was illuminated briefly by the yellow uplights outside the concert-hall. Many dismal events above pubs were recalled in which no books had been sold. A man in the training room said: "I seen a clink in the market." He couldn't feel his feet and his shoulders were aching from carrying his briefcase.

TEARING UP the old carpet had revealed a nest of paperclips, cotton buds and buttons. A young man had been apprehended on the landing attempting to remove the security door. The entrance to the bin area was flooded, so they sent for the drain doctor. Music formed part of the ambience and integrated with the structure of the vast building. They had imagined the city before ever seeing it, before being driven from the docks. The endless repetition: "Bus stopping at next bus stop – please stand well clear of doors." Everyone was absorbed: in paperback novels, a tiny, leather-bound Bible, tabloid newspapers, earphone sound-worlds, thoughts. They lost the chance, they did not gain 500 any time any network voice minutes. The quavering tone and the lack of definite articles or active verbs quickly became unendurable. Graffiti, meaningless to everyone save the original engraver, were painstakingly etched into the window glass. It took three hours to get home, drenched and cold, by train and two buses. Did they dream that they had been in a city that was an open toilet? A black man on the bus said "You need a licence to touch someone's face." "Severe fucking bonehead" – the verdict of a football supporter on the train with obvious racist sympathies. Outside the furniture warehouse, a man was heard to say "I'm going to fucking shoot you." He was a man in his forties who played guitar and sang about unattainable young women. The colour of his skin was greyish yellow, but it was surprisingly warm to the touch. The air was an unspecific threat, a kind of disembodied life form that roamed the city. Some of the young trees lining the diagonal path still had a heavy freight of blossom. Momentary, irrational anxiety as a helicopter ambulance drifted backwards in the air, roaring just yards overhead. Loud male African voices boomed from the park, whose lawn had been shaved and was yellowing fast. The festival on the park was a sort of counter-celebration, except that this was not made explicit. Eagerly, the small white dog leapt to the fullest extent of his leash, his owner quite indifferent. The small fat child danced on the pavement before his mum; later, he roared, like a pig. At close to 3 in the morning, the isolated sound of birdsong in the lane was heard. A feeding frenzy of bluetits and great tits in the early morning light outside the bedroom window. A great glass and steel building appeared almost overnight on what had previously been waste ground.


BRUNCH IN the executive lounge (steak, bacon, sausage, scrambled eggs, coffee and Bucks Fizz) before the event. Acres of polished parquet flooring, high teak panelling and a huge bay window, incandescent behind the stage. Each place had a white pad and a white pencil with the logo of the advertising agency. In the men's toilet was a machine that dispensed condoms of all flavours, including curry and lager-and-lime. T-shirted thugs placed the stacking chairs in rows as fast as people were able to thread through. A bunch were milling round waiting for the mysterious cellar room to be vacated by the Masons. In search of pianos, they went walking in the heights, marvelling, and dubbing the neighbourhood "Golden Handcuff Land". They remembered a sand-coloured evening sky pierced by the silver of building-site arc-lights and gold of street lamps. A selection of 1- and 2-bed apartments and 2- and 3-bed town houses was shortly to be released. An office the size of a football pitch, conical-topped buildings visible through polarised glass, metal of unknown provenance. How the sounds of the traffic had hard edges around them, almost as though they were being hallucinated. A supermarket trolley loaded with cabbages was being deftly wheeled out of the way of an approaching bus. People wheel wheeled objects in the street at one in the morning for goodness' sake, she remarked bitterly. On the other bus, a woman and a schoolgirl came to blows in a dispute over personal space. The bus had to terminate here because the bus driver was a novice and had lost his way. In an entertaining performance he had parodied Nietzsche and Eastern mysticism while making good use of a flipchart. Because a mother had spilt paint on the exit platform, the bus had been taken out of service. A girl on the bus: "Proper vexed – the only time I weren't vexed was when I saw you." Drenched people, multiracial and apparently mostly poor, were allowed in at last to an auction of liquidated stock. Something could have been rescued out of that sludge, but only if some objectivity about it was achieved. It was a street-market performance precisely engineered to get people to part with money for things they didn't want. A girl with a good smell but an off-hand manner sold her spare ticket to someone in the queue. But when they got to the shopping centre they decided it was one of the inner circles of hell. They asked for a cup of tea, which the owner wouldn't sell them unless they were also buying food. A dozen high cranes were employed in building the new stadium, pinpoint lights on them piercing the afternoon gloom. They cowered in the study as the deconstructors drilled and hammered terrifyingly just outside the blacked-out bathroom and kitchen windows. Hammer blows caused tiles to fall off the bathroom wall. The only viable idea was to raise the monster water tank by a couple of feet within the airing cupboard. All the trappings were slowly stripped away, until the bare boards and the light on the horizon were arrived at. Soon the snow had disappeared, and it was a sunny morning, gold light on the treetrunks, dreamy sounds of traffic. The covers had been whipped away from the kitchen window by the wind, so light came in there at last. On the balcony, major rubbish had accumulated: a sad kitchen cabinet, crumbling, an old standard lamp, a burnt-out vacuum cleaner. A pile of bathroom fittings and other debris left on the shrubbery. There appeared to be little or no furniture, though charred toothbrushes were seen through the window on the bathroom ledge. Towards dusk, the raucous calls of three crows flying frantically around and through and between the trees of the park. There was a huge yellow moon on the eastern horizon, while Mars was still clearly visible in the southern sky. Now the

Towards dusk, the raucous calls of three crows flying frantically around and through and between the trees of the park.

rain returned, in darkness outside, and a cat's brief cry, the garden partly roped off with warning tape.


NEXT DAY, another office, further south and higher, a lone hubcap framed on the wall, curry stains on the mouse mat. For weeks, the same wad of used chewing gum, showing no sign of deterioration, had remained within the men's first-floor urinal. A small dark turd was once found on the floor next to the toilet bowl in the same facility at HQ. They remembered the Muslim men with trays of brightly coloured phone cards for sale on upturned crates outside the station entrance. They remembered the performance by two female colleagues, making language do impossible things and rushing in and out of several rooms. Their sleep was disrupted in the early hours of the morning by comings and goings in the flat across the landing. The clouds were completely absent first thing in the morning, and then later came upon it stealthily and bunched and became grey. A litter of pekinese pups were taken out for exercise as usual, some on leads, the smaller ones packed into a pram. They remembered times spent partly sitting on a bench in the midst of the park's oceanic tracts of grass, circled by dogs. Two boys said there was a fire behind the men's toilets and a man with white hair confirmed that a bush was burning. A white man with a blotchy face and close-cropped hair moved in upstairs and he and his mates were heard daily, banging and drilling. He had been moved into a better room, with a view over the car park rather than of the wall of the boiler room. The day the Hoover burnt out he was seen in the pub with a couple of well-dressed strangers. They remembered waking up to golden sunshine filtering through slats and lighting up the Japanese lantern, and thinking they were in a palace, or paradise. Her new piano nestling in the bay overlooking the garden, glowing in the early morning light while sounds of kids playing and screaming drifted in. Lying face upward in the osteopath's consulting room, looking at a small square of sky above the roller blind, and deciding to cling to that. Time spent among grey, ultramarine and orange glass buildings, all of them empty, mirroring an empty world, the attractive light railway winding sharply between them. Deadheaded daffodils; sculpted bollards, rust-patined; magnolia blossom from the tree at the corner of King's on the Rye carpeting a whole corner of the grass. From the bus on a fine spring morning, watching the rush-hour crowds scurrying to work, the only sound being Ligeti's *Lux Aeterna* on the headphones. Friday evenings outside the pub: the wooden benches filling up, the sky pale, grass pale, conversation feverish, as though an event was about to happen. Clacking of shears wielded by an elderly man clipping a hedge – scent of the clippings, a ponderous screech of bus brakes at a pedestrian crossing. How the cat was buried in thin soil above obdurate clay at the bottom of the garden, and how a fox subsequently dug her up. On the floor behind was detritus, and amid this a quantity of unmistakeable droppings and an animal urine smell that had come to seem familiar. Someone had stolen the front bicycle wheel and substituted one with a bigger radius that didn't fit, and anyway had a flat tyre. The air was an unspecific threat, a kind of disembodied life form that roamed the city silently, hunting for victims, rendering them invisible, or nowhere. The city made its own music, which travelled from deep within it; there were sounds in that ocean that no human had ever heard. A foreign, wailing woman descended, not understanding the voice that said northbound trains were suspended, and then demanding to be taken to the alternative bus service. People averted their faces when a man, running for a bus, tripped on a loop of wire and fell sprawling with his briefcase in the gutter. The woman lost her temper and started cursing in a German accent: "What the fuck do you know about Frank Zappa?" was the gist of it. In the café across the road, a picture of the Niagara falls, in which the glowing waters appeared to move, provided the electricity was switched on. A crow chose its moment to divebomb a cat as it was making a break across the road – almost causing it to collide with a cyclist. Mid-winter flashed by, the sun popped out and now foxes fucked on a piece of waste ground behind the railway embankment – they heard the vixen's screams. Grey fog laid over scrub on a whitish park; suddenly a herd of deer appeared without noise, their big eyes staring,

The air was an unspecific threat, a kind of disembodied
life form that roamed the city.

while steam rose between the saplings. A large fox, greyish in the sodium lamplight, bounded swiftly across the road in front of the hotel and disappeared into the darkness of the park opposite. The Glengall Tavern, The Globe, The Greyhound, The Red Bull, The Clayton Arms, The Hope, The Heaton Arms, The White Horse, The Rye Hotel, The Clock House. In the Paper Mill, straining to hear and screaming to be heard above the music, a few of them left and those getting fewer clustered more closely. Who was the only other person in the cinema to get the joke when the Brad Pitt character pronounced the Marquis de Sade "Shah-deh", like the singer? In the lane, which was filled with bright sunshine, a crowd of Muslim men and boys in white shirts, some embracing each other, held up the traffic. The oriental shops they remembered from their previous visit seemed to have long gone, as part of the inexorable drift of tourist traps towards global corporate homogeneity. A man showed them an envelope containing what purported to be the remains of a scorpion; it turned out to be a practical joke that didn't work. It was pleasant enough in the garden at the centre of the square, normally closed to the general public, saying farewell over frascati, chicken legs and baby quiches. Too warm and stuffy to take sound into another direction in the upper room of the pub; but a self-destructing poem at least did not outstay its welcome. After brief discussion outside the pub, they concluded that dread is when you have to go to work, and angst is when you don't, but have no money. At the top of the escalator each evening, the homeless boy held up a magazine in one hand, offering it for sale as though it were the sacrament. They were exhorted to stand well clear of the closing doors; advised not to place their persons or belongings or the smooth functioning of the system in jeopardy. A great mound of rubbish lay outside the front door: old clothes, a filthy carpet underlay laden with orange brick-dust, grubby woollen rug, a motorbike helmet, an umbrella. Later, unseen in the warm dark garden, the three-legged cat betrayed its presence with a faint tinkle from its collar, a familiar and comforting sound in the stillness. The sound of a piano late at night from a neighbouring window, played by an elderly man from the Balkans known by everyone

The Rye Hotel.

locally to be profoundly deaf. It was not until he turned round to put on his coat at the end of the evening that he became aware there was nobody at the keyboard. Meanwhile, a bus blew up a few hundred yards away, killing one man, said on the news later to have probably been the bomber, and badly injuring four others. They passed a yard wherein three vans, in states of disrepair, were almost submerged in detritus of all kinds: bricks, planks, pieces of scaffolding, rusting tools, traffic cones, rubble. Another yard packed with hibernating ice-cream vans. In the centre of the city, dozens of police vehicles were parked at the kerbside and hundreds of policemen in fluorescent yellow jackets patrolled meaningfully in the intermittent rain. In the supermarket, an old woman who had what looked like a growth on her face, the skin around it being yellowy-green, giving the impression her face was collapsing. On the bus, a man with a baby's dummy in his mouth, held on a cord round his neck, said "508" with a look of bruised grandeur on his face. A young woman squatting between parked cars, jeans pulled down, peeing, being remonstrated with by an elderly homeless man, shouted back: "I don't see why they think it's so funny." Every morning the old woman with the sick dog took it out of its travelling basket in the park, where, followed by marauding crows, it would do its business briefly. A crane swung an iron ball repeatedly at a remaining brick wall, while a bulldozer busied itself on the mountain of rubble and a bonfire of planking blazed through the mist. The builders had gone bankrupt, it appeared, leaving the fire escapes half done, and the security man posted outside each day was there to stop them coming back to steal materials. Animal cries and bird calls, distant train whistle and the rush of an incoming wave, brief interludes of utter mayhem, long moments of controlled beauty – at least, that was the idea. Someone had transported a traditional river barge to moor at the quayside between the office buildings, but after some time it had sunk because nobody realised it had to be maintained. They were disappointed to discover the warehouse district near one of the many river bridges, once redolent of spices, had been transformed into a complex of boutiques, wine bars and high-priced apartments. A man with stumps for teeth, wearing a girlie T-shirt nuzzled a small black cat as he boarded the bus, speaking to it in reassuring tones and kissing it when it whimpered. They recalled the crowds were threaded, three by three, up the wooden spiral staircase with its vertical rope banister, through the surgical museum under the rafters and into the tiny operating theatre. One of the women shot water at a boiling kettle to cool its strident blast, while an "empty" film was projected onto the wall beyond, interfered with by the shadow of steam. They wore uniformly dark suits; one of them endlessly chalked scribbles on a blackboard while the smell of burning wax from two paschal candles began to permeate the space, altering its shape. (When the roof started to catch fire, that was not part of the performance.) What it felt like was baroque music or jazz at the time of its creation; that is, when the protagonists collectively had little idea of what it was called or what the boundaries were. Elsewhere, a man who looked as though he'd been put together from spare parts was amiable, as was his poetry – but he was of the school that prefaces each poem with an amusing anecdote. Ripples spread majestically across the breadth of the branches of the great plane tree across the road, swaying symphonically as the wind caught it, then moments later becoming still again before the next gust. A thunderstorm was predicted, and duly arrived just after midnight, crashing dramatically almost overhead for not more than a few minutes, flashing golden-white light through the curtains and bringing with it sudden torrential rain.

THAT MORNING an overweight man in a T-shirt and dark slacks came out of the baker's swinging a French stick sheathed in custom-made clear plastic; he tripped on a paving stone and the sheathed bread skipped. A familiar old woman in a fawn raincoat, headscarf and old wellington boots shuffled very slowly up the road past the park, pushing a shopping trolley, and stopping every couple of minutes for a long rest. There was scarcely anybody about, the houses seemed uninhabited, even the birds had been silenced, the weather was greyly oppressive; for all they knew, everyone had been carried off by a plague or a silent inva-

227

sion. She was asked whether she would prefer the Cardinal, only walking distance away but with dull food and ambience, or the New Inn, a car ride but nicer; to which she replied instantly, "I'd prefer to die." An elderly black man on the underground train picked up a copy of a newspaper that had been left on the seat, muttered half to himself, "Twenty t'ousand dead – what purpose?" more than once before tossing it aside. A man carrying a black rucksack gestured across the street at an unseen person, possibly the driver of the bus they were on, tapping his finger on his forehead to indicate insanity, and then spitting, or simulating spitting. Then he made his excuses and slipped across the river to listen to a man roaring around the room, pausing to sonically trace the contours of a Patrick Caulfield print – the attendant pretending not to be concerned. A curious setting, like a school stage, a high platform, wood panelling behind to a height of seven feet, and above that blood orange walls, and the performers coming out of doors in the scenery at the back. On the way back, he was interrupted by a young woman calling out to him, asking the time; upon being told, she immediately asked, in the same singsong, yet deadpan voice: "Can I come and live with you?" All evening, a strong smell of burning slowly became more and more pervasive; then in the morning an aluminium pan appeared on the ground next to the bins, which on closer inspection contained a mass of charred ex-food. They relived a walk through the cemetery, along the canal to a pub with a view of the great sweep of the river, buildings glinting, seagulls skimming, and then on to the customary Indian restaurant and several Kingfisher beers. It was spotting with rain and the air suddenly became laden and dense over the trees, then there was a tremendous flash of lightning maybe yards away, followed almost immediately by a huge thunderclap – after that, the air cleared. (They were told there were no trains because lightning had struck the signal box.) Another day, having locked himself out of the flat when embarking on a walk over the common to the takeaway, he had to ask the man for a plastic spoon with which to eat his biriani on a park bench. The flat had been devastated by fire – a sack of garden rubbish by the gate had been charred, and on top of it was the burnt-out frame of an armchair, which appeared to have been flung out of the window. A constant, unnamed fear was experienced – or rather, an intermittent one, disappearing from consciousness for long periods and only being triggered by apprehension of an unusual moment, such as a customer in the throng stooping to inspect his own shoe. While he was waiting under the railway bridge for the bus, a van roared up and a man leaned out, appearing to aim a missile at him, which turned out to be a black floppy disk that clattered on the pavement. "Is he a communist?" the question was posed, to which the answer, "No he ain't, he's just using religion to cover his disgusting acts", came amid the aroma of vinegar, or more properly, non-grape condiment, deliquescing on a portion of chips. Sunday morning: the Jehovah's witnesses arrived for their service in their Fords and BMWs, middle class black couples, occasionally white folk, occasionally single people, few children; they parked their cars on the yellow lines and the men took out their briefcases. They remembered the deep-voiced, square woman in a dress and wool hat who chanted about Jesus at the bus stop outside the train station daily; and how fewer people each day remarked on her presence, until at last acceptance or indifference prevailed. At one point the train was being backed up a few yards in order to then build up enough speed to get it over the next gradient; but eventually, this ploy failed, and it died about 200 yards short of the station. More than 40 people crammed into the back space of the bookshop for the launch, including those who'd wandered in off the street and stayed, and a dog that howled softly when one of the poets spoke the line "the dog's death". An Irish drunk addressed a pile of rubbish in the passage between the train station and the office building with an improvised ballad: "Oh the streets of the city / Such a dreadful sight / They're filled with papers / And other shite...." Bedding, Rugs, Kitchen Utensils, Toiletries, Mobile Phone Accessories, Kashmir Halal Butchers, Elnamic House of Fashion (To God Be The Glory), Big Girl Specialists in Large Sizes, African & European Cosmetics, Hair Products, Jewellers, African Videos & Audio (CD's, DVD's), Spiritual Products, Aromatherapy Products. Approaching the bridge, the bus was delayed in a traffic jam for some time, the reason becoming apparent when it finally crossed the bridge: an army of police had set up a roadblock, including about a dozen policemen and women armed with submachine guns. Close by the station the homeless magazine vendor, after grumbling he was doing so badly in the cold he'd "rather go back to thieving", refused a sale, muttering "I ain't got no change" as he returned the proffered coin and grabbed back the magazine. A dog on a lead, and fat marker pens lined up in his breast pocket. They considered how they never saw the young people upstairs in daylight, nor heard more than faint rumblings within; but they would come to life as midnight approached, and then there were comings and goings and door bangings until maybe five in the morning. Following the collision, the couple abandoned their car, the man aiming a couple of blows first, with a motorcycle helmet he was carrying, at the driver of the van involved in the incident, then they both ran away down the street and never came back. Alone in the gloomy, deserted ballroom, the only one to turn up at the session had started improvising on his instrument (never having done this before), and continued for about 45 minutes, afterwards reporting it to be the most liberating experience of his life. Crossing the rye at dusk, on the way back from a visit to the library, the glimmer of frosty turf all around, he passed two black men in heavy coats midway on the path, while in the left-hand distance the lights of the traffic moved without cease. In the park, a black pit bull terrier hung by its teeth from a dangling tree branch, swinging back and forth for some time before falling to the ground, then leaping up to repeat the performance; its owner, a grey-bearded man in a fawn blouson, watched proudly. He observed a crow fall upon an injured pigeon, and start tearing chunks out of it while it still flapped its wings, the movements becoming less vigorous and finally ceasing; an hour later, some remains and a cloud of feathers were visible, but the following day there was no sign. On the bus, a small boy exclaimed, "Hey, there's Leroy's girl-friend!" whereupon he and his friend wound down a window and shouted below in unison "Leroy's girlfriend!" – but on getting no response the first turned round to his friend and observed, "She ain't Leroy's girlfriend, she's too small for

Leroy!" Next evening, while waiting for a No 12 bus home, a man came straight towards them walking exactly along the line of the kerb; when he got close he stopped dead, staring at them, and when, feeling uncomfortable, they moved away, he screamed "shit" at them, then continued along the kerb. He seemed to be a businessman in a suit and tie, with shaven head and chin; then he started acting strangely, counting a great wad of banknotes, and it had become apparent that, despite his smart suit, he was wearing no socks, furthermore, that his hands were incredibly filthy, smeared with what looked like printing ink. Earlier, he had banged on the door, making a big fuss of a puddle of water on his bathroom floor, and insisting on going upstairs to harangue a pair of bemused Indian builders about the tenant, a mysterious "Mr Pensard" , while his pale blonde girlfriend, allegedly a surgeon who had once saved his life, nodded mutely. He was last seen on the platform looking anxiously at the destination indicator. Hard to recall the perceptions that burgeoned into consciousness at certain instants of the day then faded back into non-being: broken bricks at the side of the path leading up to the publishing office; the combination on the entryphone keypad, memorised as a visual pattern; the faint aroma from the toilets at the foot of the stairs. Four tanks were ranged at the back of the stage, at first covered by drapes, but then each in turn was brought forward at various points in the drama, to reveal that they contained, respectively: a model city (which burned down); a bunch of giant toadstools; a collection of flasks of specimens; and finally, pure glittering water. Bright sunshine suddenly turned to foreboding gloom; then there was a ferocious hailstorm for about five minutes, rattling loudly and alarmingly against the windowpanes before abruptly stopping, converting the street and back yard into instant snowscapes; and when sunshine eventually returned there were still thick piles of hailstones the size of gobstoppers to be seen, accumulated in shadowed areas.

THEY RECALLED how a new perfume seemed suddenly to become fashionable, such that every so often they caught a

Someone else would move into that flat eventually, and the story would start from zero again.

whiff of it in a crowded street, on a bus, in the queue for the station lift, a repugnantly fruity, overripe sort of smell, like that of rotting peaches; and how, much later, just as suddenly, it ceased to be popular and vanished completely. When the doors of the ancient lift failed to open at the bottom, the customers waited silently for almost five minutes, pretending this wasn't happening, before someone shyly suggested pushing the alarm button; upon which the alarm rang harshly and incessantly and could not be turned off throughout the entire time the lift was being winched up, almost imperceptibly slowly, to the top again. Outside the shop where they had gone to buy a new vacuum cleaner, a man had fallen to the pavement, for unknown reasons, and struck his head on the kerb; he was quite still and greyish, a dark stain and a small smear of vomit on the ground round his head, and a woman was giving him mouth-to-mouth resuscitation while a crowd stood around. The bus ground to a halt because a man in a car ahead coming in the opposite direction refused to back up and let it past, even though there was plenty of room for him to do so; becoming aggressive, he got out of his car and shouted and gesticulated at the bus driver, then got back in and started shouting into a mobile phone. At night, they watched from a window overlooking the street: the terrace on the right, the park on the left, a skip stationed at the kerb, then a vast pool of undrained water, two parked cars and a white van, a black and white cat trotting across the road, making for the Paladin shelter, all-night TV reflected in window-glass, the images leaping ceaselessly above everything. The commotion upstairs turned out to be the young solicitor and another man breaking into the neighbour's flat; it was said that he had died a couple of weeks ago, in hospital of a stroke while his now pregnant girlfriend was "up north", thus rendering meaningless all that fuss about the water leak and the building works; and as for the intrigues and threats and byzantine stories nobody had been able to get to the bottom of, all that had vanished into the air; someone else would move into that flat eventually, and the story would start from zero again. It was only a matter of time.

In the morning, sunshine, with faint streaks of high cloud; sun flashing off parked car windows opposite putting spots in everyone's vision; in the area of the park where traditionally people would walk their dogs, a man with dark skin, long dark hair, white shirt, black trousers, ambled slowly with hands clasped behind his back, like the monarch's consort on an official visit, his head bowed as though in solemn contemplation, though with no sign of a canine companion; and a blonde woman in jeans and a child in black top and white skirt appeared with a German shepherd, which squatted briefly to shit in the grass, then scampered.

In the morning, sunshine, with faint streaks of high cloud.

# ACKNOWLEDGEMENTS

### Down With Beauty

The "Prologue" and "Epilogue" appeared in earlier versions in a different context in *onedit* magazine, edited by Tim Atkins, at www.onedit.net/issue7/kene/kene.html

The "Epilogue" also appeared in *Gangway*, Issue 40 "Expatriations", guest edited by Helen Lambert, at www.gangway.net/magazine

"Us and Them" appeared in Douglas Messerli's online journal *Exploring Fictions* at exploringfictions.blogspot.com/2009/07/ken-edwards-us-and-them.html

"Soldiers", "The Story of Nobody" and "Down With Beauty" appeared in various issues of *Golden Handcuffs Review*, edited by Lou Rowan.

"A Memoir of Our Father" appeared in *Ekleksographia*, "after Oulipo" issue, guest edited by Philip Terry, at ekleksographia.ahadadabooks.com/issuethree/authors/ken_edwards.html

"Exile" appeared in *The Other Room Anthology*, 2012.

"Nothing Doing" appeared in *VLAK*, edited by Louis Armand et al.

"In Gondwanaland" appeared in *Black Market Review*, edited by Kyle Hughes, at www.blackmarketreview.com/issue2/07.html

My thanks to all the editors.

### Nostalgia for Unknown Cities

"City of Reclamation" appeared in *Golden Handcuffs Review*, edited by Lou Rowan.

"City Break" appeared in *Poetry Salzburg Review.*, edited by Wolfgang Görtschacher.

"Bruised Rationals" in an earlier version appeared in *RWC*, edited by Lawrence Upton, and was also used as a text for an orchestral piece by the author, performed by the London COMA Ensemble on various occasions.

A shorter version of "City on the Marshes" appeared in *Kiosk*, edited extracts as a field report in *Ecopoetics*, and a more complete version in the language art anthology *The Dark Would*, edited by Philip Davenport.

My thanks to the various editors, and to Gordon and Saskia for providing the space in which the bulk of "City of Grain Elevators" was written. The first edition of the entire work was published by Reality Street in 2007.

*KE, 2013*

# REALITY STREET titles in print

## Poetry series

Kelvin Corcoran: *Lyric Lyric* (1993)
Maggie O'Sullivan: *In the House of the Shaman* (1993)
Allen Fisher: *Dispossession and Cure* (1994)
Fanny Howe: *O'Clock* (1995)
Maggie O'Sullivan (ed.): *Out of Everywhere* (1996)
Cris Cheek/Sianed Jones: *Songs From Navigation* (1997)
Lisa Robertson: *Debbie: An Epic* (1997)
Maurice Scully: *Steps* (1997)
Denise Riley: *Selected Poems* (2000)
Lisa Robertson: *The Weather* (2001)
Robert Sheppard: *The Lores* (2003)
Lawrence Upton *Wire Sculptures* (2003)
Ken Edwards: *eight + six* (2003)
David Miller: *Spiritual Letters (I-II)* (2004)
Redell Olsen: *Secure Portable Space* (2004)
Peter Riley: *Excavations* (2004)
Allen Fisher: *Place* (2005)
Tony Baker: *In Transit* (2005)
Jeff Hilson: *stretchers* (2006)
Maurice Scully: *Sonata* (2006)
Maggie O'Sullivan: *Body of Work* (2006)
Sarah Riggs: *chain of minuscule decisions in the form of a feeling* (2007)
Carol Watts: *Wrack* (2007)
Jeff Hilson (ed.): *The Reality Street Book of Sonnets* (2008)
Peter Jaeger: *Rapid Eye Movement* (2009)
Wendy Mulford: *The Land Between* (2009)
Allan K Horwitz/Ken Edwards (ed.): *Botsotso* (2009)
Bill Griffiths: *Collected Earlier Poems* (2010)
Fanny Howe: *Emergence* (2010)
Jim Goar: *Seoul Bus Poems* (2010)
James Davies: *Plants* (2011)
Carol Watts: *Occasionals* (2011)
Paul Brown: *A Cabin in the Mountains* (2012)
Maggie O'Sullivan: *Waterfalls* (2012)

## Narrative series

Ken Edwards: *Futures* (1998, reprinted 2010)
John Hall: *Apricot Pages* (2005)
David Miller: *The Dorothy and Benno Stories* (2005)
Douglas Oliver: *Whisper 'Louise'* (2005)
Ken Edwards: *Nostalgia for Unknown Cities* (2007)
Paul Griffiths: *let me tell you* (2008)
John Gilmore: *Head of a Man* (2011)
Richard Makin: *Dwelling* (2011)
Leopold Haas: *The Raft* (2011)
Johan de Wit: *Gero Nimo* (2011)
David Miller (ed.): *The Alchemist's Mind* (2012)
Sean Pemberton: *White* (2012)
Philip Terry: *tapestry* (2013)

*For updates on titles in print, a listing of out-of-print titles, and to order Reality Street books, please go to www.realitystreet.co.uk. For any other enquiries, email info@realitystreet.co.uk or write to the address on the reverse of the title page.*

REALITY STREET depends for its continuing existence on the Reality Street Supporters scheme. For details of how to become a Reality Street Supporter, or to be put on the mailing list for news of forthcoming publications, write to the address on the reverse of the title page, or email **info@realitystreet.co.uk**

Visit our website at: **www.realitystreet.co.uk/supporter-scheme.php**

## Reality Street Supporters who have sponsored this book: